HER LOVING HUSBAND'S RETURN

MEREDITH ALLARD

Copperfield
PRESS

PROLOGUE

In seventy years so little has changed. Then, the gate was taller than the tallest person, electrified, eager to shock to the death. Looming over the fence were eight high-standing towers with armed guards with submachine guns who looked down upon the people as though they could be, should be shot for amusement's sake. They were at one with the enemy across the Pacific Ocean, many decided. They had to be. They were traitors. They were spies. How else can we separate the good ones from the bad ones? How else can we know the loyal ones from the conspirators? We must round them up like cattle and pen them here where they're safe from us and us from them.

Above the barracks, higher than the gates, beyond the guard towers, were the mountains. Always the mountains. They encompassed everything within their distance—one vast, jagged, granite wall stretching toward the heavens from the deepest valley in the Americas, cascading Vs flecked with icy snow, unmistakable even through the wintry clouds. The mountains were everything everywhere. If the gates, the guard towers, and the armed military police weren't enough to remind you that you were a prisoner here, the mountains shouted your helplessness. You are here, the mountains said, and we will trap you here forever.

I remember when the bus stopped in Manzanar near the guard station, a lonely shack at the edge of the camp, one window on either side, misshapen rocks slapped together with mortar, and a pagoda-style roof. The guards spoke to the bus driver and barked directions as though the people inside were orange-clad prisoners linked by irons, but they were only families—fathers, mothers, children, grandparents. I remember the anxiety in those inside the gate, their quick-scanning eyes wide as they drew as close to the barbed-wire fence as they dared, searching those on the other side for missing family or friends. I remember the fear in those outside as they stepped off the bus and shivered in the bitter desert cold. Their reaching hands grabbed family members and they stared without seeing the nighttime landscape of brush and tumbleweed that promised blinding dust storms, the horizon flat until the mountains. Always the mountains. The people from the buses were herded inside, shouted at, tagged and numbered. Already they were losing themselves. When the gate slammed and locked behind them they looked toward the outside as though they would never be free again.

So, yes, I have been here before. I have walked this arid wilderness. I have heard the sand blow a maddened howl in the night. I have seen the white-glow moonlight reflect the saw-toothed horizon. Through it all, the mountains have remained the same. After all, what is seventy years to a mountain range that has watched millennia pass away? Now, the gates are taller since they guess we can jump anything less. Now, the gates have a silver coating, the electricity and barbs deemed no longer necessary since they guess the barbs cannot pierce our preternatural skin and the electricity will do nothing. Now, the military police carry guns with silver bullets, which we secretly laugh at. Now, I am the one who has been carted away, considered too unpredictable to be out among polite society. Yet the barracks, the mess halls, the natural barrier of the mountains between us and everyone else in the world... so much of it is the same. There are nights when I cannot make the distinction between then, when I was here from compassion, and now, when I am the one encaged. But do not worry for me, my love. Now, with this silver-coated gate and these imposing mountains between us, I am reminded all too strongly how I cannot be without you. Soon, Sarah. I will hold you in my arms soon. Be patient this little longer, my love, and I will return to you. I will.

CHAPTER 1

Sarah Wentworth sat on the edge of her bed and wept, her husband's letter fallen to the floor. Even with the heavy black marker censoring some of his words, this note from James in his curling, calligraphy-like hand was the first message she had from him. She had been without him twenty-four days, twelve hours, and seventeen minutes. Was it only that long since they sat huddled in the Boston train station, pressed together against the madness? Was it less than a month since he leaped from the speeding train like the graceful hunter he was, when he rushed back to her, held her close, and kissed her passionately because this kiss had to last?

The first days were the hardest since she didn't know where they were taking him. After public debates and private posturing, social media finger-pointing, and reality show name-calling, it was decided the undead, as they were called, would be held in relocation camps similar to the ones used for 100,000 Japanese-Americans during World War II. After numerous frustrations of the bureaucratic sort, Sarah learned that James was sent to a location close to the old Manzanar site in eastern California near the Nevada border. Now that she knew where he was, now that she had a sense he was safe, she thought she should feel better. But it was too hard, looking for him in the night, expecting to hear his sweet, strong voice, wanting to feel his hands on her, but he wasn't there. She clutched James' wedding ring, hanging from a gold chain around her neck, glad she kept it since she was afraid they would take it from him in camp and he would never get it back. She grabbed James' letter and reread it, savoring every word as if for sustenance.

"Even gone you're up to your old tricks," Sarah said aloud. "Of course you were at Manzanar during World War II. And of course I knew nothing about it until now." She held the letter closer to her face, searching again for any sign there was more to find. James hasn't changed in over three hundred years, Sarah thought. He's always so literal, always the professor searching for rationale and reason. Would he add a secret message somewhere in that letter? The camp authorities probably blocked out nothing, paranoid for whatever reason, and this is all there is.

For now, she reminded herself. For now.

Sarah survived life without James one day at a time, reminding herself to eat, sometimes reminding herself to breathe. At night, she wore James' t-shirts to bed, allowing herself to feel closer to him by wearing clothes that had touched his body and lingered with his scent. She was still wearing his sky-blue t-shirt though it was nearly two in the afternoon. She couldn't bring herself to take it off. She touched the cotton, long and wide on her since James was so much taller and broader, and it was thinning in places from frequent washing—it was his favorite t-shirt after all—but she didn't care. She realized she had been functioning in perpetual numbness since James was gone. On the outside she seemed fine—taking Grace on long strolls around the historic streets of Salem or sitting with her in Winter Island Park near Salem Harbor by the rocky shore bordered by green grass with white and yellow wildflowers. Some days they examined the fort or admired the scenic view of Pickering Light House. Other days they enjoyed the soothing bay breezes under the umbrellas at the outdoor tables at Pickering Wharf. Sarah kept busy with mundane tasks as well, going grocery shopping, cleaning the old wooden house from the over-hanging attic to the new modern kitchen, normal things at normal times. During the day she was mostly all right. She was used to being without James then, used to looking at their closed bedroom door, checking the sky to see how much more the sun had to drop before their bedroom door opened and he was there with his ready "Hello" as he took her into his arms and kissed her lips.

The nights were nearly unbearable. After Grace was put to bed, after Olivia turned into her makeshift lodgings in the great room, then the loneliness was overwhelming. To fill the empty hours, she turned to her old comfort—reading. She was working her way through the classics, many of them first editions from the vast shelves of books in the great room. Now she was rereading *Romeo and Juliet*, an odd choice, maybe, for the sad ending, yet she found comfort in Shakespeare's most beautiful love poetry. Some mistook the phrase star-crossed lovers as something positive—we're so in love we're star-crossed—but Sarah knew the phrase referred to Romeo and Juliet's certain deaths at the end. In Shakespeare's day, people believed the position of the stars when you were born determined your destiny. The star-crossed lovers were fated for destruction—it was written in the stars after all. But Sarah and James weren't star-crossed, she knew. While they had their share of difficulties along the way, no matter the obstacles, they were destined, not for destruction, but to be together. In the darkness, in the lonesome hours when she was reading in their bed, Sarah knew this separation would pass and she would see her husband again. Maybe Romeo and Juliet reunited in another life in another way, Sarah thought. Maybe they found their way back to each other again the way James and I did.

Sometimes, in the sleepless hours when she lay awake, she was haunted by horrors—a finger-pointing, pock-faced monster wielding a heavy chain over his head like a cowboy lassoing cattle, a gloom-infested dungeon, death and dying, not just her own, but her daughter's too. She was afraid for James, still not entirely sure what he faced in the camp, and she couldn't escape the vision of some military guard sticking her husband's paranormal chest with a wooden stake or depriving him of the blood he needed. There were nights when she felt hell, all the stages of it, grasping at her with sharpened claws, ready to drag her back into the nightmares. Other nights she dreamed that she stood over James while he sat at his seventeenth-century wooden desk while he worked, reading something or writing something, while she rubbed his neck and shoulders and he said how human he felt when she touched him. She dreamed she felt his hands under her nightgown, touching her, everywhere, and she dreamed she felt his mouth on her, everywhere. Sometimes she would reach for James in her sleep and in the mornings she awoke clutching his pillow close to her body as though it were him.

She sighed as she set the letter aside and stood from the bed, her legs and arms tingling as she stretched toward the gabled ceiling. She peeked around the door of her daughter's room, needing to check on Grace even if she was napping. Sarah walked to the crib, on her toes so she wouldn't creak the three-centuries-old wooden floor. She smiled at her angelic baby with the golden curly halo so similar to her father's, still awed whenever she thought of how she and James were reunited with the Grace they had been missing. Sometimes, Sarah wondered where the note came from, the one that pointed out that this was their Grace, but at that moment all she could think of was her husband and her daughter and she was amazed at the pure love she felt for them.

Content that her daughter was sleeping peacefully, Sarah slipped into the great room. She looked around the gabled house and saw the wooden walls, the remodeled stainless steel kitchen, and the fireplace where the cauldron used to hang. She saw the flat-screen television, the vast collection of books on the shelves, and James' seventeenth-century desk. She sat in his chair and sighed. She could feel him suddenly, as though he were there with her. She looked out the diamond-paned casement window, opened the door, and let the cooling Massachusetts sea breeze wash over her, soothing her unsettled nerves. It was June now, and the looming humidity was a guess in the air. She stepped outside, checking back to make sure her tailless black cat didn't run past the open green door, close enough to hear Grace if she cried. Sarah was at home in Salem near the coast among the historical buildings and the landmarks from colonial days, but nothing felt right without James. The crooked oak tree near the curb slumped toward the grass, weighted and heavy. While it was always gnarled, now it looked sickly, as though it had seen its time, it had done its work, it had lured Sarah when she first came to look at this house nearly two years before, and now it could go home. Sarah wasn't ready to lose the tree, and she decided to call a tree doctor to help it.

She went back inside, closing the door behind her. She had that restless leg syndrome again, a permanent fixture since James was gone. She wanted to go for a walk along the Salem streets, her usual panacea to deal with the excess energy, but she didn't want to wake Grace and she couldn't leave the baby alone. Instead, she paced the great room—to the bookcase and back, to the kitchen and back, to the ladder leading up to the attic and back. If she climbed to the attic she could dig through the seventeenth-century artifacts from her previous life with James, thinking it would bring her some comfort. True love never dies, she thought. Look at what we survived in the past. We will survive this too.

She jumped at the sudden knock. She looked through the window, but there was no chain-wielding monster, only Thomas Masters, the Maine doctor who treated her after the car accident. The doctor who put his career on the line after he learned James was James. Sarah opened the door, and Thomas stepped inside.

"How are you feeling?" he asked.

"Back to normal, at least as far as my injuries go. I'm not sore anymore, and I'm not dragging through the day. The scar from surgery is healing."

More than her injury, more than her pain, she remembered James' anguish at her suffering, his thought that he could save her by turning her. For that moment, with Thomas standing beside her taking her pulse, she wondered if she should have let James have his way that night. Then she would be with him now and they would be together.

But she thought of Grace sleeping peacefully in her crib, and she knew she made the right decision. She had to be there with Grace. She had to be human. And if James had turned her, she could never go back to before. Even delicate, even fragile, even struggling through every night without James, she had to stay as she was. She nodded at her thoughts. She was right to say no.

She noticed the stethoscope around Thomas' neck when he pulled the knob from under his shirt collar. He listened to her chest and nodded. "I'm officially releasing you from my care as of today, which is a joy, Sarah. I wasn't sure you were going to make it when they first brought you to the hospital."

"You've done more than your part," Sarah said. "You promised James you would look after me when he was gone, and you have."

"That's why I'm here, Sarah. I wanted to tell you in person that I'm leaving for California today. My wife and kids are in the car outside. My mother-in-law is driving us to the airport. I have a new position in San Francisco at Saint Francis Memorial Hospital. I found a supervisor from the hospital in Maine willing to give me a good recommendation even after the stunt I pulled with the ambulance."

"I'm going to miss all of you," Sarah said. She waved at Thomas' family waiting outside. "Sometimes the best thing you can do for yourself is go somewhere new. It's a chance to start over. That's why I moved here from Los Angeles. I wanted to begin again after my divorce."

"I didn't know you were married before James."

"It's a long story." Sarah sighed. "I know James would want me to thank you for everything you've done for us."

"I'm sure James will be home soon."

"I hope so."

Thomas reached into his jacket pocket, pulled out a crumpled post-it note, and handed it to Sarah. "This is our new address in San Francisco. Please keep in touch, Sarah."

"I will. James is in California now."

"It's three hundred and forty miles from San Francisco to the

Owens Valley. It's a seven-hour drive. I'd offer to go, but I heard they're not letting them have any visitors."

Sarah nodded. "I tried to get permission to see James but they said no one with a pulse is allowed near or past the gate."

"You definitely have a pulse."

"Thanks to you."

Sarah walked Thomas outside. She hugged Thomas' wife and children, greeted Thomas' mother-in-law, and said her heartfelt good-byes. As Thomas walked toward the car, Sarah grabbed his arm.

"I've been meaning to ask you," she said. "You didn't have to protect James after you realized he wasn't breathing. You didn't have to commandeer an ambulance to help me escape the hospital. Why did you help us?"

"Because you needed help."

Thomas shrugged as though it were the most obvious answer in the world. He sat in the passenger's seat beside his mother-in-law, waved at Sarah, and as they drove toward Derby Street Olivia pulled her silver Prius up to the curb and got out of the car. Sarah marveled at her Wiccan friend with the close-cropped, silver-threaded red hair, her hoop earrings, her ringed fingers, her coin necklace, her peasant-style skirt, and her Greek sandals. Always the gypsy, Olivia looked every bit the fortune teller she could be, and she grabbed Sarah's hand and led her into the house.

"What are you doing out here, dear?"

"I was saying goodbye to Thomas and his family. He has a new position in San Francisco and they're leaving today."

"San Francisco? I thought they settled here after they left Maine. Why would anyone want to leave Salem to live in San Francisco? I suppose San Francisco is a nice enough city—I've been to Wiccan gatherings there—but Salem has everything you need, the soothing sea, a quiet, small-town pace, Boston, one of the greatest cities in the world, just twenty minutes away by train. I would never leave Salem. It's the best place in the world."

"Sometimes people need a fresh start," Sarah said. "Thomas gave up his position at the hospital in Maine to help James and me after the car accident. Maybe he thought it was a good idea to put some distance between himself and the East Coast."

"People try to escape their past by running away, but it never works. Wherever you go, there you are. Unless you make peace with your past, it will always follow you."

"Are you saying I was trying to escape when I came here after my divorce?"

"You weren't running from anything, Sarah. You were running toward James."

Sarah looked once more down the road where Thomas and his family disappeared.

"All right," Olivia said. "Maybe California isn't that bad. Maybe." Her steel-gray eyes narrowed, and she studied Sarah with that detective seeking clues look. She pulled Sarah closer. "Is everything all right?"

Sarah saw the motherly concern, and she was thankful for her wise, wonderful Olivia. Olivia put her arm around Sarah, and they walked into the wooden gabled house together.

"Before Thomas left, I asked him why he helped us," Sarah said. "He took a huge risk. He didn't have to care."

"What did he say?"

"He said he helped us because we needed help."

Olivia nodded. "That's right."

"But how does someone give up everything, his job, his reputation, possibly risking jail, to help two strangers who happened to end up at his hospital?"

"Think about the way James helps others, Sarah. For centuries he has helped those in need. He helped the Cherokee on the Trail of Tears. He helped my family during the Great Depression and World War II. And he did what he could for the Japanese-Americans who were incarcerated during World War II."

"He could never make peace with the way I was treated during the Salem Witch Trials," Sarah said. "He still feels the injustice of it."

"Which is why he helps others who have been treated unfairly.

And, as a result, whenever he needed help he received it. It's the law of karma. You get back what you put out into the world."

"I know about James' involvement with the Japanese-Americans during World War II," Sarah said. "I got a letter from him today, and it was the first time he told me about being at Manzanar."

"A letter from James? Let me see."

Sarah grabbed the letter from the dresser in her bedroom, and Olivia read it slowly, savoring every word as Sarah had done earlier.

"Why is some of this blacked out?" Olivia asked.

"I thought maybe there was a hidden message, but James wouldn't leave cryptic clues."

Olivia held the letter close to her face as she inspected it. "It looks like he was pressing down with his pen when he wrote," she said. "Let's see if we can find what's under the marker." She held James' handwritten letter up to the light bulb in the lamp near his desk in the great room. She turned the letter over to the back and tried to read James' words under the censor's thick marker, squinting at the lines. Sarah looked over Olivia's shoulder, hoping to see something, anything, but James' handwriting was too faint under the black boxes. Olivia opened the long top drawer in James' desk and pulled out a sharpened pencil. "How about this?" She turned the letter over to the blank side and rubbed the pencil over it. Like the black magic messages Sarah used to send in crayon when she was in elementary school, the imprint of James' handwriting was faint but visible. It was backward since the letter was turned over, so Olivia pulled her mirror from her bag and held it to the paper.

"You're so sneaky," Sarah said.

"I saw it on a television detective show." Olivia winked at Sarah. "I always wondered if it worked." They read James' letter in its entirety, and neither saw anything that should have been censored. James mentioned the buses at Manzanar. He described the mountains. He said he realized more strongly how he cannot live without her, and to be patient a while longer. He will return to her. He will. What was there the authorities didn't want her to see?

"Do you see anything else?" Sarah asked.

"I don't, and I'm disappointed. I was hoping for a code to a vault or a safe. You know, a million dollars hidden somewhere forbidden and we could go on an adventure to find it."

"You've been watching too many of those detective shows," Sarah said.

Olivia folded the letter and placed it in the drawer. "At least he's settled enough to write to you, Sarah."

"James has always been good about writing to me. Even when he thought I was gone from him forever, he wrote to me."

Olivia took Sarah's hands in hers. "I have a feeling before long you'll have more letters than you'll know what to do with."

"I'll have everything but him." Sarah dropped her head into her hands. "I know now, Olivia. I know how James felt all those years he missed me, thinking he would never see me again. I don't know how he survived the loneliness for three hundred years. It's not even a month, and I..."

Sarah did her best to shake her sadness away. Grace would wake from her nap soon, and Sarah didn't want her daughter to see her that way. She needed to stay strong for Grace.

"All in good time, Sarah."

"This is not a good time."

"I know, dear, but everything works out right in the end. If it's not right, it's not the end. Your love for James and his for you has survived centuries. It will survive this." Olivia kissed Sarah on top of her dark curls and hugged her close. When she pulled away, she studied Sarah, her detective seeking clues look again on high alert. She must have decided Sarah was all right because she nodded. "How is vegetarian chili over a baked potato for an early supper?"

"That's perfect. Thank you."

"It's only supper, dear."

"Thank you for everything, Olivia. For your support. For your love. For moving in here to help Grace and me."

"Jennifer, my ever-stubborn daughter, doesn't want my help now. She says she can handle it, which I question, but she pushes me away whenever I try to help. That frees me up to be here with you."

Sarah smiled as Olivia disappeared into the kitchen. She sat in James' chair again, pulling his letter from the desk drawer, studying it more, wishing she had his hunter's sense of smell. She knew he could smell her scent from a distance, and she wished she could do the same.

"Maaaaaa!"

Sarah rushed to Grace's room and peeked around the open door. She saw her daughter standing upright in her crib. Grace was pulling herself up now, and she smiled at her mother.

"Maaa," Grace said.

Sarah scooped her daughter from her crib, smothering the little face in kisses, brushing the silky golden curls from her flowery, jewel-like blue eyes, laughing and smiling and not even having to pretend because this was pure joy for Sarah, holding her daughter in her arms, making her giggle, watching her grow. They would celebrate Grace's first birthday the following week, and they would have a little party, Sarah decided. She needed to maintain this normalcy for her daughter. Nothing was normal with James gone, but Grace would suffer as little as possible in the meantime.

Sarah carried Grace into the kitchen where Olivia stood over the stainless steel stove, stirring the chili in a black pot.

"You look like a witch stirring your concoction," Sarah said.

"I am a witch." Olivia winked at Sarah, then pointed at the empty fireplace. "Too bad you removed the cauldron. I could have brewed a concoction or two in there."

"You are one of the most powerful witches."

Olivia swatted her hand in the air, sweeping the idea away. "Nonsense. Every witch is as powerful as she wishes to be, no more and no less."

"Another Oliviaism," Sarah said.

"A what?"

"An Oliviaism. I'm keeping track of all of your wise sayings, and I'm going to compile them into a book called Oliviaisms."

"Oliviaisms. I like it." She tasted the chili in the pot. "Are you hungry?"

Sarah nodded. She sat Grace in her high chair, then seated herself at the long wood table near the fireplace. As Sarah tasted the vegetarian chili, she thought fondly of the night she made blood soup for James on Christmas Eve. She stared dreamily out the window, remembering how James loved the soup and how Geoffrey intruded in his boisterous way. She wondered how Geoffrey was doing in California along with Timothy, Jocelyn, and Chandresh. Her world was hard enough without James, and it was even smaller without her friends.

"Thinking about James?" Olivia asked.

"How did you know?"

"You always get that dreamy, far-away look when you're thinking of him. And you have this sweet smile on your lips."

Sarah mashed some cooled chili on her plate and fed Grace a small spoonful. "I thought you were reading my mind."

"I can't read minds, Sarah. I read energy. It's a good thing I can't hear everyone's thoughts. I have a friend in Louisiana who's telepathic, and it's a dreadful thing, I can tell you. You don't need to know everything about everyone standing around you. You certainly don't want to know what everyone is thinking. People think the strangest things at the strangest times."

"But when I first started working at the library, Jennifer knew what I needed before I knew I needed it. And you always know what to say to help me. Isn't that reading minds?"

"It's intuition, Sarah. My intuition tells me things I don't catch with my five senses. Jennifer listens to her intuition too." Olivia gathered the empty bowls and put them into the sink. "Your intuition is strong, Sarah."

"Why do you say that?"

"You were drawn to Salem your whole life. Why Salem of all places? You felt your intuition, followed it, and when you arrived here you found James, who waited over three hundred years for you to return."

Sarah shook her head. "I grew up in Boston, which is twenty minutes away, and yet I never made it here as a child. I married a man

14

I never loved and lived in a city I didn't like for ten years. It wasn't until I was divorced I finally came here."

"What good would it have done to come when you were a child? Even if you and James had crossed paths, he wouldn't have looked at a girl to be the ghost of his beloved wife. Being stuck in your bad marriage, needing to get away. It gave you the impetus to make a change, and where did you go? Here, to Salem, the place you were drawn to all along. Just because you felt drawn to Salem didn't mean you had to come. Most people don't listen to their intuition. Most people make decisions deliberately against what their intuition tells them. You could have gone anywhere, but you listened to that voice inside your heart that called you here, and within nights of your arrival you crossed paths with James and discovered your purpose, to reunite with him, and your daughter. Now you're with Grace, and James will be home soon." Sarah shook her head. "He will, Sarah. Then you'll both be exactly where you should be, all because you listened to your intuition. You've returned."

"James said your ancestor Miriam told him he'd return. He said it was her prophecy."

Olivia stopped, stone solid. When she recovered herself she scrubbed the bowls in the soapy water as though nothing had happened. When the dishes were washed and dried she turned to Sarah.

"She said he would return? Miriam used that exact word?"

"That's what James said."

Olivia was a statue again, and for a moment Sarah thought she had fallen into a trance.

"Are you all right, Olivia?"

Olivia smiled in her warm, motherly way.

"I'm fine, dear. You know, we older folks get forgetful sometimes. Yes, he's right. I remember now. Miriam did tell James he would return. And he will."

Sarah turned away, not wanting Grace to see the pain she felt as a tightening behind her eyes. In the great room, Sarah flipped on the flat-screen television, turning to the children's programming Grace loved. Funny red monsters, hungry blue monsters, orange and yellow best friends, Grace would sit mesmerized watching them and babbling along with their songs. Sarah sat cross-legged on the woven rug and pulled Grace into her lap. She watched the television as though it were the only thing in the world to see.

Olivia returned the dishes to the cupboard and joined Sarah and Grace in the great room. She sat on the sofa and watched television with them, laughing when Grace laughed at the puppets' crazy antics. When the show was over, Sarah stretched her limbs, her back aching from sitting on the floor. She handed Grace to Olivia and went into the kitchen for some ice water, her mouth dry.

"Daaa!"

Sarah's hand went to her heart. "No, Grace. Daddy's not here now, but he'll be home soon."

Grace pointed at the television screen. "Daaaa!"

Sarah shook her head. "No, Grace."

"Wait, Sarah."

Olivia moved closer to the television. She leaned toward the flat screen, her eyes squints, her face taut. "Sarah! Come see!"

Sarah looked where Olivia pointed, to a news story about the relocation camps.

"It must be a repeat," Sarah said. "They've been there nearly a month now."

"But look!"

On the screen Sarah saw footage of a group of undead getting off a chartered bus within the boundaries of the camp that was their home for now. The prison-like nightlights were on full blast, giving an eerie glow to the blue-white men and women as they gathered near the silver-coated gate. Sarah turned up the volume and listened.

"...because this is near the location of the Manzanar camp where over ten thousand Japanese-Americans were held during World War II. When asked why this location was chosen as a detention center a second time, officials said the area, in the vast desert of California's Owens Valley, provides an isolated location where they can keep their detainees secure. This camp is known as Camp Dracula."

"Camp Dracula?" Sarah said.

Olivia shrugged. "It is a camp for vampires."

The camera panned the well-secured encampment. The long, neat lines of barracks, the prison-like guard towers, the sterile blankness of the desert environment. If the footage were in black and white it could have been filmed in the 1940s. The scene cut back to their nighttime arrival at the camp. The camera panned the faces, and Sarah gasped.

"Daaaa!" Grace said. She clapped her hands and giggled. "Da!"

There he was, James, nearly a head taller than those around him, surveying the scene with his usual level-eyed calmness. He didn't look worried. He didn't look afraid. Sarah leaned close to the television, wanting to kiss him through the screen. Suddenly, nearly too quick for her to see, James looked into the camera with a grin on his lips. Sarah sighed aloud. It was his message for her. He was all right.

"Look at him, Sarah," Olivia said. "He's smiling for you."

Sarah touched her husband's beautiful face on the screen, his gold hair in his eyes as always. "I know," she said. And then he was gone.

When the news program repeated later that evening, Sarah recorded it, and after Grace went to sleep Sarah watched it again, and again, and again. James was on screen for a few seconds, but Sarah didn't care. She would watch him smile at the camera over and over until this nonsense was done and her husband was home where he belonged. Finally, when she couldn't watch it any longer she turned the television off, walked into her bedroom, pulled out a pen and some paper, and she wrote. What was she writing? She didn't know. First, she thought it was a diary. Then, she thought it was a letter for James she hoped would get through to him in the camp. Finally, she thought it was simply venting everything she was feeling then, which left her uncomfortably full. Letting the words leak out was a way for her to feel like she was touching James while he was three thousand miles away. It was a way to feel him beside her when he wasn't there.

When she reread the words she had written, she realized she wasn't sure what she wanted to say. She gave up writing, for that moment, and looked at the darkening late afternoon sky, realizing it was earlier and brighter in California. James was still sleeping. She wondered what he would be doing when he woke up later, and she wondered when he would be home.

For the record, please state your full name with your place and date of birth.

My name is James John Wentworth. I was born in London, England on April 19, 1662.

You're three hundred and fifty years old, is that correct?

Yes.

Marital status?

Married, and I have one child.

A child?

She's adopted.

I see. Where is your wife?

At home.

She's?

Human.

Where is your place of residence?

Salem, Massachusetts.

And what is your profession?

I'm a university professor, formerly of Salem State University.

What do you teach?

English literature.

Thank you. I'm hoping you can help me, Mr. Wentworth.

Doctor Wentworth.

Excuse me? (Papers shuffle.) I see, yes, Doctor Wentworth. We're trying to determine where the vampires have been getting their blood to survive. We need to be certain you're not a threat to the community. I'm sure you understand.

What exactly are you asking me?

I'm asking where, when you were living in Salem, Massachusetts, you got your blood from, Doctor Wentworth.

I got my blood from the hospital.

The hospital?

Yes.

Which hospital?

I was getting it from Salem Hospital, and then I switched to Massachusetts General Hospital.

You took blood from the patients?

(Sighs.) From medical assistants who got it from the blood bank.

So in a way you were taking it from the patients because the blood you took wasn't available to humans who may have needed it.

Donated blood has an expiration date. I was taking blood that would have been wasted because it was no longer useful in transfusions.

Do you have contact names for the medical assistants who acquired the blood for you?

I can give them to you if it's necessary.

It may be necessary. Have you ever hurt anyone to get the blood you need, Doctor Wentworth?

Of course not.

Not ever? You've been undead for how long now?

Since 1692.

That's three hundred and twenty years. There weren't a lot of hospitals with blood donation facilities three centuries ago.

Animal blood works as well.

Does it?

You're feeding us blood from slaughters here. I've never had a problem finding butchers willing to sell blood.

So you've never hurt anyone, bitten anyone against their will, or killed anyone, accidentally or not, to get the blood you need?

Never.

You can be honest, Doctor Wentworth. The crimes you committed years ago are long past the statute of limitations.

I am being honest. I haven't committed any crimes.

I have the feeling you're being less than forthright, Doctor Wentworth. Do you have something to hide?

I have nothing to hide. I've committed no crimes. I want to go home to my wife and daughter. I made a mistake coming here. I was naïve about what would happen though I've seen enough to know better. I hoped we'd learned a lesson or two since World War II, but I can see I was wrong. I thought if I surrendered myself when the government asked I'd help to show we're not any different from anyone else and we can be trusted.

Except you're dead.

I'm speaking to you now.

You have no pulse.

One could argue you have no heart.

Really, Doctor Wentworth.

I'm being imprisoned without being charged with a crime, and while I'm not a law professor I know enough about the Constitution to know it's illegal to hold people indefinitely without charging them. It's the Fifth Amendment to be exact. I can quote it for you if you like...

You're not being imprisoned, Doctor Wentworth. We're simply detaining you and the others until we understand what we're faced with. We can't let anyone who might be a threat to society out among innocent Americans. We can't take a chance that a...

Vampire?

Yes, that a vampire might begin feeding on innocent humans at whim.

(Laughs.) Do you think the ones who are here, the ones who will-ingly surrendered themselves, are a threat to society?

I'm asking the questions, Doctor Wentworth. Have you ever murdered anyone for their blood?

You already asked that question.

Doctor Wentworth, the sooner you answer the questions, the sooner we're done here.

(Sighs.) No, I've never murdered anyone for their blood.

Are you certain?

Have you ever murdered anyone?

No, Doctor Wentworth, I have never murdered anyone.

Are you certain?

Of course.

There's my answer. When can I go home?

As soon as we know how we're going to handle this situation. I'm sure you understand this is unprecedented in history.

It isn't unprecedented at all. You don't understand. I need to go home to my wife. It's too hard being here without her. We need to be together.

Everyone here misses their family, Doctor Wentworth. Assuming everything checks out, we'll get you home as soon as we can.

It's not as if I have a choice in the matter.

CHAPTER 2

*W*henever I awake in the darkness, in those first moments of consciousness when I open my eyes, I think I am home, in our house, in our bed, your strawberries and cream scent everywhere, Grace's cinnamon a warm undertone. Every night is a harsh reminder, static on my skin, when I'm fully awake and I realize I'm not home at all but in this hastily built windowless bungalow in the middle of the Sierra Nowhere desert. Every night I look at the thin, bare walls that shake and rattle with the coiling winds, the haphazard wooden desk, the army cot with the feather-thin mattress that sags under my weight, the army surplus pillow and blankets. The only light inside is from a single fluorescent bulb hanging from the ceiling. During the war the families were given black potbellied stoves for heat, but since we are what we are they decided we don't need to keep warm, which is true enough. I have been cold for over three hundred years, and it is only with you I feel warm again. My cramped quarters are at the front of the trailer divided from my roommate by an unpainted wooden board, as good as nothing to one like me who can hear miles away. And who do I hear snoring on the other side of the partition?

Geoffrey. Yes, I am bunking with Geoffrey. He haggled the authorities until they put us in the same barracks, much to my chagrin. He goes on and on about returning, only to laugh and say I wouldn't know what he means *about returning, would I? Only I know all about returning and how I must return to you. I am ready to strangle him, though I suppose that is nothing new.*

Tonight after I awoke I pulled the rough gray blanket close to my chin. I didn't want to get out of bed, but then I thought of you, your sweet, full-lipped smile, your softness, your warmth, and I shook off the sadness. I survived over three hundred years without you. I survived sunlight for you. I can survive this if this is what I need to do to get home. Being here now, I cannot help but remember when I was here before, how I came to be here before, and the similarities between then and now.

I can hear your voice, Sarah. I can hear you complaining about how I never tell you anything about my past, that you want to know everything about my life from the years we were apart. "Another night," was always my response. Another night is here, my love, so I will tell you a story.

*When I awoke the night of December 7, 1941, I had no sense that had been an extraordinary day. The world changed while I slept, and yet nothing felt wrong, nothing looked upside down, inside out, tossed round and round. Everything looked as it should for a December Sunday. It was a typically mild winter night in Southern California, the air cooled though not cold, at least not by Massachusetts standards. The earth was scented with wet and rain, the sky grayer without visible starlight. Everything was in its place, no odd sadness in the air. I pulled my notes together for my Monday night classes at UCLA, where I taught then, and I slid the notes into my briefcase. I drank what I had in the fridge, then turned on the cherrywood Zenith radio as I often did. I knew virtually no one in Southern California, and I wanted it to stay that way. I always knew it was dangerous to make ties with anyone, too problematic in case anyone guessed my secret (a paranoia which has been sadly proven true), so I stayed within the solitude of the four walls of my dwelling with no company but my memories of you and the radio programs that connected me to the rest of the world. I listened to it all—*The Adventures of Ellery Queen, *the crime melodrama* The Whistler, *Kate Smith,* Big Band music, Truth or Consequences, *and news programs. You would have loved the comedy shows, Sarah, like* Abbott and Costello. *You've always loved to laugh. After lifetimes of silent, lonely hours, the radio helped me feel as though I had company. It was a marvel to me—a live human on* the other side of the speaker—and I was thankful for the distraction. But that December night, after the static crackled into the room, I heard the urgency in the announcer's voice. It was a wavering voice, an unsteady voice, though it struggled to remain impassive. These are merely the facts, the voice said, and the facts are the facts.

"...when the Japanese bombed Pearl Harbor at just before eight a.m. this morning..."

Pearl Harbor? I didn't even know where to find Pearl Harbor on a map. Is it part of the United States, I wondered? When I settled myself enough to listen, I sat in the wing chair and tried to concentrate, needing to understand.

"... over two long hours, Japanese bombs killed or wounded nearly four thousand Americans, damaging eighteen ships, including all eight battleships of the Pacific Fleet, and destroying over three hundred and fifty aircraft. Over one thousand lives were lost when the battleship U.S.S. Arizona exploded and sank off the Hawaiian shore..."

"This must be some kind of hoax," I said aloud. "Of course the United States hasn't been bombed." But the more I heard the panic in the announcer's voice, the more I believed. Where will this lead, I wondered? Who will play scapegoat now?

Then I listened to a rebroadcast of the President's speech from earlier that day:

"...December 7, 1941—a date which will live in infamy—the United States of America was suddenly and deliberately attacked by naval and air forces of the Empire of Japan...

"I regret to tell you that very many American lives have been lost. In addition, American ships have been reported torpedoed on the high seas between San Francisco and Honolulu...

"Japan has, therefore, undertaken a surprise offensive extending throughout the Pacific area. The facts speak for themselves. The people of the United States have already formed their opinions and well understand the implications to the very life and safety of our nation.

"As commander in chief of the Army and Navy I have directed that all measures be taken for our defense. But always will our whole nation remember the character of the onslaught against us..."

．　．　．

CLASS WAS *quiet a week after Pearl Harbor. The students were taking their last quiz of the term before their comprehensive final exams, and they were concentrating on Shakespearean quotes and quibbles. I can always tell by their faces as they scan the papers whether or not they've studied. The prepared ones are relaxed, easy as they write their essays, knowing where to look in the text for their references, knowing what they want to say. The unprepared are slumped, staring at the tips of their pencils, cursing me under their breaths.*

"To be or not to be..." I heard one student murmur. I nodded at the words.

I heard quick-time steps racing across campus, and I pretended not to hear the hurry come closer and closer, not that my students were paying any attention to me. Suddenly, one of my students, Keiko Sato, pushed open the door and rushed into the classroom. She could hardly speak for her panting.

"Professor Wentworth," she said. "I'm so sorry. Can I still take the quiz?"

"Of course, Keiko," I said. I pulled another quiz from my briefcase, along with a sheet of notebook paper. She nodded, her sharp, observant eyes on the floor, her cheeks pink in embarrassment, but I wasn't concerned. She was a smart girl, Keiko. Even with her late start I knew she would finish before most of the others. She took the paper to an empty desk near the back of the room, and several heads popped up when she passed. I heard a snicker from a scowl-faced boy in the center, but a stern look from me stopped him. The students settled again while Keiko worked with the relaxed demeanor of one who has prepared. I went back to grading their essays on "Distinguishing Tragedy from Comedy in Shakespeare's Hamlet *and* Measure for Measure."

After thirty minutes, some students began handing in their quizzes and leaving. One student, a young woman about twenty years old, turned to Keiko and said, with a voice syrupy sweet, "Did you know Japan was going to bomb Pearl Harbor?"

Keiko looked up, confused. "Excuse me?"

"Do you know what your soldiers did to innocent Americans in Hawaii?"

"My soldiers?"

"The Japanese soldiers."

"I'm from Los Angeles," Keiko said.

"Thank you, Jessica," I said to the young woman. "That will be all for tonight."

Jessica turned away, flipping her white-blond locks behind her. I could hear her heavy-heeled shoes clunk on the floor as she stomped down the hall to the stairs. I watched Keiko, trying to gauge her feelings, but she was impassive, concentrating on her work. A few other students flashed icy-cold or poker-hot glares in Keiko's direction, but she didn't look up. I wandered around the classroom checking on the students' progress, and I noticed Keiko had finished her work. From my glance I saw that not only had she finished, but her answers were spot-on. Yet she remained staring at the paper as though she were still working, her pencil retracing words she'd already written. Finally, after everyone else handed in their papers and left, when we were alone in the room, she stood.

"I'm finished, Professor," she said.

"You finished about thirty minutes ago."

"I thought it was better if I waited. I don't want any trouble."

"Did you have trouble getting here? Is that why you were late?"

Keiko didn't answer. I shook my head because already it was starting, the finger-pointing, the accusations, the false pretenses, the better-you-than-me decisions.

"Did someone hurt you?" I asked.

"They just shouted things."

I looked out the window at the December night sky, the street lights leaving the campus dull and shadowy. I didn't see anyone who looked like they were loitering, anyone who looked like they were waiting, but I knew Keiko was afraid.

"Where do you live?" I asked.

"Not far. My parents, my grandmother, my brother, my little sister, and I live in an apartment off campus."

"Let me escort you," I said.

Keiko gathered her book bag and handed me her quiz. "You're very kind, Professor Wentworth, but I'll be fine. I walk home by myself all the time."

"The circumstances are different tonight," I said.

Keiko nodded. "Thank you, Professor."

We walked across the campus, past the brick buildings, the trees, other

students on their way from their night classes. I thought I should say something to break the silence, perhaps ask Keiko what she thought of the quiz, did
she get anything useful from the class, some new insight into Shakespeare she
might not have had otherwise. Perhaps she needed help preparing for the
final? I guessed she wouldn't need help, so I said nothing.

Finally, she said, "I'm an English major."

"I didn't know that," I said.

"I'm going to be an English teacher. Or I was going to be an English
teacher."

"There's no reason you can't teach."

"People are mad at the Japanese because of Pearl Harbor."

"You're American."

"There are a lot of people like that girl in class who don't see any differ-
ence between those responsible for the bombing and me."

I wanted to say something that would give her hope, something that
would give her heart, but I couldn't think of anything because I was afraid
for her. I had seen it too many times before. Wanting to change the subject, I
said, "Teaching English might not be as fulfilling as you think."

"What could be better than teaching people to love reading?"

"It sounds wonderful, doesn't it? But most students aren't as self-moti-
vated as you are. I've been teaching for a long time, and most people are
bored by anything that doesn't have any obvious connection to their immediate reality, which is true of most English literature. Literature is full of
stories that seem so foreign and abstract from our own lives, so a lot of people
don't attach much importance to them."

"But the classics are classics because of what they have to say about
human nature. We can make connections between then and now. There's
value in studying stories from days when ladies wore corsets and men wore
top hats. Now, ladies wear pantsuits and men wear fedoras, but human
nature hasn't changed. We still want the same things people have always
wanted."

"That's an A for you," I said. Keiko nodded, a grin brightening her
features.

We arrived at her apartment building, a white stucco structure behind a
gate. "Thank you, Doctor Wentworth," she said. I saw an older, gray-haired

woman watching us through a street-facing window. Keiko nodded toward the woman. "That's my grandmother."

"See you in class on Wednesday," I said. As I turned away, I heard the gate open, and Keiko's grandmother said something in Japanese, to which Keiko's voice dropped in answer. I heard my name, and I nodded goodbye.

After Pearl Harbor, people walked on eggshells, afraid to step too heavily for fear of setting off another attack. People sat spellbound by their radios, scanning every newspaper headline they could find for news about the bombing. Moviegoers sat motionless in their seats as newsreels sputtered black and white scenes of the carnage before their eyes. Gossip, half-truths, and wishful thinking were accepted as news, and after the shock, when the numbness went away, everyone looked for someone to blame. On the surface, everyone seemed friendlier. People stopped their cars for those in the crosswalk without zooming around them, honking their horns as though they were put out by the simple act of slowing down to let the pedestrian pass. People smiled at each other. People nodded at strangers passing on the sidewalk. Unless you were Japanese-American. For Japanese-Americans, there was a coldness in the air unexplained by the winter sky, and many didn't know where to turn for warmth.

Fortunately, for me, my love, warmth is not an issue. I will write again as soon as I am able. Kiss our Grace for me.

CHAPTER 3

*S*arah sat on the sofa in the great room reading James' latest letter. There were so many similarities between then and now, but what did it mean? History had a habit of repeating itself, she knew. Again, she wondered if James was trying to tell her something not obvious in his words. Nothing had been censored in this letter, and Sarah wondered why. The information about the after-effects of the bombing of Pearl Harbor was well known, she supposed, available in most American history textbooks, so there was no point in blacking it out. They already knew James was more than three hundred years old, so there was no reason to hide that. She watched Grace bang some wooden blocks on the floor, then turned on the television hoping for another glimpse of her husband, maybe a different scene from the one she had already watched many times. She couldn't get the sight of James, smiling and sure, from her mind. But instead of a new report about the camps, the angry woman was on the air, yelling at this man, squinting at the unfortunate guest over there, confrontational even when the talking heads acquiesced. If you agreed with her you were right, if you disagreed you were wrong, and up was up and that was that and she didn't care what you thought anyway. So there.

"Have you ever heard of the Fifth Amendment of the Constitution of the United States of America?" she asked in her aggressive southern drawl. "When I was prosecuting cases, I became well acquainted with the Fifth Amendment, as any American attorney should be. Are you well acquainted with the Fifth Amendment, Mr. Tomes?"

"I graduated from Harvard Law School, I believe..."

"Did you? Because from the nonsense you're talking I'm thinking you don't remember it all that well. The Fifth Amendment says no person shall be held to answer for a capital or otherwise infamous crime unless on a presentment or indictment of a grand jury..."

"That's no person. The undead are..."

"Are you still wallowing in the semantics of whether or not the vampires are people? Mr. Tomes, have you ever looked into the eyes of a vampire, shaken their hands, had a conversation with one? Because I have. I've spoken to many of them, and they are indeed people."

"Even if they are people, the Fifth Amendment specifically states no person shall be held to answer for a capital, or otherwise infamous crime, *except in cases arising in the land or naval forces, or in the militia, when in actual service in time of war or public danger.*"

"Are you seriously trying to say the vampires are war criminals? That they're a public danger?"

"Are you sure they're not a public danger? Are you willing to put your family at risk by living next door to an undead if you're not sure of the risk they represent?"

"I'll have you know that I do live next door to an undead, or I did until this unlawful round-up sent her to one of those camps. This brings me back to the Fifth Amendment, which also states that citizens will not be deprived of life, liberty, or property, without due process of law. We are incarcerating law-abiding Americans without due process of law."

"The undead are being investigated one by one..."

"One by one?" A sarcastic laugh. "Good thing they're immortal since it's going to take a hundred years to get background checks on all of them."

"You must understand this is an unusual situation. Never before have we been faced with an influx of alien influences."

She closed her eyes. "Zzzzzzz. Bore me to tears, why don't you? Never before have we been faced with an influx of alien influences? There was a time in this country when signs saying *Irish need not apply* hung in shop windows. During World War II we incarcerated thousands of innocent Japanese-Americans, and years later we paid them paltry sums. In 1988, Congress passed the Civil Liberties Act, also known as the Japanese-American Redress Bill. That's more than forty years after the Japanese-Americans were wrongfully detained. Are you familiar with the Japanese-American Redress Bill, Mr. Tomes?"

"Of course I am."

"Why don't you show us how familiar you are? What did the bill say?"

"The bill acknowledged that a grave injustice was done and it mandated that Congress pay each victim of internment or their heirs $20,000 in reparations."

"Along with the reparation payment, President Clinton sent a signed apology to the interned Japanese-Americans on behalf of the American people. It took nearly fifty years for the Japanese-Americans to get some kind of closure for their unnecessary distress, thanks to the tireless efforts of their leaders and advocates."

Sarah turned off the television and stared at the blank screen. She looked at Grace, now playing with her stuffed bear, hugging it and kissing it and babbling to it in her little language spotted here and there by something like a word. Sarah realized she had received two letters from James so far and hadn't sent any to him in reply. He must be worried by now, she thought. He must want some word that she and Grace were all right. She sat at James' seventeenth-century desk and studied it for the first time since she moved back into the gabled house. That desk, along with the house itself, had been a wedding present from James' father, John, in 1691. The desk was solid European oak with hand-dyed hide lining the top, solid brass handles, hand-carved moldings on the side panels, and knobby feet. There were eleven drawers, five on either side and one long drawer at the top, and the bottom right drawer had a handmade lock for which she now held the key. That was where many of the secrets from James' three centuries were held. That was where she found his letters to her during his time with the Cherokee on the Trail of Tears, and there were other letters to her from the 1840s on. There was an odd gap between letters during the 1940s, the years of World War II, to be exact, though there were so many letters in the drawer that Sarah was still making her way through them all. Reading them brought her comfort while James was gone, seeing how often he thought of her even when he thought she was lost to him forever. But James knew she would love the letters, which is why he gave her the key before he left. Look at everything he's written to you, Sarah thought. Stop procrastinating. Write to him now.

She opened the long drawer at the top and pulled out some paper. She shuffled through his pens, he still had several feather quills and ink wells, and found a ballpoint pen. She stared into the blank paper as if it were a void, a too-large space of nothing where words would never make sense. Why was she so apprehensive about writing to James? Whenever she thought about trying to put her feelings for him into words she felt like a pot of water boiling over, too hot to hold in, unable to be contained. How could she explain how much she missed him? How she was going through the motions every day for Grace? And then she'd realize James wouldn't want to hear that at all. She would only worry him more than he already was, and James had always been a great worrier. Then, in the trepidation brought on by her wordlessness, she would dust the bookshelves or sweep the floor. But she couldn't procrastinate anymore. She had to send something, anything, to James. She glanced through his letters, often written about what he did that night, so she decided to do the same. What did she do that day?

A brisk knock at the door shook Sarah from her reverie. She glanced through the window and saw Howard Wolfe, a former colleague of James' from Salem State University—a biology professor and one of James' closest friends. Over time Sarah learned to overlook the fact that Howard grew hairier, and more horizontal, whenever there was a full moon. He looked tired, Howard, his salt and pepper hair longer from missed trips to the barber and curling near his ears, his salt and pepper beard straggling near his throat. Sarah opened the door and Howard stepped inside.

"How are you?" Howard asked.

"I'm hanging in there," Sarah said.

Howard saw Grace playing on the floor and he leaned over her. "I like your bear, Grace," he said. Grace babbled in reply. He turned to Sarah. "How is she?"

"She spotted James on the television yesterday."

"I saw it." Howard shook his head. "Timothy wasn't there. I would have liked to have seen him."

"Don't worry, Howard. James is watching out for Timothy."

"I know."

Sarah walked into the kitchen. The stainless steel appliances would always feel new to her whenever she thought of the black cauldron that had been her primary means of cooking in centuries gone by. She poured some freshly squeezed lemonade for Howard and herself and topped the glasses with sprigs of mint leaves. She brought the drinks to where Howard sat on the sofa, his gaze following Grace's every move.

"She's precious," Howard said. "You're so lucky, Sarah."

Sarah smiled at her daughter. "You're lucky too, Howard. How lucky you are that you found Timothy in the forest that night. You found your son like James and I found our daughter."

Howard nodded, and they watched Grace, who waved her stuffed bear at them.

"I'm glad you stopped by," Sarah said. "It's nice talking to someone who understands."

"Olivia has been staying with you."

"I'm so grateful for everything she does for us. But you know what it's like to have someone you love rounded up and taken away."

"Yes, I do." Howard sighed. "Some days I feel like this is a temporary obstacle, this too shall pass. There were days when I thought the only reason I was able to get through the hours was because I had my classes at the university, but now we're off for summer. I should have taught summer school classes."

Sarah looked dreamily at Grace. "I miss the university. I miss the library. I fell in love with James again there."

Sarah was so caught up in memories of James—the first time she saw him outside that house, the first time she saw him in the lecture room of the library, the first time they walked the old-time Salem streets together—she forgot about Howard until Olivia walked through the door. Olivia stopped, her hand on the knob, her mouth open at the sight of Howard next to Sarah on the sofa with Grace playing on the floor near them. Olivia nodded.

"Hello everyone," she said. "How are we this afternoon?" Olivia watched Howard with a gaze that would have pierced someone only human.

"I was just leaving," Howard said. He turned to Sarah. "Nice to see you, Sarah. Olivia."

Olivia opened the door for Howard and found Jennifer with her hand in the air ready to knock. Jennifer's eyes narrowed at the sight of Howard leaving. Howard nodded at her as he walked to his car near the curb.

"How is Howard?" Jennifer asked. Sarah heard sarcasm in her friend's voice.

"He's the same as I am," Sarah said. "He has good days and bad days."

Jennifer flipped her auburn hair behind her shoulder. "You shouldn't encourage him, Sarah. You can't forget James."

Olivia held up her hand. "It's all right, Sarah. Jennifer knows you haven't forgotten James." Olivia turned to her daughter. "She isn't encouraging him, Jennifer. He shows up sometimes. He understands what Sarah is going through."

"I lost someone in the round-ups too," Jennifer said. "Just because Chandresh and I were only dating..." She stopped as though she didn't know how to end that sentence. "Don't forget about James, Sarah, that's all."

"Do you think I could ever forget about James? Do you think I'm so fickle that a few weeks away could make me forget him for another man? He didn't forget about me in over three hundred years. I won't forget about him either."

Olivia shook her head at her daughter. "What is this about, Jennifer?"

"I know how James pined for Sarah before her return. I know how he never considered being with another woman, how he never looked at anyone else because he held his love for her so strongly in his heart. I don't want him to get hurt."

"You think I would hurt James?" Sarah stepped away from Jennifer, wondering who this stranger was she was speaking to.

Olivia shooed her daughter toward the door. "I think you've had a long day, Jennifer. It's time to go home and rest. I'll call later to see how you're doing."

Jennifer left without another word.

"What's wrong with her?" Sarah asked.

"She must be tired. Don't think about it for another minute, dear. No one who has seen you and James together, no one who knows your history, could ever doubt that you two were made for each other. Don't forget, Jennifer misses Chandresh. She has a different way of showing it, that's all."

Suddenly, Olivia looked around the great room as though she were searching for someone. "Did you say something?" she asked.

Sarah shook her head. "Did you hear something?"

Olivia closed her eyes, her head tilted toward the door. "No," she said, opening her eyes. "I must have imagined it. I do that sometimes. When you read energy occasionally you think there's a disturbance that turns out to be nothing. Never mind me. Go take a hot bath, Sarah. Relax. Dinner will be ready soon."

Sarah kissed the top of Grace's gold curls and went into the bathroom. She turned on the faucet, undressed, and lowered herself into the hot, bubbling water, remembering all the times James had joined her in that tub. She couldn't get Jennifer's recriminating glare out of her mind until she focused on James' face, his golden halo hair, and his secret-dark eyes, and she found comfort imagining him there beside her. She remembered how she had begged for the night hours to begin when he was home because, finally, she would see him again after the long daylight hours, like Juliet waiting for Romeo after their wedding because she expected her beloved to arrive cloaked by the shadows:

Come, night; come Romeo, come; thou day in night:
For though wilt lie upon the wings of night
Whiter than new snow on a raven's back
Come, gentle night; come, loving black-browed night.

Like Juliet expecting to see her Romeo, Sarah opened her eyes and James wasn't there. Romeo had been banished to Mantua for killing Tybalt. James was banished to California for being James. Sarah covered her face with her hands, calming herself. Unlike Romeo, James was immortal, and not even Friar Laurence's herbal potion could harm him. But Sarah needed to reach out to him. She needed him to know she was thinking of him.

Tonight I will write my letter to him, she decided. Tonight I will let him know what is happening here while he's gone. And he will know he is always on my mind.

CHAPTER 4

*J*ames laughed aloud when he received the letter from Sarah. He caught her scent and thought he was imagining it, sweet strawberries and cream wafting across the arid desert night, similar to the way her fruity fragrance hovered in Salem's salt-sea air. When the mail was delivered James had a letter, and he was embarrassed he had ever doubted her feelings for him. Odd thoughts had crossed his mind since he was incarcerated, and he was thankful for this proof that his Sarah was thinking of him.

It was a simple note, not very long, not long enough. James imagined he heard Sarah's voice narrating her words so he could pretend she was talking to him. She wrote about herself and how she felt recovered from the car accident that nearly took her life two months before. She wrote about Olivia and how she had moved into the wooden gabled house, there to help however she could. Sarah wrote about how the baby spotted him on the television, how she shouted his name—"Daaaa!"—when she saw him on the screen. When Sarah wrote about Thomas and how he left Salem for a new position in San Francisco, James wasn't as happy anymore. He had been comforted by the idea that Thomas was checking on Sarah. James was grateful to Olivia, always their wise, wonderful Olivia, but he felt better knowing a medical doctor was tending to Sarah. At the end of the letter Sarah wrote about Howard and how he was stopping by, how they shared stories, how they each understood the other. More uncomfortable thoughts flittered through James' mind, and he wondered if Sarah even missed him anymore. He was there, in California, three thousand miles away, and in a pinch of sadness he wondered if she would be better off with Howard. Howard wasn't human, not entirely so, but he wasn't incarcerated. James dropped his head into his hands, admonishing himself for his depressing thoughts. Sarah would never forget about him, he knew. She couldn't. James scanned the letter again, thinking that at least nothing was censored. James heard from others in the camp that most of their letters from outside arrived with either heavy black mark-outs or entire sections scissored away. He wondered how intact his letters were arriving home to Sarah.

"I need to get home," James said aloud.

He heard shuffling behind the wooden plank that separated his quarters from the rest of the barracks.

"We all need to bloody well go home."

"Hello, Geoffrey."

"Good evening, James. How was the interview?"

"The interrogation?"

"If you prefer. How did it go?"

"He tried to get me to confess to murdering for blood."

"Which of course you didn't do."

"Of course."

"Very good." James heard more shuffling as Geoffrey drew closer to the plank wall between them. "I have to admit, I was a little worried about that need you have for truth, justice, and the American way."

"I'm not Superman," James said.

"Near enough. I was afraid you might want to unburden your soul."

"I want to go home more than I want to unburden my soul."

"Good boy."

James realized he wanted privacy. He wanted to be far from everyone and everything to think in silence, but there was nowhere to hide. Geoffrey was a thin board away, and he could hear everything James did as well as James could hear him. James expected Geoffrey to be able to hear his thoughts inside his head since they lived in such close quarters. "Are you writing something?" Geoffrey would ask if he heard James' pen scratching on paper. "Reading again?" Geoffrey would ask if he heard pages turning. And ten minutes later, "I can hear you brooding from here, James. Come keep me company. Your little human person thinks I'm funny. I'll tell jokes. Van Helsing and a vampire walk into a bar..."

Geoffrey didn't understand James' need for solitude. James craved the aloneness, having no one to answer to, no one to entertain, and he was uncomfortable in the world without it. He had always needed the time. Sarah understood, even in their first life together, and she left him his time at his desk to read, think, and write in peace. She never begrudged him his time alone. She knew him so well. But here, in the middle of the Owens Valley, with barracks upon barracks set up in neat little rows in the dust-blown desert, there was nowhere to hide. James paced the small space in his quarters the way he often paced at home, back and forth, back and forth, trying to numb himself with the movement, keeping his body busy, struggling to focus on Sarah. Again, he thought of Sarah keeping company with Howard, and he realized he was jealous. He was jealous because Howard was there, in his house, near his wife, when he, James, couldn't be. James tried to picture her, her dark curls, her full lips, her sweet smile, her inquisitive chocolate-brown eyes. He was so rattled at the thought of Howard alone with his wife he couldn't even hold his wife's beautiful face in his mind. Overwhelmed by it all, James sat on the floor of his room and wept bloody tears that left him shaking, as though he would never see anyone he loved again. He felt forgotten, lost to Sarah, to Grace, unnecessary and unwanted. They could get along without him. He had a vision that he died when Elizabeth died. There was nothing left of him but a memory. He was dust, bones, and skull, a three-hundred-and-fifty-year-old corpse. Or perhaps he never existed, merely a figment of someone's imagination. The despair was overwhelming. James hadn't felt this much grief since Elizabeth's death in

1692. He tried to stop his tears, but they would be shed that night with or without permission. They had been held back too long.

"Are you crying, James?"

"Go away, Geoffrey."

"You are. You're crying. Oh no. My little man is crying."

"Little man?"

Geoffrey pushed the partition aside and it knocked against the wall, the thud reverberating across the dry night to the mountains and back. "My little man is crying. Don't cry little man. I'll make it all well. There there."

James wept as though he would never stop, embarrassed at being so emotional in front of Geoffrey, who, in a swift gesture, sat on the floor and swept James onto his lap as though James were no more than a toddler, holding him, rocking him, cradling him as though he were a lost little boy found. James tried to climb off Geoffrey, who wouldn't let him go. "There there," Geoffrey kept saying. "There there. I know this is hard, but everything is going to be all right. You'll see, Jamie."

James looked into Geoffrey's eyes. "Only two people in the world have ever called me Jamie. My father and my wife."

Geoffrey shrugged. "I must have overheard your little human person calling you that one time. I thought it might make you feel better."

"Coming from my father or Sarah, yes. Coming from you…"

"Don't start that again. We were having a nice bonding moment here. I'm trying to comfort you."

"Why?"

"What do you mean why?"

"I always think you have some ulterior motive and I'm wondering what you want from me. Why did you follow us to Maine? Why did you talk me into coming here? And why do you care if I'm upset because I miss my wife?"

"I thought we were friends, James. Do I need another reason to care?"

James shrugged. As much as he hated to admit it, he was

comforted by Geoffrey's presence. There was something inchoate about Geoffrey, some connection James couldn't name that drew him to the vampire with the almond-shaped black eyes, the long face, and spikes of gray in his red-brown hair. James thought of his father suddenly, and he shook his head.

"What is it?" Geoffrey asked.

"I was thinking about my father."

Geoffrey looked around the room. "Do you see him?"

"Of course not. He died over three hundred years ago."

"So did I. So did you. But we're here."

"My father wasn't turned like we were."

"Just as well. It's bad enough there's the two of us." Geoffrey took James' face in his hands and looked closely at his vampling. "No more tears, that's good. How do you feel?"

"Better."

"Good. Get off me. You're heavy."

James sat on the floor beside Geoffrey and closed his eyes. Everything was an unfathomable mystery, never to be understood. He thought his life was explained in an Ancient Greek text he couldn't decipher.

"I wish I could undo everything I've done," Geoffrey said. "I wish I had been honest with you from the beginning. I wish I could return you."

"I need to return," James said. "I miss Sarah too much."

Geoffrey studied James from the top of his gold-blond hair to the tips of his black Vans shoes. "Returning means more than going home." Geoffrey leaned into the wall as he waited for James' reaction.

"Of course it does," James said. "It means to be reunited with those I love. It means Sarah and I will never be apart again. I can't live without her, Geoffrey. I thought I could suffer through this separation because I suffered all those years without her. I thought since now I know she's alive, she's out there and she loves me, that I could handle the madness until it passed, but it won't be over any time soon, will it?"

Geoffrey shook his head. "We're only in the first stages of it, I reckon." Again, Geoffrey studied James as though he were unsure about a decision he made. "How badly do you want to go home?"

"More than I have ever wanted anything in my life."

There were no windows in the barracks, so James opened the door to see the barrenness outside, the brush, the meddlesome mountains, always the mountains, the natural barrier beyond. He closed his eyes as he thought of Sarah. "I should be home with my wife and daughter. I never should have left." He turned to Geoffrey, who was still sitting on the floor, his long legs spread carelessly in front of him, his arms crossed in front of his chest. "Why did you convince me to come?"

"Because I was afraid you were going to run, and I was afraid they were going to come after you. Do you want to spend the rest of your life running, looking over your shoulder, paranoid about everyone?"

"I've lived that way since you turned me."

Geoffrey nodded as though he agreed. "But when we chose to come here, your little human person, the one you were abooing and ahooing over a moment ago, was hurt. She couldn't run. She couldn't hide."

"She's better now. And now when I want to run I can't because I'm caged here."

"This returns me to my question. How badly do you want to go home?" Geoffrey closed the door, but James knew how little that helped. Those living in the barracks around them could hear as well as he could. Geoffrey grabbed James' arm and led him to the corner, dropping his voice to a whisper as though he read James' mind. "What if there were a way out?"

James leaned into the thin wall as he considered. A way out? A way to get home to Sarah? His mind skimmed the possibilities.

"When my wife was in jail in 1692, I wanted to break her out and escape with her somewhere far from Salem where the madness would never touch her again. But by the time I got to the jail she was..." James couldn't continue. The ache from that memory was still too much.

"You were too late that time because you were dealing with a

44

human person. What if we break you out instead? You're hardly a human person."

James shook his head. "Geoffrey…"

"I know what you did in Germany."

James walked to the other side of the barracks, needing to put some space between himself and the ridiculous vampire. "How do you know I was in Germany? Even Sarah doesn't know I was in Germany."

"More secrets? Honestly, James, you must learn to be more forthright with her."

"How do you know I was in Germany, Geoffrey?"

"I told you. I've been keeping track."

James sighed. "The mountains are too daunting."

"Why? They're one hundred million-year-old hunks of granite."

"But we need to get past them. Prisoners couldn't escape Alcatraz because of the San Francisco Bay. We have to get past the Sierra Nevada mountains."

"Remember one thing, James—we're already dead."

"I've been dead since the night you turned me."

"What does it mean to be dead, Professor?"

"For us or them?"

"For anyone."

"You no longer breathe. Your heart no longer beats. You have no pulse."

Geoffrey nodded. "You've already made it clear you want to get home to your little human person. Now I ask you, what are you willing to do to get there?"

James heard footsteps outside the barracks, and he shook his head at Geoffrey. Geoffrey made a zipper sign in front of his lips and opened their door.

"Ready to hit the mess hall?" Geoffrey asked. His eyes bulged, his cheeks puffed, and he looked ready to gag. He spoke loudly enough for their preternatural neighbors to hear without strain. "I hope they've got our tin cups cleaned and ready for a pint of pig's blood. Yum!" He retched with great dramatic effect.

"Let me find Timothy," James said.

Geoffrey waited outside watching others trek to the mess hall. Many chatted as they walked, some laughing and smiling, others sullen and forlorn. James found Timothy in his bungalow on the other side of camp, his blue jeans and green cotton t-shirt rumpled, his dark hair unkempt, his cheeks hollow. Timothy shrugged when he saw James, and they walked toward the mess hall, though Timothy stopped when he saw Geoffrey. James had noticed Timothy's stiffness around Geoffrey before. When they were on the train to California, Timothy sat some distance from Geoffrey though he watched the older vampire with fascination. As they sped past the California border, while Geoffrey was engaged in conversation with Jocelyn and Chandresh, Timothy leaned close to James and said, "I think that's him, James. That's the one who turned me."

James had been waiting for Geoffrey to make a similar observation —that Timothy was another vampling—but so far nothing. Geoffrey's lack of recognition struck James as odd, especially since Geoffrey kept track of James' every movement from the night outside the Boston jail until that moment in the camp.

"Let's go," Geoffrey said. "We don't want to miss the delicious hog's blood."

"Where's Jocelyn and Chandresh?" Timothy asked.

"We'll find them in the mess hall," James said.

Timothy kept his gaze on the back of Geoffrey's head while he walked three steps behind. James looked from Geoffrey to Timothy, unsure what to make of it all.

FOR THE RECORD, *please state your full name with your place and date of birth.*

My name is Jocelyn Marie Endecott and I was born in New York City on December 7, 1941.

You were born the day Pearl Harbor was bombed?

Yes.

Marital status?

I'm married to my husband, Steve, and we have a son, Billy, who's two years old.

Is he adopted?

Yes.

Is your husband human?

Yes.

Where is your place of residence?

Salem, Massachusetts.

Are there many of your kind in Salem, Massachusetts?

I don't know.

What is your profession?

I'm a dentist.

A dentist?

Yes.

You...

Take care of patients' teeth? Yes.

What do you do with their blood?

With their blood?

Yes. When people have dental work there is often a fair amount of blood. What do you do with it?

If I do my job well, there shouldn't be a lot of blood. When there is blood, I dispose of it the same way other dentists dispose of it.

Have you ever attacked a patient for their blood?

Absolutely not.

Never been tempted? Never wanted a taste?

Never.

We're trying to determine where the vampires have been getting their blood. I'm sure you understand. If you're not getting blood from your patients, where are you getting it?

(Silence.)

Where do you get your blood from, Doctor Endecott?

My husband.

Excuse me?

(Louder.) My husband.

You take blood from your husband?

47

(Sighs.) Yes.

Why?

Because he wants me to. Because he loves me.

Do you bite your husband?

Yes.

Why?

Because he likes it. (Silence.) It's consensual. I'm not doing anything to him he doesn't want me to. I love him.

If we asked your husband if the biting and the blood-letting were consensual, he would corroborate your story?

Yes.

(Pen scratching on paper.) Have you ever hurt anyone to get the blood you need to survive, Doctor Endecott?

No.

Not ever? You've been a vampire for how long?

Since 1967.

And since then you've never hurt anyone, bitten anyone, killed anyone, accidentally or not, to get the blood you need?

No.

You can be honest, Doctor Endecott. The crimes you committed years ago are long past...

I have the right to an attorney.

You're not being charged with anything, Doctor Endecott. You haven't been arrested. We're simply asking a few questions.

You're trying to get me to admit to crimes I didn't commit. I'm a dentist. I want to help people. I have never hurt anyone.

But you bite your husband for his blood.

I have nothing further to say.

Are you refusing to answer our questions?

I have nothing further to say until I have legal representation.

(Shuffling papers.) You may leave, Doctor Endecott.

CHAPTER 5

I have heard how others here have received letters from home with lines inked or removed with scissors the old-fashioned way. These very words may be removed. Yet it was such a relief to see your handwriting, to wallow in your sweet scent, to know for myself, in your own words, that you are thinking of me as I think of you. I look at the barracks and I think of our old-time wooden home and I think of you in it. I look at the others, some of whom are families who are the same and were able to stay together, and I wish we were the same and allowed to stay together. I look at the mountains and I think of the barriers between us. The new picture of Grace is priceless. I didn't know whether to laugh or moan—she has grown and I have missed so much. I have it taped to my wall, along with the one of you and Grace I brought with me. Send more pictures, both of Grace and yourself, as many as you can. I cannot have enough of them. I talk to you in the lonely nighttime hours, and seeing your face comforts me.

Being here is like being in a warp, trapped in a time that is both then and now. When I turn this way I see the pale-skinned men and women who only come out at night. When I turn there I am in Manzanar again. The camp now is virtually the same as the camp then. Manzanar means "apple orchard" in Spanish, and it was built in a former farming community left desert-dry when the water was rerouted to Los Angeles two hundred miles *away. Manzanar itself covered five hundred and forty acres, surrounded by a barbed wire fence and eight watchtowers. There were sixty-seven blocks, thirty-six residential blocks consisting of twenty-foot by one-hundred-foot barracks constructed of wood frame, board, and tarpaper. There were two staff housing blocks, an administrative block, two warehouse blocks, a garage block, and military police. Within the thirty-six residential blocks were a mess hall, a recreation hall, communal bathhouses, a laundry room, an ironing room, and a heating oil storage tank. The hospital in Manzanar became the largest in the country, and there was a Bank of America branch and a Sears Roebuck catalog store. Churches, shops, canteens, beauty parlors, barber shops, and a photography studio were all located on the grounds.*

But why, I asked myself? Why did the Japanese-Americans have to recreate their lives in Manzanar? Because Pearl Harbor was an external excuse for an internal prejudice many held against Asian people, a hatred that festered for generations. In the early nineteenth century, Chinese immigrants to the United States contributed their muscle power to building transportation systems, mainly the thankless, backbreaking work of laying railroad tracks. Japanese immigrants arrived on American shores around the same time. Japanese men worked as agricultural laborers in California, and Japanese women came as "picture brides" to marry men they had never met in person. When the Asian groups grew large enough for notice, they grew large enough to be feared.

"They're taking American jobs," some said.

"They're taking honest American wages from honest Americans."

Yet who among the honest Americans were looking to work for subsistence wages doing muscle-tearing, bone-wearying, heavy-laden work, digging, and digging, and digging, bent over all the daylight hours, hoeing, sowing, weeding, and watering?

By 1907, discrimination against the Japanese led to calls restricting the "Yellow Peril," as some called it. By 1913, the Alien Land Law prevented Asian Americans from owning the land they worked. They became aliens ineligible for citizenship—a special status applied only to Chinese and Japanese immigrants. Groups against Japanese farm workers sprang up throughout California. The seeds of prejudice against Japanese Americans were already long-planted and well-fermented. It is a fertile ground, bigotry, where weeds and thorns grow aplenty.

Who is Other? Who is Us? Who are They? What right, some ask, do They have to infringe on our rights? Who are They to take our jobs? Our neighborhoods? Our businesses? Everything wrong in human nature stems from Fear. Fear of the unknown. Fear of consequences. Fear of unfairness. Fear of They. Fear of what They might do to Us.

In Salem in 1692, They were anyone accused of witchcraft. In the 1830s, and throughout the nineteenth century, They were the Native Americans. In Germany and throughout Europe, They were the Jews. In 1941, after Pearl Harbor was bombed, They became Japanese-Americans. Japan was the despised enemy, but Japanese Americans were the target. Who leaped directing anger onto those in Japan who masterminded the attack to law-abiding citizens of Japanese descent? Perhaps they were born in this country, some said, but They looked like the enemy. "They all look alike" is a pejorative phrase so common it's trite. And since They looked like the enemy, They must think like the enemy, act like the enemy, and believe everything the enemy believes.

Days after the bombing of Pearl Harbor, newspaper headlines made Japanese-Americans out to be the most untrustworthy creatures ever to step foot in America. First, They were accused of spying on behalf of Japan in Hawaii. Then Their sabotage spread to the mainland U.S.A. Everyone accepted gossip as gospel and rumors as truth.

Two weeks after Pearl Harbor I sat alone in my apartment. It was cave-dark, lights off, curtains drawn, windows closed. In those years, you had been gone generations by then, I had grown used to being alone. The ache of missing you was always within me, as it pains me now knowing you are too far to take into my arms, but over time I developed a numbness that didn't wane until the night I saw you outside our house again. After Pearl Harbor was bombed I felt my aloneness acutely because whenever I heard of anyone suffering from madness I grew troubled and restless. I turned the dial on the radio, hoping to find a news program with something positive to say, something hopeful I could hold onto, someone saying this prejudice against Japanese-Americans wouldn't evolve into foolishness after all. But all I found were more false accusations, more finger-pointing, and more name-calling.

Already some wanted the forced evacuation of the Japanese-Americans along the West Coast because of the proximity to the Pacific Ocean, and, by connection, Japan. According to the learned-sounding man on the radio, "Those evacuated would be the Japanese living along the Pacific Coast in states like California, Oregon, and Washington. It's for their protection. There's a lot of anger towards the Japanese right now, and people become violent when they're angry. In addition to an angry public, the Attorney General in California claims Japanese-Americans have infiltrated every strategic spot in the state."

"There are some reports that the Attorney General was incorrect in his assertion," said another voice. "There's no proof that any Japanese-American citizen..."

"Do you think the Attorney General would lie?"

I turned off the radio and turned on the phonograph instead. I pulled out the heavy vinyl recording of Vivaldi's "Four Seasons" and listened to the soothing seventeenth-century music because, when the melody played, I was transported to the days when we were together before the hysteria in Salem. I opened the door and looked out into the gray winter night. No one was there, and I felt my solitude like a slap in the face. I grabbed my newspaper from the lawn and sat at my Formica table. I scanned the headlines and wished I had left the paper outside. On the floor of the House of Representatives, Congressman John Rankin shouted, "I say it is of vital importance that we get rid of every Japanese...Damn them! Let us get rid of them now!" I crumpled the paper and tossed it into the bin outside my door because I didn't want the words in my home. I thought of Keiko, who hadn't been in class that night, and I hoped she was well. I looked at the black Ericsson telephone with the rotary dial on my kitchen counter and I wondered if I should call her. Already news of violent acts against Japanese-Americans was surfacing, and I looked through my briefcase and found the class list with my students' phone numbers. Then I realized it might seem odd to the family, a random call from a random professor, and I put the list away and shut my briefcase. I could have told them the truth, I thought. I could have told them how I had seen it all before, and I worried for them.

Two nights later, the night of the final exam and our last class of the term, I called Keiko's number and asked if she would like me to walk her to class. She gratefully agreed. She met me on the sidewalk outside her building —I don't think she told her family I would be escorting her—and we walked in silence toward UCLA. As we drew closer to campus we passed a newspaper stand, and there flashed the beginning traces of the anti-Japanese propaganda, sweeping aside rhyme and reason, leaving ugly-faced hatred behind. I saw the headline of the San Francisco Examiner *proclaiming, "Ouster of all Japs in California near!" We passed posters pinned onto lamp posts that showed a grotesque caricature called Tokio Kid with a monster face, pointy ears, over-wide smile, and fang-like teeth, more like a vampire than I have ever looked. The poster read* Tokio Kid say "Much waste of material make sooo happy! Thank you." *Throughout the city were caricatures of Japanese men holding bloodied knives to frightened Caucasian women's necks.* "Keep this horror from your home! Invest 10 percent in war bonds!" *the posters proclaimed.*

"We're at war now," Keiko said as we stepped past the traffic lights on Westwood Boulevard toward campus.

"Pearl Harbor means neutrality is no longer possible for the United States," I said. "Now we're in the war alongside our Allies against Japan."

"Against Germany too," Keiko said. "Have you seen the newsreels about what's happening there?"

I thought of Beth and Samuel, Miriam's descendants in Germany, Olivia's cousins, and without having been to the moving pictures I knew all too well what was happening there. As we neared our classroom I hoped Keiko hadn't noticed the propaganda. While we walked she kept her eyes straight ahead, not right or left, up or down. She stared at the horizon, toward campus and our classroom where she would be safe, where her life would have some normalcy, at least for two hours.

I insisted on accompanying Keiko home after the exam. I quizzed her on the way, trying to gauge her take on the test, and she knew everything about Hamlet, Othello, *and* Richard III.

"Sounds like you did well," I said.

"I hope so. I studied enough." She smiled for the first time that night. Then her face fell flat. "They're selling war bonds," she said.

"Yes," I answered.

"Those posters...they're from the government, aren't they?"

It was my turn to look away. I didn't want to admit that the propaganda was indeed from the government, meant to dehumanize, antagonize, and create fear of the Japanese nation, and, by proximity, Japanese-Americans. The government sold war bonds to support the war effort, but it also created a sense of unity among Americans. This war is right. This war is just. We must stop these vampire animals from their desire to overtake the world. Japanese-Americans were portrayed as wickedness personified—a sinister threat to everything good about the American way of life. Americans were encouraged to work harder, avoid absenteeism at work, recycle scrap to support the war effort, grow victory gardens, and buy war bonds. Keiko waited for a response, but I could only shrug.

Passing houses on her block, I noticed the ordinary-looking woman before Keiko did. The woman was standing before a square, one-story stucco house with a white-fenced porch like you see everywhere in Los Angeles. She looked like someone's middle-aged mother—white-frilled apron and starched gray shirtdress, her short, curled hair framing her rigid face. Her lips were two flat lines, and her hard eyes latched onto Keiko as we passed. Her long finger pointed toward the sign nailed to her roof: "Japs keep out—you are not wanted here."

Then she pointed to another sign across the street: "This is a white man's neighborhood."

Keiko disappeared into her building without another word.

CHAPTER 6

Sarah pushed Grace in her stroller along Derby Wharf toward the Salem Maritime National Historic Site, enjoying the late afternoon summer sunshine, allowing herself to be comforted by the sound of the soothing laps against the rocky shore. Even after nearly two years back in Massachusetts, the sea in the bay never grew old for her. Children ran along the shoreline, splashing in the gray-blue calm, waving at their mothers, laughing at each other. Sarah smiled at them, then at Grace, who was fascinated by the other children, watching them as though they were floating fairies or horned unicorns, as though she didn't know what they were but they were magical anyway.

"Am I keeping you too isolated?" Sarah asked her daughter. "You don't see other children now since Steve's taken Billy to Canada to be with his family. Maybe I should look into putting you into another school. Or maybe we should go to California to wait for Daddy. I didn't like California much when I lived there before, but that was before I found Daddy again." Sarah stared into the distance where the Atlantic Ocean swelled. "But I love Massachusetts. This place has so much meaning for your father and me."

Sarah watched the white Salem Ferry as it sailed past, one of many boats cruising on this perfect day.

"Maybe we should go for a ride on the boat tomorrow. You'd like that, Grace, wouldn't you?"

Grace smiled, and Sarah stopped walking to stroke her daughter's gold hair from her flowery topaz eyes. "You look so much like your father. You got your thick gold hair and your jewel-blue eyes from him. Your father's eyes used to look like yours. And that is definitely your father's smile." Sarah sighed. "He'll be home soon." Her voice was barely audible over the boats zipping through the harbor. She pushed the stroller toward Derby Street. "Should we go to the Witches Lair to see Olivia?"

Sarah stopped at her favorite candy store, one of the oldest shops in Salem, and bought some saltwater taffy for herself and a cherry-flavored lollipop for Grace. As they walked toward Pickering Wharf Sarah saw Howard headed in their direction. He was leaving the bank, sliding an envelope into his pocket, and he stopped walking when he saw her, as though the candy shop was the last place in the world she should be.

"Sarah?" he said.

"You look like you're intent on something," Sarah said. "Is everything all right?"

Howard looked into the window of the candy shop. "I got a letter from Timothy today. I think he's depressed again. He wasn't all that happy before this happened, and now..."

"James is keeping an eye on him," Sarah said.

"I'm glad James and Timothy went to the same camp."

"When did you get your letter?"

"This morning. Have you heard from James yet?"

"Two letters so far. Paper and pen letters. Reminds me of the days when people used to take the time to handwrite notes to each other. I've written him one letter so far, and I'm sending another this afternoon."

"Which way were you headed?" Howard asked.

"I was on my way to the Witches Lair. I thought maybe Olivia could use some help this afternoon. It's the busy tourist season."

"Is she still living with you?"

Sarah nodded. "I've been blessed with the friends I have here. Olivia, Jennifer…"

"Me."

Sarah laughed. "Yes, Howard. You too." She looked at the darkening sky as the sun dropped in the west, painting the sky fluorescent pink and gold. The seagulls settled, the traffic cleared, visitors left for the trains, and there was that Massachusetts calm she loved. "I used to love this time of day," Sarah said as she watched the tourists leave the House of the Seven Gables. "The sun dropping away means it will be dark soon, and when it's dark…"

"You would see James like I would see Timothy."

Sarah nodded. "Now it gets dark and I remember it's still light where James is in California, and he won't be awake for another three hours." Howard still looked distracted, and she had a feeling he needed to be somewhere else.

"It's nice seeing you, Howard."

"I'll come by soon, Sarah."

As Sarah pushed Grace toward Congress Street she wondered if she should go to California after all. She wanted to be closer to James, as close as she could be, as close as James was to her when she was the one who was imprisoned and he was free. James sat outside the Boston jail for days trying to find someone to help them. What was she doing to help him, she wondered. She was taking care of his daughter, keeping his home ready for his return, and keeping herself strong, which she knew was the most important thing to him, but what was she doing to get him free? She hired an attorney willing to fight for James, Timothy, Jocelyn, Chandresh, and Geoffrey pro bono because he believed so strongly in their case. Could she be of more use in California? Sarah didn't know what to do. On the one hand she wanted to stay home, she needed to be home, but if it would help James to be closer to him, then she would go.

Sarah stopped on the deck of Pickering Wharf among the gray-blue buildings with the white trim. She sat on a bench across from the coffee shop, rocking a sleeping Grace in her stroller, sipping her iced coffee, admiring the cobalt-blue sea reflecting the cobalt-blue sky, and casting glances toward the Witches Lair. She pushed Grace's stroller toward Derby Street and watched the summer tourists with their cell phone cameras pointed everywhere, at the harbor, at the shops of Pickering Wharf, at the Derby House, at the Custom House, at the West India Goods store, and she remembered when these sights were new to her and she marveled at everything old in Salem. After Grace awoke, she meandered through Pickering Wharf back to the Witches Lair. She opened the door and the tinkling bells rang, bringing Olivia out from behind the counter. Olivia kissed Grace's cheek, and Grace laughed at Olivia's coin earrings as they clanged in gypsy music.

"Hello, ladies. Out for a walk this beautiful summer day?"

"We went to Derby Wharf," Sarah said. "I thought Grace and I might go on the Ferry tomorrow."

"I'd love to come," Olivia said. "I haven't been on the Ferry for years. Let me get things settled at the shop tomorrow morning, and we can go around noon."

"Sounds like a plan," Sarah said.

Olivia laughed at Grace's candy-red lips. "I see you stopped for candy."

"I can't resist their saltwater taffy. I ran into Howard there."

"How is he doing?"

"He thinks Timothy is depressed again, even more now than before."

"I'm sure James is looking out for Timothy."

"That's what I told him. But Olivia?"

"Yes, dear?"

"Who's looking out for James?"

Olivia hugged Sarah with the motherly compassion Sarah loved her for. "James has always been self-sufficient, Sarah. You know that. He has his stoic way of charging through whatever obstacles end up in his way. Whatever the problem, whatever the issue, James looks at it with his level-headedness, he figures out what needs to be done, and he does it."

"But he pretends things don't bother him when they do. James feels things deeply. He always has. He doesn't wear his emotions where anyone can see, and he tries to keep his real feelings to himself, even from me sometimes." Sarah smiled. "I can usually figure out when he's hiding something from me, though. I know him so well."

"I wouldn't worry about him. James has the strength to get through this the way he's had the strength to deal with everything he's had to handle in his lifetime."

Sarah began to speak but stopped herself until she had the words straight in her mind. "I was wondering if you could do another psychic reading," she said. "You haven't tried since Maine after the accident. Could you try again?"

"But why, dear?"

"I want to know what you can see. Even if it's hard. Even if it's painful. When you did the reading when I first moved to Salem you knew James would find me even if you didn't realize it was James at the time. What can you tell me now, Olivia? I want to know."

"All right. But Sarah?"

"Yes?"

"You need to be prepared for whatever I say. Remember, I go into a trance when I'm connected to the spirit world, and sometimes I start speaking in tongues. Like with the first reading, I'm not able to edit what I say so I'll say whatever I see. I need you to understand."

"I want to hear it, whatever it is."

"All right," Olivia said.

Sarah looked out the window and sighed.

"What are you thinking?" Olivia asked.

"I'm remembering my life with James in the seventeenth century. I loved cooking dinner in the cauldron while he was out working with his father on their importing business. And the dusk. I had forgotten that."

"Forgot what?"

"I loved dusk then too because when the sun dropped that meant

James would return from his father's. I guess dusk has always been my favorite time of day."

"It is beautiful when the sun drops, especially along the shore."

"Are you really such a powerful witch?" Sarah asked.

Olivia laughed. "Where did that come from? I've told you, I do my best, that's all."

"Why do people think you're so powerful?"

"I've cast a few spells other witches have attempted and failed. Since I was able to make the magic happen, other witches see me as more powerful."

"What kinds of spells?"

"Some weather spells. I've brought about rain once or twice, and I've helped people when they were ill."

"That sounds powerful to me," Sarah said.

"You're powerful too, Sarah. You just don't know it yet."

Sarah slid her hand over the books on the bookshelf.

"That's where we first met," Olivia said.

"I was looking through a book about dream interpretation."

"And what dreams they were."

"I want to work here," Sarah said. "I need something to do during the day. I need something to focus on. Jennifer said I could go back to the library, but I don't want to commit to the shifts right now. I thought if I worked here I could bring Grace and help you at the same time. It's the least I can do since you've done so much for us."

Olivia looked toward the storeroom as she considered. "The truth is I could use the help since Belinda left." Olivia extended her hand. "Congratulations, dear, you're hired. Welcome to the Witches Lair."

"Thank you," Sarah said. It was a quiet afternoon in the shop with only two customers roaming the aisles browsing around the meditation aids and tarot cards. "What would you like me to do?"

Olivia pointed to the stool behind the counter. "Sit. You can keep me company."

"This isn't what I had in mind," Sarah said.

"All in good time. I'm expecting a new shipment tomorrow that will need to be categorized, organized, and shelved. For now, sit."

One of the customers, a young mother carrying her toddler in her arms, asked for Olivia's help with the prices of the beaded bracelets. As Sarah studied the crystals and silver crosses set out in baskets near the register, she thought she heard her name. Olivia was still helping the young mother, so Olivia hadn't spoken to her. She looked at Grace, but it wasn't Grace's baby voice she heard. Besides, Grace wouldn't call her by name. I must have imagined it, Sarah thought. When she saw a shadow, she turned but there was no one there.

Olivia rang up the purchase, dropped the bracelets into a plastic Witches Lair bag, and handed it to the young mother. When the woman and her toddler left, Olivia asked, "What is it, Sarah? You look like you've seen a ghost."

"I think I have. I heard my name, and I thought I saw someone in the shadows, but it must have been the flickers from the candlelight."

Olivia stilled her breath and closed her eyes as she became stone-like behind the cash register. When she opened her eyes, she looked around, the store empty of customers, and watched the shadows on the wall.

"What is it?" Sarah asked.

"Do you feel that?" Olivia looked at the door as though she expected someone to walk in. "There's a presence here."

"What is it?"

Olivia closed her eyes again, listening. "I don't know. I can't get a feel for it."

"It knew my name." Sarah checked behind the bookcase and the display cases, hoping to see someone she knew and trying not to be afraid.

"I don't feel it any longer, so it must be gone," Olivia said.

"What do we do now?"

"We wait to see if it comes back. I wouldn't worry, Sarah. I didn't feel anything angry, like it meant you harm."

Sarah nodded even if she wasn't convinced. She looked at Grace, who was still fascinated by the store, pointing and babbling at the shiny beads on the counter. "Aren't those pretty, Grace?" Sarah said. "When you're bigger I'll get you one for yourself. You're too little now and I'm afraid you'll choke on the beads." Grace nodded as though she understood every word.

Olivia turned the sign on the door to closed. "I think it's time to go home," she said. She held the door for Sarah and Grace and locked the shop behind them.

"Do all witches have the ability to feel presences?" Sarah asked.

"I wouldn't say all. It's impossible to classify all witches the way it's impossible to classify any group of people. I happen to have a gift for prophecies, a knack for casting certain spells, and I'm more sensitive to the presence of spirits than others."

"Do you consider yourself Wiccan or a witch? I'm never sure what to call you."

"Wicca is simply an older name for witchcraft. The problem is that witchcraft has been called so many different things over the years and no one is sure what it means. What do you think when I say the word witchcraft?"

"To me witchcraft means magic," Sarah said. "Which both you and Jennifer have."

"Yes, we do. But we don't want that going around any more than James wanted people to know he was a vampire because he was afraid of what people…" Olivia let her words trail away. "I'm sorry, Sarah. I wasn't thinking."

"It's all right, Olivia. James was right. It would be the Salem Witch Trials all over again if people discovered your magic. People would assume all witches are evil the way they're assuming all vampires are evil."

"For some people, magic is synonymous with Satanism. Yet most witches don't believe in Satan. We certainly don't work for Satan."

"During the Salem Witch Trials people believed the witches got their magic from Satan."

"My magic is all my own. I inherited it from my ancestor Miriam."

"Is all magic hereditary?" Sarah asked.

"Magic can be hereditary, as it is for Jennifer and me, though others learn to wield spells over time. Others try but never catch on. You don't need magic to become a witch."

"How does someone become a witch?"

"There's an initiation process."

"How do you know if they're going to be good witches or bad witches?"

Olivia laughed. "This isn't *The Wizard of Oz*, Sarah. We don't believe in good or evil. We believe some forces must be balanced. There's no one truth, though people like to tell themselves there are absolute truths because it helps them feel better. By thinking of life as having irrefutable answers, we think we can understand things that are beyond our understanding."

"But you're so wise," Sarah said. "I thought you knew everything."

"If I have any wisdom at all it's that I'm at peace knowing I don't know everything. I don't need to understand every mystery in the universe. I want to marvel at every miracle I experience around me every day."

They stepped onto the lawn in front of the old wooden house with the two gables on the roof and the green front door. Every time Sarah saw the house again, even if she were only gone for an hour, it called to her, welcomed her, and she felt there was nowhere else in the world for her to be. Olivia unlocked the door and held it open while Sarah pushed Grace's stroller inside. As Olivia put her handbag on James' desk, she saw his letter there.

"Is that another letter from James?" Sarah nodded while Olivia glanced over the paper. "Nothing was blacked out this time."

"They must have decided they don't need to censor information about James' account of World War II. I'm pretty sure there are no secret messages there."

Olivia held the letter up to the lamp near James' desk but saw nothing unusual. "Are you still thinking about secret messages?"

"I keep thinking of the dreams I used to have," Sarah said. "This morning I pulled out my old journals, the ones I used to document my nightmares. Those dreams were messages to me even if I didn't realize it at the time. I keep hoping there's something more to James' letters the way there was something more to my dreams. Some deeper meaning." Sarah shrugged. "I know I'm being silly. Thinking

James is up to something helps me think he'll be home soon. But James is so logical and straightforward. It's not like him to be tricky."

"I wouldn't be so sure." Olivia bent over the stroller, lifted Grace into her arms, and kissed the top of the baby's golden curls.

"If there's any good that came from this, James is being less secretive," Sarah said. "He's telling me about what happened to the Japanese-Americans after Pearl Harbor. When he was here it was like pulling teeth to get him to tell me about his past. Now he's three thousand miles away and he's telling me all kinds of stories."

Sarah took Grace from Olivia's arms and held her daughter up, tickling the baby until she laughed. Sarah brought Grace to the television, it was time for her favorite children's puppet show, and they sat on the floor and watched together until Sarah turned to Olivia.

"What did you mean?" Sarah asked.

"About what?" Olivia was in the kitchen rummaging through the refrigerator. "What do you want to eat?"

"We can warm up the leftover pizza," Sarah said. "What did you mean about not being so sure James wasn't up to something?"

Olivia pulled the pizza from the refrigerator, placed it on a pizza stone, and slid it into the warmed oven. "James can be sneaky, Sarah. What about the stunt he pulled when he went into the sun to fool that reporter who started this whole mess?"

"The plan to expose him to as little sun as possible was mine."

"Yes, but the idea of going into the sun in the first place was his. He was a vampire willing to go into the daylight at noon to make a point with that pesky little man. What about how James uses fake IDs, birth certificates, and diplomas? That's being sneaky."

"But he needed to stay hidden."

"He hid the fact he was a vampire from you for some time."

Sarah nodded. "Yes, there's that."

"And there have been other times when James has had an idea or two to get himself or someone else out of a scrape."

"Tell me," Sarah said. "I want you to tell me about James." Olivia nodded, and Sarah hugged Grace close. "Olivia is going to tell us a story." Grace watched Olivia as closely as Sarah did, her jewel-blue eyes wide.

Olivia pulled the warmed pizza from the oven and set the slices on plates, which she put on the table in front of Sarah and Grace. Sarah wasn't interested in the pizza. She only cared about what Olivia had to say. Olivia sat at the table and leaned forward as though she were telling a secret of great importance.

"After Miriam helped James learn what it meant to be a vampire, he felt indebted to her, to her children, and to her children's children through the generations. For all his wanderings over the years, he never lost touch with my family. Every generation has known James from 1693 until now. In my family, the immortal James Wentworth is a legend, a fairy tale that's true. When we're children, we learn about the beautiful blond man who saved our ancestor Miriam from certain death at the hands of willful, drunken men. We learn how he lives on, and on, and how he visits each generation in their turn. And then, when he does arrive to say *Hello, how are you, can I help you? Miriam said I would be here for her future generations, as she said you would be here for me* we're amazed that he's real. He exists, and he is even more beautiful in person than we ever imagined. The first time I saw James I was ten years old. He hadn't visited my family in over twenty years, since my mother was a little girl, and I was in awe of him. I was amazed by the stories I heard from my mother about how he helped her family during the Great Depression."

"I remember you and Jennifer telling me that James helped your family during the Depression and World War II," Sarah said.

"That's right. When he visited my mother's family in 1933, my mother was eight years old. F.D.R. was President, and America was in the midst of a long and severe economic depression. By 1933, eleven thousand of the twenty-five thousand banks were insolvent, and since so many people lost so much money, Americans lost confidence and reduced their spending, which reduced production, creating an unending circle of scarcity. Sound familiar?"

Sarah nodded. "The more things change, the more they stay the same."

"Precisely. Before the Depression, my grandfather had a thriving restaurant here in Salem. It wasn't anything fancy, but it served hearty German comfort food, recipes from his grandmother. He made the best chicken soup you ever tasted, and he was so proud his restaurant was kosher. Then my grandfather lost his savings when the stock market crashed in 1929, and as the economy worsened people had less money to spend on eating out. Finally, in 1932, my grandparents had to close the restaurant, and there was no work to find anywhere. About thirty percent of the American workforce was unemployed then. By 1933, her family was destitute. They had barely enough to get by. And then one night the white-skinned blond man appeared. He was so pale my mother thought he was translucent, like an apparition. But he was no evil spirit. He explained who he was, and my mother reached her hand out to touch him to see if he was really there or was she dreaming. Remember, she was only eight at the time. James jerked away, he was used to avoiding human contact, but then he realized my mother didn't mean any harm. He held his hand out, and she touched his skin, and she laughed when she felt his coldness. She wasn't afraid. She sensed in her child-like way that this tall blond man was no one to fear. When he realized how destitute they were he was mortified. He was living in Italy at the time, in Florence teaching at the university there, and while the European economy suffered when the United States economy suffered, he was largely buffered from the reality of the Depression. He lost some money in the stock market, he told my grandparents, but he learned from his father, John, an astute businessman, not to put all your eggs in one basket, so his portfolio was diversified and invested in places other than the stock market. When James learned how my mother's family suffered, he paid off my grandparents' debts, he paid their rent for six months, he bought them groceries. When my grandfather protested, afraid he would never be able to pay James back, James insisted it was a gift for Miriam's descendants.

"*She gave me a gift when I needed it most,* James said. *She helped me learn to live with myself when I thought I was too dead to live anymore. She gave me hope that one day I would return, and that has given me strength throughout the years. The least I can do is help her future generations, as her prophecy said I would.*

"But my grandfather was a proud man. He didn't want to take more than he could give, and he could give nothing then. Finally, after James had been back in Salem for about a month, my grandfather put his foot down and said no more charity even though my grandparents still weren't able to find work, no matter how hard they tried. Factories were producing less, restaurants were closing, and even work like cooking or sewing for other families was hard to come by since everyone was making do with less. James found a way to work around my grandfather's reluctance to accept more money by finding him a job as a janitor at Harvard. It wasn't the most glamorous job, but it was the first time in three years my grandfather was paid a living wage."

"There's nothing sneaky about that," Sarah said. "James knew people at Harvard. He got his PhD there, and he taught there in the 1920s."

"James thought putting a good word in for my grandfather would help him get the job, but there was something like one hundred candidates for three positions. My grandfather had no janitorial experience so he was passed over. Then James worked his magic."

"His good word helped?"

"He snuck into the office of the man doing the hiring and added my grandfather's name to the hired list. Four men were given positions instead of three. My grandfather couldn't believe it when they called to tell him he had to report to work at seven a.m. the next morning." Olivia smiled. "Is that sneaky enough for you?"

"Are you trying to tell me not to trust my husband?" Sarah asked.

"James will do whatever he thinks he needs to do to accomplish his goal."

"What did he do for your family during World War II?"

Olivia grimaced. "We'll have that story next time, dear."

"Olivia…"

Olivia threw her hands into the air in acquiescence. "I had cousins who were trapped in Germany during the war. They had been rounded up and herded into Bergen-Belsen, which was a holding camp. They were waiting to be shipped off to Dachau, the forced labor camp where they would be separated men from women, boys from mothers, daughters from fathers, and sent to work to their deaths. But then orders came through which said my cousins, Beth and Samuel Baum, their three children, and five of their friends were to be sent with Officer Kluge Jaeger to Buchenwald instead. While others boarded the train for Dachau, my cousins were left behind at Bergen-Belsen until Officer Jaeger led them away."

Sarah's hand went to her heart. "Led them away to where?"

"To here, dear. The United States."

"Why would Officer Jaeger lead them here?"

"Because Officer Jaeger was James."

Sarah felt the room spin beneath her as if she were Dorothy caught in the tornado-filled Kansas sky. Finally, she asked, "James was an SS officer?"

"Of course not, Sarah. He only pretended to be. Once he was in Germany he got his hands on an earth-gray officer's uniform as well as identification naming him a generalleutnant, the two-star rank of a division commander. I'll never forget the pained look on James' face when he described how sickened he felt putting the uniform on. He spit on the Nazi insignia on his arm. He nearly backed out of his plan, but he kept thinking of Beth and Samuel. He was very brave, Sarah. Who knows what could have happened if something went wrong?"

"Who knows?" Sarah repeated, her head still whirling in the storm.

"Since they believed James was a ranking officer, they didn't question his orders. He looked the part, he had the uniform and his orders seemed legitimate. He was blond, tall, broad-shouldered, strong. If others asked what was special about these ten, why were they being sent somewhere else, James answered *We have other plans for them.* As James boarded his group onto an SS bus, he barked at them, sneered at them, and pointed his Bergmann MP 18 submachine gun at their faces. James nodded at the driver, an SS infantryman he paid off with a handsome sum, and they were soon past the Bergen-Belsen gate. When they were safely away, he explained who he was and why he was there. He showed them his unloaded machine gun. Beth, Samuel, their three children, and their five friends grasped James' hands and wept over him, this pale-cold angel man who was saving their lives.

"*Dry your eyes,* James said. *We still have three more checkpoints to pass through before I can smuggle you onto the train that's going to take us to the boat that's going to take us to America. And we need to do it all in the dark.*

"They thought James meant it would be easier to smuggle them in the shadows. They didn't ask why he was so pale and cold to the touch. They didn't care. He was there for them, and he was a gift from God as far as they were concerned. Angels from heaven are white, aren't they, they asked. But James didn't feel much like an angel. He felt like he failed, Sarah. He kept thinking of the many others he left behind, and he had to fight the urge to go back for them. He wanted to be an undead Harriet Tubman, leading people from inhumanity into the Promised Land."

"How did they get through the checkpoints?" Sarah asked.

"Ten was a small enough group that they didn't draw attention to themselves. If anything had gone wrong..." Olivia couldn't finish the thought. "Whenever they passed another checkpoint, James small-talked the guards, dropping juicy tidbits of gossip about other officers he picked up along the way, distracting the guard examining his orders. He didn't want anyone looking too closely. He didn't want anyone calling to check. Kluge Jaeger means Clever Hunter in German, and James didn't want anyone to know what a clever hunter he was."

"James speaks German?"

"Also French and Italian and he learned Japanese while he was in Manzanar, I believe."

Sarah sighed. "Why do you know my husband speaks five languages and I don't?"

"You know James, Sarah. He's so modest about himself. And he's been alive a long time. He needed something to fill those long night hours. In this case, he spent some hours helping my relatives escape a concentration camp."

"Where did James get the documentation from?"

"All he ever said was he knew someone. He got them whatever they needed to immigrate here. He got them visas and passports. Everything had to be in order because the United States government wasn't sympathetic to Jewish refugees even during the crisis."

"How could they turn away people escaping Hitler?" Sarah asked.

"You know how Sarah. In this case, they were afraid of increasing immigration during an economic downturn because there would be more people scrambling for fewer jobs. And xenophobia is nothing new. Anti-Semitism is nothing new. Franklin Roosevelt did nothing to rescue the European Jews until 1944, and even then it was only because he was under pressure from his government and an American Jewish community that wouldn't silently watch the slaughter from afar. When the displaced people arrived from Europe they went to the refugee shelter at Fort Ontario in Oswego, New York, but James managed to get my family past that obstacle as well. My cousins settled in Maine, and then my grandmother's sister Anna moved to Maine to be close to them. You know Anna's family Theresa and Francine Silvers."

"I know them well," Sarah said. She gave a silent blessing to her dear friends, Olivia's cousins, who gave her family shelter from an impending storm.

"My family prospered here," Olivia said. "Thanks to James."

Sarah pushed the plate of cold pizza aside and rested her head on the wooden table. She didn't know whether she wanted to kiss her husband or pinch him somewhere it would hurt.

"How could he keep this from me?" Sarah asked. "He led ten people out of a concentration camp in Nazi Germany and he didn't think that was something I would want to know?"

Grace patted Sarah's hair away from her face and Sarah laughed.

"You're looking at me with your father's eyes," Sarah said. "And you know I can't stay mad at him for long. He has a way of making me see his side of things."

"Don't be mad at him, Sarah. I'm sure he was going to tell you about it. As soon as he's home."

Sarah thought of her beautiful, brave husband and she decided she wanted to kiss him. "Yes," she said. "As soon as he's home."

FOR THE RECORD, please state your full name with your place and date of birth.
Timothy Bryston-Wolfe.
Where and when were you born, Timothy?
I was born in Boston, Massachusetts on August 20, 1994.
What do you do when you're in Boston, Timothy?
I live in Salem. I'm a student.
Where?
Salem State University.
How long have you been this way?
Since I was fourteen.
Is your whole family...like you?
Like me?
Supernatural.
You mean a vampire?
Yes.
My whole family is dead.
(Pen scribbling on paper.) How did they die?
In a car accident. I would have died too, but another vampire turned me. He's here.
Who's here?
The vampire who turned me.
Are you sure?
I'm not positive, but I think so.
Did you ask to be turned?
No. I don't think so. I don't remember much about that night.
Are you afraid of him?
Of who?
The vampire who turned you.
(Pause.) I'm not afraid of him.
Has he turned many people into vampires?

I don't know. He might be the one who turned James.

James?

Wentworth.

Do you know James Wentworth?

James helped take care of me when I was first turned.

Are you glad the vampire turned you into this?

(Pause.) I don't think so.

Why?

Because I'm stuck here answering your stupid questions. I wouldn't be here if he hadn't turned me. I'd be home with my dad studying to become a landscape designer.

Your father? I thought you said your whole family was dead.

My adopted dad, I mean.

Is your adopted dad a vampire too?

(Laughs.) No. He is definitely not a vampire.

He's human?

Okay.

Okay?

Yes, he's human. What else could he be?

I don't know, Timothy. What else could he be?

Nothing. I said he's human, all right?

All right. If he's your adopted father he must know you're a vampire.

He does.

And he doesn't care?

He loves me the way I am, the way I love him the way he is. It's called unconditional love. There are some people, human and vampire, who are capable of loving someone the way they are no matter what they are, even if it's different from themselves.

(Shuffles papers.) If we asked you, could you identify the vampire who turned you?

Why?

It's a simple question, Timothy. Could you identify him?

I'm not sure.

But you said the vampire who turned you was here, and he's the one who turned James Wentworth.

I said I'm not sure it was him. I had just been in a terrible car accident that killed my parents and my little sister. I was dying myself. I
said…

I can play back the recording to see what you said, Timothy.

(Sighs.) I don't know why it matters. What's done is done. It's not
like he can take it back.

Would you ask him to take it back if you could?

If it would stop you from asking me these questions, and if I could
go home, then yes. I would choose to not be a vampire anymore.

CHAPTER 7

*J*ames was used to waking up to the buzzsaw sound of Geoffrey snoring, an ungodly rasping that irritated James to no end. James opened the door, saw the deepening dusk, and went back to bed. He wanted to be alone with his thoughts of Sarah.

The buzzsaw snoring stopped, and Geoffrey knocked on the thin wooden wall between them. "What are you doing over there? You must be awake by now. You're quite the lazy boy lately, James."

James pulled the blanket over his head. "Go away."

"I will not go away. I am like a bunion or a boil. I am here, and the more you ignore me the more painful I become."

"Don't I know it," James muttered.

"What was that?"

"Nothing."

James reached for his jeans and pulled them on, listening to Geoffrey hum a tune on the other side of the partition. James grabbed his green t-shirt and slid it over his head, closing his eyes while he concentrated on the melody, certain he knew it from somewhere.

"What is that?" James asked. Geoffrey stopped humming. "Geoffrey?"

"It's a song."

"I know it's a song. What song?"

"A little ditty from when I was a boy. *We Be Three Poor Mariners* it's called. We were quite the dancers then, the English. In those days we were known on the Continent as the Dancing English."

"I think I've heard that song."

"Like it or not, young man, you're English, and you were born in London."

"We've had this conversation before. Yes, I was born in London, but now I'm American."

"Very well, abandoner of all that is cultured and civilized. But whether or not you're American now, you were English then, and you probably heard the song when you were a boy."

"Sing it," James said.

"Am I singing to the wooden partition or the army cot? Come round where I can see you properly, James. I feel like a hallucinating patient in the psychiatric ward talking to walls and whatnot. And no smart comments from you about whether or not I should be in a psychiatric ward."

James slid the partition aside and sat in Geoffrey's wooden chair.

"So where's my song?"

"Aren't we demanding today?"

Geoffrey stood up straight, pushing and pulling his lips into exaggerated vowels, widening his almond-shaped black eyes as though the sounds would come from there instead of his mouth. Finally, Geoffrey nodded. "All right, here goes."

Geoffrey knelt before James and gestured widely with his arms as he sang:

We be three poor mariners
Newly come from the seas
We spend our lives in jeopardy,
While others live at ease.
Shall we do dance the round,
The round, the round?
And he that is a bully boy,

Come, pledge me on this ground,
This ground, this ground!

Geoffrey stood to his full height, crossed his arms in front of his chest, and danced with gestures that mimicked looking out to sea, pulling up his trousers, tugging on the ropes, and steadying himself against the elements. James laughed at Geoffrey's rhythmic movements.

We care not for those martial men
That do our states disdain.
But we care for those merchantmen
That do our states maintain.
Shall we do dance the round,
The round, the round?
And he that is a bully boy,
Come, pledge me on this ground,
This ground, this ground!

Geoffrey bowed. "Bravo," James said.

"I'm glad you approve, James. They said this was one of King Henry the Eighth's Mirth songs, one of the best-loved dance songs of the day."

James felt the memory of the song so close to the edge of his consciousness, yet he couldn't push it to the surface. It was a painful feeling, like a splinter under the skin—you want to get it out but it's stuck too far inside. He felt the way Sarah looked when he brought her the book of Anne Bradstreet's poems after she arrived in Salem. She had a long tucked away memory stored inside her then too, the memory of "To My Dear and Loving Husband," and it was Martha's past-life regression that helped Sarah remember what it meant. Then James remembered.

"My father used to sing that song to me," he said.

Geoffrey deflated. From bouncing around the room singing and dancing, now he looked confused.

"Did he?" Geoffrey asked.

"He even taught me that same dance, a sailor's hornpipe."

Geoffrey held his hand out to James. "Show us what you can do."

James stepped away. "I can't dance, Geoffrey."

"Of course you can. We're the Dancing English, remember?"

"I'm..."

"Misled by revolutionary rhetoric. You're right. We have had this conversation before. Now dance."

"Geoffrey."

Geoffrey grabbed James' hand and began the same movements he had done during the song, crossing his arms in front of his chest, kicking his legs scissor style, mimicking tugging on ropes, swabbing the deck, and pulling up his pants. James resisted at first, feeling silly, but Geoffrey sang "We Be Three Poor Mariners" again, and James remembered enough to sing along:

We be three poor mariners
Newly come from the seas
We spend our lives in jeopardy,
While others live at ease...

Geoffrey collapsed on the floor, he laughed so much, and James did the same.

"Thank you, Geoffrey. I needed that."

James heard Jocelyn and Chandresh's voices outside and opened the door. When he saw their faces he knew something was wrong. He saw Chandresh, his tall, muscular frame, his strong, manly face twisted in concern. Jocelyn, her long strawberry-blond hair pulled into a ponytail, looked equally worried. They were both dressed casually, in t-shirts and jeans, since camp life didn't require anything else.

"What is it?" James asked.

"It's Timothy," Jocelyn said. "We're worried about him."

"He's listless," Chandresh said. "I don't think he's drinking enough. I tried to bring him to the mess hall tonight, but he wouldn't come. He said he drank too much last night, but I didn't see him there last night either."

"He's upset because he thinks he said too much at his interview," Jocelyn said. "He's afraid he gave the interviewer too much information."

"About what?" James asked.

"He wouldn't say," said Jocelyn.

"Last year he was feeling down because he's getting older and he still looks like he's fourteen," Chandresh said.

Geoffrey appeared outside, nodding toward Chandresh and Jocelyn. "That shouldn't bother him here," Geoffrey said. "Everyone here is stuck in a time warp at whatever age they were when they were turned." He smiled at James. "How old were you when you were turned?"

"You should know. You were there."

"I don't recall requiring identification to see if you were legal. How old were you?"

"Thirty."

"As old as that?"

James shook his head. "Maybe I should talk to Timothy. Jocelyn, when you get to the mess hall, keep a cup aside for him."

"I will, James."

James walked across camp to Timothy's barracks, which the young-looking, dark-haired vampire shared with two others who looked the same age as Timothy on the outside—in their early teenage years—but were in reality much older. James knocked on the door, and when no one answered he let himself inside. In the unlit room he saw Timothy on his bed, his matted hair visible above the thin army blanket. James sat beside Timothy and brushed the dark hair away from the pale face.

"Timothy? Have you had anything to drink tonight?"

Timothy shrugged.

"Timothy, please."

"Leave me alone!"

Timothy flashed away, and James followed him outside. It was a dark night, not much moon, the stars receded into the black void of the desert sky. A human wouldn't have been able to see Timothy hidden behind a nearby barracks, but James spotted him easily. Timothy looked so young, James thought, younger than the fourteen he was the night he was turned. James sat next to Timothy, but Timothy turned away.

79

"Everything will be all right, Timothy."

"Nothing will ever be all right!"

James remembered the time, all those years before, when he saw his father after he was turned. His father tried to comfort him with the same words, and James responded as Timothy had. When you feel like everything you love in this world has slipped through your fingers, you believe nothing will ever be better again. This is the way it is, and this is the way it will always be. James smiled at the memory, but Timothy didn't understand.

"What are you laughing at?"

"I'm not laughing at you, Timothy. I'm remembering when my father told me everything would be all right and I was so sure it wouldn't. But my father was right. Everything fell into place. And everything will fall into place again—for all of us."

"For you maybe."

"For you too."

"No!" Timothy paced the dusty desert lane between the buildings. "It's not the same for me. I'm too young looking."

"Everyone here has the same problem in one way or another. And while you stay the same on the outside, on the inside you learn more every year."

"You don't understand. You're a man. You have a house. You have a job. You have a wife and a baby. I'll never have any of that."

"Why not?"

"Because I look like I'm fourteen! I'll always look like I'm fourteen!" Timothy waved his arms like he was flagging James down. "Who's going to marry someone who looks like a teenager? I'll never be able to work or live by myself. I'll be a kid forever, and I'm done being a kid."

"Timothy..."

"Go away, James. You don't understand. You have Sarah. No one will ever love me the way you and Sarah love each other."

James put a comforting hand on his friend's shoulder. "When we're out of here, you won't need to hide anymore. Remember how you were always talking about wanting people to know the truth? You wanted to tell Kenneth Hempel from the beginning. You got your wish. They know. You can be yourself when this is done."

Timothy wiped a red-blood tear away with the back of his hand. "You were right, James. They didn't understand. They put us here."

"Madness rears its ugly head occasionally, but it always settles down."

"And then what will become of us?"

"We'll go back to our lives."

"And that will be that?"

"I think it will take time, but it will get better."

Timothy sat on the ground, holding his legs close to his chest. "But what will my life be like when I get out of here? Who's going to hire me when I look like I'm fourteen? Besides, I can only work after dark. Who's going to hire me when I can only work after dark?"

"I work after dark," James said.

"You're a professor who teaches night classes. I don't want to be a professor."

"You were taking horticultural classes before we were brought here," James said.

Timothy nodded. "I want to be a landscape designer. When my parents were alive I used to help my mom with her garden. I loved helping her plan where the new plants and flowers would go every year, helping to care for the perennials, choosing which vegetables to grow, deciding on the color scheme."

"You could finish your classes and get your horticultural degree after we're released. And if you're wondering who would hire you, Sarah would. She's been wanting to redo the garden at our house with the flowers and herbs we had in the seventeenth century. When we were married the first time, she used to love to grow things, and she wants to start again."

"Like the garden they have at the House of the Seven Gables?"

"Exactly. She's been talking about finding a landscape artist since she saw Jocelyn's new house last year, but I know she'd rather hire you."

Timothy looked at James for the first time that night, and James saw a flash of hopefulness behind the nocturnal-black eyes.

"Maybe I could make blueprints of the layout while I'm here," Timothy said. He brightened at the thought. "I can plan it now, and we can start planting in the spring. You think we'll be out of here by spring, don't you?"

"I hope so."

"Maybe you could send the plans to Sarah."

"I'm not sure the plans will get through. They've been censoring the letters coming in and out of camp. They might assume it was an escape route or something like that." James looked around the barracks and saw the area was deserted. The others were in the mess hall, he remembered. "Don't forget Jennifer's garden. You know how much she loves roses, and Olivia has a vegetable garden in her back-yard. Once you get our gardens going, I'm sure there will be a lot of people who will hire you. Besides, some people might appreciate having a gardener willing to come at night since most people work during the day."

Timothy nodded, his pale skin glowing iridescent in the night sky.

"Will you come with me to the mess hall?" James asked. "Will you drink something?"

Suddenly, Chandresh, Jocelyn, and Geoffrey came out of the shadows. They hid so quietly even James was startled to see them.

"Ready to hit the mess hall?" Geoffrey asked. "I'm ready for an unfresh pint of blood."

As they walked between the barracks, Timothy tried to flatten his wrinkled blue jeans and his rumpled t-shirt. His dark hair was unkempt, his cheeks hollow and stained pink from his blood tears. He walked behind the others, stealing glances at Geoffrey. While Geoffrey was talking to Chandresh and Jocelyn, Timothy leaned close to James and said, "I made a terrible mistake. I've caused problems for everyone."

James stopped walking, letting the others move further into the distance, not that they noticed, engrossed in their conversation as they were. "Is that why you've been so upset the last few nights?" James asked. Timothy nodded. "What happened?"

"At my interview I said I thought the vampire who turned me is here. I pointed him out to you before. The one living with you now—Geoffrey."

After Geoffrey and the others disappeared into the mess hall, James said, "I remembered what you said, and I've been wondering myself if Geoffrey turned you."

"I thought I recognized him at your wedding, but he didn't seem to know who I was so I thought maybe I was wrong. You said he knew he turned you, and he's been keeping track of you for over three hundred years. He didn't seem to know me from anyone else."

"And you told that to the interviewer?"

"Not all of it. I said I thought the vampire who turned me was here, and that the same vampire turned you too. When the interviewer asked me if I could point out the one who turned me I said I wasn't sure it was him, I just thought so. I don't want to get anyone in trouble, James. I didn't mean to start anything."

Could this be bad news for Geoffrey, James wondered. For any of them? When they interviewed James, the interviewer was more intent on getting a confession that James committed a violent crime for the blood he needed rather than asking about who turned him. James was surprised when he realized he was worried for Geoffrey—annoying, infantile, ridiculous Geoffrey. As much as James hated to admit it, Geoffrey's presence had been a comfort to him in the camp. Geoffrey had become a...what had Geoffrey become? Still a nuisance with his blustery ways, but he made sure James was all right, and he helped to keep James' spirits up. It was as if Geoffrey were trying to make up for the time he left a newly paranormal James to fend for himself.

"I said other things too," Timothy said.

James glanced through the open door into the mess hall and saw Geoffrey, Chandresh, and Jocelyn with their tin cups waiting in the long line for their drinks.

"What other things?" James asked.

"The interviewer asked if I would have the one who turned me take it back if I could."

"Take what back?"

"Being a vampire."

"What did you say?"

"I said yes."

James nodded. He saw Geoffrey watching them through the window, and he said, intending Geoffrey to hear, "I think all of us would rather be human right now." Geoffrey shrugged in James' direction.

"Is it bad, James?" Timothy asked. "I tried to watch what I said, but the guy kept hounding me."

"He's hounding all of us. That's what interrogators do. They hound you until you say something you didn't mean to say, and then they find a way to twist it against you. They're doing it to all of us."

"Did you say anything you shouldn't have?"

"I'm sure I did."

They walked into the large, open space of the mess hall with warmed vats of pig blood on one side and folding tables and chairs scattered around. They grabbed a tin cup from the shelf near the door and joined the line with the others. James watched Geoffrey with a new suspicion, unsure what to make of him now. James decided he would have to unravel the mystery of who turned Timothy another night as the white-skinned, blank-faced attendant ladled some foul-smelling reddish-brown slop into their cups. They took their usual seats at the far end in the corner of the mess hall alongside Geoffrey, Chandresh, and Jocelyn. James glanced at the others at the tables around them.

"What are you thinking, James?" Geoffrey asked.

"I'm thinking they can hear us as well as we can hear them."

"They can," Geoffrey said, gesturing to those drinking around them. "They're already dead too. But they can't." He gestured at the human guards stationed near the doors. The guards' eyes were narrow, scanning the room, taking in every undead at once. Geoffrey shrugged. "They're afraid of us, you know, the way they avoid eye contact and keep their voices quiet when they're speaking to us. They keep a respectful distance, as though they don't know what to expect from us. They're holding those big guns loaded with silver bullets as though their weapons could do some damage to us. What do they think we are, werewolves?"

Timothy held his hand out to cover Geoffrey's mouth. "Don't say anything about werewolves."

"Very well, Theodore," Geoffrey said. "Icksnay on the erewolvesway."

"My name is Timothy."

"I beg your pardon. Of course." Geoffrey turned to James. "What were you going to share, James?"

James shook his head. "Nothing yet. I'm still working through a few ideas."

"Do tell," Geoffrey said. "I've always loved how proactive you are."

James looked again at the others of their kind drinking their stale blood, grimacing at the odor or the taste, whispering amongst each other, not appearing to eavesdrop though how could it be helped when you have a hunter's senses? He heard their conversations easily enough, about the putrid liquid in their cups, the families they missed on the outside, how imposing the mountains look, what have you heard about the court cases fighting for our release, we get no information here, when will we be able to go home?

James nodded. "Soon," he said.

They finished their drinks in silence.

CHAPTER 8

Sarah started her first day at the Witches Lair in the storeroom unpacking boxes and taking inventory. It was easy work, counting items, checking them off the list, recounting, then shelving, but it kept her mind occupied, her hands busy, and she had Grace beside her, which was best of all. She was still reeling from the stories Olivia told her about James. James breaking into Harvard to get Olivia's grandfather a job. James disguised as an SS officer in Nazi Germany to break Olivia's cousins and a few of their friends out of a concentration camp. Sarah pictured him, strong and sure, walking through Bergen-Belsen as though he were supposed to be there, his handsome face impassive, barking orders in German, leading the lucky few away. She was proud of his courage and furious with his brazenness. True, he was…nocturnal. But did that mean he could never be hurt? She realized she didn't know, and given his current circumstances she was afraid for him. He did seem all right in his letters. Sarah's head ached whenever she tried to make sense of it all. What would his bald-faced audacity bring him to now? She shivered whenever she considered the possibilities.

The bells on the shop door jingled and she heard muffled voices.

She turned around and Olivia and Jennifer stood beside her in the storeroom.

"Enjoying your first day?" Jennifer asked.

"I have a nice boss here like I did at the university. How are things at the library?"

"Hectic while we move into the new library building. I wish my strong boyfriend and your strong husband were here." Jennifer brushed a lock of auburn hair from her face, her eyes closed tight. "We could still use you back at the library."

"I don't want to leave Grace now," Sarah said. "Your mom doesn't mind if I bring her here, and I don't think the students or faculty at Salem State University would be too happy if I brought a year-old baby with me to work."

"I know. But I miss seeing you there."

"I miss you too. Last time I saw you I thought you were angry with me."

Olivia nudged her daughter with her elbow, and Jennifer nodded. "I'm sorry, Sarah. I overreacted. I don't know what's wrong with me."

"I think we have the same problem," Sarah said. "I miss James, and you miss Chandresh."

With Grace in her arms, Sarah followed Olivia and Jennifer into the hub of the store. Olivia leaned against the door that opened to the rose-trellised gazebo with the fast-spitting cherub fountain where they held their Wiccan ceremonies. She closed her eyes, her hands clasped before her chest as though in prayer.

"What is she doing?" Sarah whispered.

"She's going into a trance. Has something happened here?"

"Yesterday I heard someone say my name and I thought I saw a shadow, but there was no one there. Your mother said she felt a presence."

"I feel it too."

They watched Olivia, whose eyelids fluttered open and she breathed in deeply. She took another look around the empty aisles of the store, then walked to the front door and turned the open sign closed.

"What is it?" Jennifer asked.

"Not what. Who. But I'm not sure. I'm not able to make contact since it disappears so quickly. I think it's trying to communicate with Sarah. Can you sense anything, Sarah? Do you hear or see anything the way you did yesterday?"

Sarah looked around the shelves and shook her head. She closed her eyes the way Olivia did whenever she fell into a trance, but she didn't feel anything. "Nothing," she said.

"All right," Olivia said. "Maybe we can catch it next time. It still feels friendly to me, Sarah. I don't think it wants any trouble, so I wouldn't worry." Olivia busied herself behind the cash register, handling the afternoon's closing business. "Have you heard from Chandresh yet, Jennifer? Sarah has already received two letters from James."

Sarah held her breath, ready for the showdown. She knew Jennifer wouldn't take well to Olivia's question no matter how innocently it was meant. Sarah wasn't surprised when Jennifer's smile dissipated into a petulant frown.

"I haven't heard from him yet. I'm sure he's busy."

"I'm sure he is, Jennifer."

"What does that mean?"

"It means I'm sure he is," Olivia said. "What do you think it means?"

Jennifer stood tall, her hazel eyes flashing in her mother's direction. "Say it, Mother. I know you're still not happy I'm dating Chandresh."

Olivia slid the cash tray into the register and locked it for the night. "I'm still not sure if your reasons for dating him are the best, that's all. I'm your mother. I'm allowed to worry. It's what mothers do."

"I'm dating Chandresh because I like him."

"And?" Olivia looked expectantly at her daughter.

"And?"

"What about James?"

It was the same question Jennifer had spewed at Sarah, and now it was directed back at Jennifer by her mother. Jennifer flashed a worried look toward Sarah, her eyes thin, her lips narrow. "This isn't a good time, Mother," she said. She turned to the crystals in the basket near the register and organized them from smallest to largest as though they were the most important thing in the world.

"What about James?" Sarah asked.

Olivia swatted the air with her hand. "Jennifer's been in love with him since she was five years old. She's been married twice to tall, blond-haired men, but they never were James enough for her so the marriages didn't work. Now she's dating Chandresh, who's known James since the 1830s, and I hope she's dating him because she likes him for who he is as Chandresh, not because he's a vampire like James or because they've been friends for nearly two hundred years."

Jennifer dropped the crystals and they bounced in dull thuds against the crimson carpeting. She didn't deny her mother's words. She didn't protest. She sat on the ground and scooped the crystals back into the basket, avoiding eye contact with anyone. Finally, she said, "Nothing ever happened between us, Sarah. He always said I was too young for him, but I knew. Even before you returned to Salem I knew he loved you too much to think of anyone else."

Olivia looked from Jennifer to Sarah. "I shouldn't have said anything. There I go running my mouth without thinking again."

Jennifer's hands fluttered by her sides as if she were flapping her wings, struggling to propel herself high into the sky so she could soar far away from the Witches Lair. Sarah tried to lighten the mood.

"Is that why you were married four times, Olivia?"

Olivia laughed. "No, dear. I was merely trying to find a man who wasn't a fool."

Jennifer didn't seem to hear them. She stayed rooted to the ground, her flapping arms not fast enough to whisk her away. She grabbed her bag and unlocked the door.

"You don't need to leave, Jennifer," Sarah said.

"Where are you going, Jennifer?" Olivia asked. "You need to lead the ceremony we're having tonight. We're casting our spells to protect James and the others."

"I can't stay," Jennifer said.

"You're the high priestess of this coven," Olivia said. "You must stay."

"You don't need me. You're the powerful witch here. You always have been. You stepped down as high priestess because you thought you should since I was next in Miriam's line."

"I stepped down because it was time." Olivia looked at the clock behind the register. "It's nearly six o'clock. The others will be here soon."

"I can't do it tonight." Jennifer looked through the window into the late summer twilight, the sun casting a rainbow over the harbor, Pickering Wharf cleared of customers after closing time while a few lingerers ate clam chowder outside Capt's Restaurant.

"Jennifer." Olivia's tone was terse. "You have a responsibility to your coven that doesn't depend on your personal feelings. How you feel right now is irrelevant, quite frankly. We've called everyone together tonight to help James, Chandresh, and the others. There is no reason for you to leave now except for your guilt at not telling Sarah about your feelings for James sooner."

"Don't leave because of me," Sarah said. "I'm not angry with you."

"There, you see? Sarah isn't mad at you, though I don't know why she isn't. You've been a pain in the ass lately, dear, if you don't mind my saying."

Sarah saw a smile break across Jennifer's face, and Jennifer exhaled. "I need to change into my robe," she said.

"It's hanging up in my office," Olivia said.

As Jennifer disappeared into the back of the store, Sarah wheeled Grace in her stroller toward the door. She smiled at Olivia. "I'll see you at home later."

"Where are you going? Stay for the rituals, Sarah."

The door jingled, and four women dressed in white robes entered the shop. Olivia greeted them with a hug and a kiss, then opened the door leading to the patio with the cherub fountain. There was a brown wooden picnic table pressed against the wall, covered with a white linen tablecloth, a silver tea service, porcelain tea cups, and plates of cakes and pastries.

"Please, ladies, help yourselves."

"Are we going to have the Rising Sun of Hope ceremony?" one of the women in white asked. "Or Healing of a Wounded Tree?"

"Rising Sun of Hope? For vampires? And they're not really trees, dear, though they are very strong."

"What about the returning spell?" asked another, older woman in white, her long white-gray hair pulled into an elegant chignon. "If you led the ceremony, Olivia, and we all worked together, maybe we could cast it. Then they wouldn't have to stay locked up anymore. They would be…"

Olivia stopped near the door and shook her head at the woman who was speaking.

"Emma, you know no one has ever cast the returning spell."

"But if anyone can, Olivia…"

Sarah saw fear in Olivia's eyes.

"What is the returning spell?" Sarah asked.

When Emma began to reply, Olivia held up her hand.

"It's a very old spell from a long, long time ago that some witches tried to cast but couldn't. But that doesn't concern us now. Tonight we're here to bring strength to James, Chandresh, and the others."

Sarah followed Olivia into the store and saw ten more ladies in white robes, including Martha, who grabbed Sarah in a tight hug, her flapper-style black bob swinging in the swiftness of her movements. "I didn't know you were going to be here, Sarah. And Grace!" Martha swept Grace from her stroller, and Grace giggled. "How are you, Gracie? Oh, Sarah, she's growing so fast." Martha hugged Grace closer, her southern-style laughter filling the air with glee, and Grace slid her arms around Martha's neck.

"We weren't going to stay," Sarah said. "We don't want to get in the way."

"You're not in the way, Sarah," Martha said. "The ceremony tonight is for James, Timothy, Chandresh, and Jocelyn. You should stay."

"But Grace…"

"Grace is fine. Right, Grace?"

Jennifer joined the others outside, her ornately embroidered medieval-style white robe flowing over the cobblestones, her auburn hair loose around her shoulders. "You should stay, Sarah. Please."

"Yes," Olivia said. "Stay, Sarah."

"I don't have a white robe," Sarah whispered.

"You don't need one," Olivia said. "You have James in your heart."

Jennifer lit the patchouli incense cones in the soapstone lotus burner and the women gathered around her. This wasn't the Jennifer who had been annoyed by her mother only moments before. This was Jennifer in her element, presiding over her coven, and leading the ritual. This was the Jennifer who performed Sarah's second wedding to James. This was the Jennifer who hired Sarah to work at the library at the college, and this was the Jennifer who was Sarah's first and best friend in Salem. Sarah realized suddenly how much she missed this Jennifer.

"Now we need to clear our minds," Jennifer said. "Other thoughts, other worries, other concerns must be left aside. We are here with one mind and a single purpose. We gather together to help our friends. To give them the strength they need to carry them through these difficult times. They are already blessed with physical endurance. They are made by magic to last through the ages. But now they need emotional and spiritual resilience so they can do what they need to do to come home." She smiled at Sarah. "And tonight we also bring strength for those of us at home as we carry our struggles of living without the ones we love." Jennifer looked at the cobblestones beneath her feet. "And I include myself in that as well."

Jennifer invoked the goddesses in the four directions. "Hail and welcome," Jennifer said. "Hail and welcome," the group echoed behind her.

Jennifer drew a large circle on the ground with an athame, a sacred knife, and marked the directions with candles on tall metal candelabras—yellow in the east to represent air, blue in the west to represent water, green in the north to represent earth, and red in the south representing fire. When the space was defined, Jennifer said, "The circle is cast, and everyone who enters the circle does so with love for our friends and loved ones who cannot be here now." Olivia took Sarah's hand, and Martha took Grace's hand, and they stepped into the sacred space. Grace was spellbound by the candlelight and everything happening around her.

Jennifer began: "Now, as we stand together under the night sky, we know the darkness for our friends never ends. They are trapped where others do not understand. Tonight we will help the light return to their nights so they can return to their homes, their lives, those they love most in the world. Tonight in this circle we celebrate their immortality, and we do our part to impart strength as they work through their struggles. In this circle we have only positive energy and power." Olivia swept the circle with a straw broom, clearing away the negative energy. Jennifer walked to the candle stationed north and said: "Guardians of the North, I call upon you to watch over the rites of this coven. Powers of endurance and strength, guided by Earth, we ask you to keep watch over us within this circle so that we may bless our friends in need."

It was fully dark now, and everything was still, the only movement from the nighttime bay breeze kissing the roses with whispers, leaving the sweet scent of flowers to mix with the salty sea air. The whiteness of the women's robes reflected light from the glowing licks of the candles at the four cardinal points while the waxing crescent moon pointed toward them like a heavenly blessing. Everything and everyone was silent, even Jennifer, who stood before them with her eyes closed, her face rigid with concentration, her body upright like a soldier at attention. Olivia's eyes were also closed the way they were whenever she went into a trance. Sarah wondered if Olivia was going into a trance now.

Jennifer took her mother's hand on her right and the hand of the woman to her left. The others in the circle joined hands, creating a bond between them. Jennifer said: "James is my good friend. I'll keep him close until the end. Evils dwell within our world. Protect him from the unknown cold. This orb of light I send unto him will keep him safe until the end. James is my close friend. Protect him until the very end. So mote it be."

The others in white chanted after Jennifer, creating what sounded like a mystical echo down a mountain range, a hushed, spiritual sound, like softly sung Gregorian chants or oft-repeated meditation mantras. First Jennifer's voice, then Olivia's voice, then the other voices. Sarah joined too, though she substituted "my dear and loving husband" for friend. They repeated the spell for Chandresh, Jocelyn, Timothy, even Geoffrey. Then, on a piece of white paper with a black marker, Jennifer drew a five-point star. She lit a white candle using the candle in the north and placed it in the middle of the star. She waved her arms to the scattered stars above and said, "Give protection to my friend, James John Wentworth. So mote it be." The others repeated the spell ten times, and again they did the same for Chandresh, Jocelyn, Timothy, even Geoffrey. When they were finished and the magic spells wove themselves around the women, casting them in a golden aura, Jennifer stood in silence, allowing the magic to rise into the Salem sky. "Go west," Jennifer said. "Far west, to the California horizon, in the desert, in the camp where our loved ones wait. To help us here at home, we will cast a Witches Ladder spell."

Jennifer held up one yard each of red, blue, and purple ribbon. "The red ribbon represents the passion with which we hold our missing loved ones in our hearts. The blue ribbon represents the peace we need, in our hearts and in our minds, as we continue our nights without our loved ones by our sides. The purple represents wisdom, which is what we gain in times of sacrifice and struggle. Here we create a talisman that will allow us to surrender our pain to the universe, allowing us to survive these difficult times with dignity so we may be ready for our loved ones when they return."

At the word return, Olivia's eyes popped open and fixed on Sarah. Jennifer braided the three ribbons together, one knot at a time, chanting, "By knot of one, my spell's begun. By knot of two, it will come true. By knot of three, so mote it be. By knot of four, this power I store. By knot of five, my spell is alive. By knot of six, the spell for our endurance and strength exists. By knot of seven, events I'll leaven. By

knot of eight, it will be our fate. By knot of nine, what's done is mine."
Jennifer walked to Sarah and handed her the braided cord, bowing as
their hands touched. "The power has been stored here, Sarah. I
haven't forgotten James calling in his second wish at the train station
when he asked us to protect you. This is for you. To help you."

Sarah was touched by Jennifer's gift, and she held the talisman
close to her heart, believing she felt James' eternal love there in the
ribbons. Jennifer repeated the spell two more times, creating a
talisman for herself and one to give Howard at another time. Grace
reached for the braided ribbon in her mother's hand and giggled at
the touch of the smooth strips.

"Well said, Grace," Jennifer said. "The circle is open but always
unbroken. Hail and farewell."

"Hail and farewell," the others echoed.

The ceremony was over, the circle undone. Jennifer blessed the
food, and everyone meandered to the linen-covered table where the
cakes waited. Olivia placed a mesh ball of Darjeeling tea into the
teapot and poured boiling water over it. The women chatted while
they waited for the tea to brew, the enclosed mysticism brought about
by the ceremony evaporated into a group of white-robed friends
passing a pleasant summer night together. Emma and two other
women in white robes clustered around Martha. Sarah heard one of
the women say something about the pretty dark-haired woman and
her blond-haired, blue-eyed baby. She couldn't make out everything
they said, but from their frequent glances her way she guessed they
were talking about her.

"That's Sarah Wentworth," she heard Martha say. "Her husband
James is in Camp Dracula in California."

Emma's gray eyes grew wide. "Sarah Wentworth? The..."

Martha nodded, her black bob bouncing. "The reincarnation? Yes."

"And that's the baby?"

"From the Wentworths' first life together, yes. She was never born
in that life, but now she's here. They were reunited last year."

Emma grasped Sarah's hand. "It's wonderful to meet you, Sarah

Wentworth. I've heard so much about you." Sarah smiled, unsure what to say to this Wiccan woman who seemed to know her.

"What's it like knowing about your past life?" a younger blond-haired woman asked. "I've tried a few times to get in touch with my previous lives but I've never been able to connect with them. Do you have flashbacks? Can you remember everything from then?"

"I remembered a lot after the past-life regression," Sarah said. "I remembered my husband and a lot of our life together—the good and the bad." Sarah grimaced at the memory of the pock-faced monster and the prison from her nightmares. "I remembered our unborn baby." She kissed Grace's cheek. "But I didn't remember everything at once, and sometimes, even now, something will trigger a memory from the seventeenth century. I don't feel any different than I did before the regression. I still feel like myself. The memories are like my memories from this life. They're inside me, but they don't overwhelm me, not now that I know what they are."

"Is it true you died here during the witch hunts?" Emma asked.

"Yes," Sarah said.

"That must have been frightening."

"It was. And now my husband is locked up because of other people's hysteria."

Martha shook her head. "It's not the same, Sarah. James is immortal, and you were all too human."

Grace yawned, and Sarah held her daughter close to her heart.

"I should get Grace home."

Sarah thanked the ladies for everything they did for James and the others, and then she said good night. Walking home, pushing Grace's stroller down Derby Street near the bay, the waxing crescent moon higher in the sky, she thought of her husband, awake since it was dark in California now, and she wondered what he was doing, what he was thinking, and she hoped that some of the magic from the women in white had already traveled his way.

.   .   .

97

FOR THE RECORD, please state your full name with your place and date of birth.

Chandresh Mankiller, born March 26, 1808.

Mankiller?

Mankiller.

Is that a threat, Mr. Mankiller?

You asked for my name. My name is Mankiller.

Is that a special name for a vampire?

It's a special name for the Cherokee. Mankiller was the name given to those who guarded the people from invaders. My father was of the Paint tribe, he was a medicine man, but I chose to make my own path and my father supported my decision.

Marital status?

I'm not married.

So you're single?

I'm not married. I would have become engaged if I hadn't been forced to come here.

And your would-be fiancée?

Is human.

Any children?

I had two children, my daughters.

Where are they?

They died in 1838 during the Trail of Tears.

And they were human?

Of course.

Where is your place of residence?

Primarily, I live in Oklahoma, however lately I've been residing in Salem, Massachusetts.

Mr. Mankiller, we're trying to determine where the vampires have been getting their blood. We need to be certain you're not a threat to the community. I'm sure you understand.

I understand.

So where do you get your blood?

Wherever I can find it.

Where are places you might find it?

Blood banks at hospitals. Slaughterhouses. The older I get the less blood I need, so it becomes less of an issue as the years pass.

How often do you feed now?

Perhaps once or twice a week.

Is that all?

Yes.

Is it the same for other vampires? The older they get the less they need to feed?

I would imagine so. I can't say for certain. I don't know every vampire in the world.

Have you ever hurt anyone to get the blood you need to survive, Mr. Mankiller?

No.

Not ever? You've been a vampire for how long now?

Since 1838.

You've already stated that's the time of the Trail of Tears.

(Chair shuffles.) Yes.

Were you a vampire during the Trail of Tears?

(Pause.) Yes.

Why would you walk the Trail as you are?

I didn't begin as a vampire. I was turned during the journey.

We've been asking vampires about the vampires who turned them.

What do you want with him?

Him? (Pen scratching on paper.) Do you know him?

(Pause.) I don't know him. I don't remember anything about it. The last thing I remember I was dying on the trail, and when I woke up I was what I am now.

Try to remember, Mr. Mankiller. What can you tell us about the vampire that turned you?

Why do you want to know?

We're curious about the process of how one becomes a vampire. Do they ask before they turn you? Do they infect unsuspecting and unwilling victims? We need to understand why vampires might choose to turn a human being into...into...?

Yes?

We need to know that humans are safe living in a world alongside infectious beings like yourself. If a human doesn't want to be a vampire, then humans shouldn't be forced to become vampires because of their proximity to the likes of your kind.

I can't speak for anyone else. I don't know why some vampires choose to turn people and others don't. I have never turned anyone so I can't speak about it.

Have you ever heard of a human being who was turned against his or her will?

(Silence.)

Mr. Mankiller, have you ever heard...

I heard your question.

And your answer?

I have never heard of a human being turned against his or her will.

Were you turned against your will?

I was turned because my father wanted me to be turned. I was dying, and he wanted me to live.

Do you consider this living, Mr. Mankiller?

I did until I was locked up here. First the government orders my people to walk a thousand miles to Oklahoma with little food to eat or water to drink. You can't imagine the horrors I saw on the Trail. Now I'm detained here for no reason other than the government doesn't know what to do with my kind. What else can you take from me?

Thank you, Mr. Mankiller. That will be all.

CHAPTER 9

W *hen the President of the United States believes the lies, what do you do? Where do you go? You go where they tell you to go.*

On February 19, 1942, President Franklin D. Roosevelt signed Executive Order 9066, which permitted the military to circumvent the Constitutional safeguards of American citizens in the name of national defense. The order set into motion the exclusion of "enemies" from the West Coast, since now Japanese-Americans were "enemies." Most of the people ordered to evacuate were U.S. citizens or legal resident aliens, sent away without due process of law. Without a trial of their peers. The writ of Habeas Corpus—the legal right to a trial in court with a judge before imprisonment can take place—was suspended. The government justified its action by claiming there was a danger of those of Japanese descent spying for the Japanese nation. Japan was on the other side of the Pacific Ocean, after all, a mere 5,500 miles across the water from Los Angeles, California to Tokyo, Japan. What if They pass secrets to Japanese submarines? So the Japanese-Americans were made to go away.

I remember the night Keiko and her family were evacuated. I walked from my apartment and saw them, with other families, standing by the busy Los Angeles curb. They were subdued and confused, watching while Southern

Californians continued their routines and procedures—people walking or driving their Studebakers home from work, stopping at the corner diner for coffee, chatting with neighbors, children running home from a friend's house with their book bags flapping behind them—without regard for those standing near their bags tossed into untidy piles on the sidewalk waiting for the buses to take them away. The men and boys wore fedoras, boxy suits, and wide-legged trousers while mothers and their daughters wore trench coats over knee-length dresses and sensible shoes. The mothers spoke softly to their children, not wishing to alarm them, and some managed to look relaxed while they chatted. The fathers kept their distance, looking here, looking there, pacing up and down the block, staring somewhere far, wondering where their families were going and whether they would be able to protect them wherever that was.

When Keiko noticed me she looked through me as though she didn't know who I was. In that moment I was just another white man pointing, ridiculing, prompting fear of the "Yellow Peril" in our midst. They were an easy scapegoat for Pearl Harbor, these law-abiding families. Who is afraid of these people, I wondered? These soft-spoken mothers, straight-backed fathers, wise-looking grandparents? Not knowing what waited for them was the worst of it, yet their faces remained aloof, not giving away their inner turmoil for public viewing.

"Keiko," I said. "Are you being evacuated today?"

She nodded. What could she say? The evacuation signs were posted across the city, all along the California, Oregon, and Washington coasts: Western Defense Command and Wartime Civil Control Instructions to all Persons of Japanese Ancestry Living in the Following Areas... And there, in black words on the white paper, were the instructions on how these families were to leave their lives behind so they could be rounded up and held away from the rest of the country like lepers from Biblical days, as though the imaginary "Yellow Peril" were contagious. Keiko kept her eyes averted as though she were embarrassed for me to see her there. And I wondered again, what can she say?

She watched her mother stare down the street. Finally, when she realized I wasn't leaving, Keiko said, "Some families had a forty-eight-hour warning to move out, but we only had twenty-four hours." She nodded to where her mother still stood on the curb, sizing up the darkness as though she were willing the bus to appear so they could get this internment started already. "My mother is worried because we didn't have time to store our belongings. Our furniture, our pots and pans, and everything else is still in our house. My mother is sure everything will be stolen as soon as people realize we're gone. And Peppy..." Keiko's sadness broke through her hard-won stoicism.

"Who is Peppy?" I asked.

"My poodle. We're not allowed to bring any pets. He's my best friend."

"Where is he?" I asked.

"He's with our neighbors, but they can't keep him because their daughter is allergic. They're bringing him to the shelter tomorrow." Keiko turned away, her eyes closed tight. In a moment she turned back as though everything were fine. "It's all right," she said. "My mother is sure a nice family will adopt him." Her smile didn't reach her eyes.

To casual bystanders, the stoicism of the people might have seemed hard, but I recognized that look too well. The families waiting on the curb had the same aloofness the Cherokee had when they were lined up to begin the hellish walk to Oklahoma. Keiko's little sister, Cho, was standing near their mother looking like a doll dressed in big girl's clothes in her tweed coat and matching man-style hat. Cho clutched a sack bag and her doll, a blond-haired, blue-eyed baby doll, who was also dressed for the winter weather. Some of the people started to shiver from the colder February night air. The more time passed the more they looked serious, and though they tried to maintain their nonchalance, as though this were any ordinary night, you could see the sadness starting to cloud their eyes, even the children, who looked more like wizened old people than youngsters buoyant with energy.

"Are we going to prison, Professor Wentworth?" Keiko asked.

"They say it's an internment camp," I said.

"What's an internment camp?"

The professor in me wished I had an answer that wouldn't frighten her. I looked into Keiko's eyes and I saw it, the concern about what was waiting for them in these camps that were unknown elements in this nightmare. Were they going to prison, I wondered? I wanted to give Keiko an emphatic no, of course you're not going to prison, you've done nothing wrong, but I couldn't lie to her. Will there be bars there, I wondered? The waiting people didn't know. They had been told next to nothing about what was waiting for them.

I saw Keiko, her staring mother, her downcast sister, her pacing father, her distracted brother, and her drooping grandmother. I had to do something for them, no matter how small.

"Which neighbor has your dog?" I asked.

"Mrs. Triston. She lives in the greenhouse behind our apartment building."

"I'll get Peppy," I said. "I'll keep him until you come home."

"We might be gone awhile."

"However long it takes," I said.

I looked for Keiko's mother, but Mrs. Sato had disappeared into the crowd and I didn't see her. "If I can get the keys to your house I can store your belongings and keep them safe," I said.

"My father has the keys."

Mr. Sato was still pacing, ten steps to the right, ten steps to the left, ten steps to the north, ten steps to the south, creating a box of tension only he could enter. Keiko said something to her father in Japanese, though I made out "Professor Wentworth," "English," and "UCLA." Mr. Sato bowed deeply in my direction, which I returned.

"You don't need to bow as deeply as he bowed to you," Keiko whispered. "He's showing you respect as a university professor."

"But your father deserves respect as well," I said.

Keiko smiled for the first time that night. "Trust me with this one, Doctor Wentworth."

Mr. Sato fished through his pockets, digging out the house keys. He handed them to me and bowed again.

"Thank you, Professor," he said. "I can't tell you how much you're helping my family by doing this." He looked toward his wife, who was standing on her toes at the edge of the curb, still willing the bus to appear. "My wife will appreciate this more than you know. She has so many things...things that have meaning to her...things from our family."

"I'll take care of all of it, Mr. Sato. Even Peppy."

Keiko smiled again.

"When we come home, I will do whatever I can to repay you, Professor," Mr. Sato said. "You don't understand what this means to us."

"I understand more than you realize," I said.

He bowed again, more deeply than before. I looked at Keiko, and she bowed slightly from the shoulders, and I followed her lead.

I heard the fraught engines of the buses before they appeared down the street. In a matter of moments three chartered buses parked by the curb, the brakes squealing as the heavy vehicles pulled to a halt, the accordion doors slapping open. Military officers barked orders and the people snapped from their reveries. Mothers searched for their children, fathers pulled their family's luggage from the haphazard pile, and families pushed around others to stay together. They had heard the stories from other round-ups where families sometimes ended up at separate camps, even mothers from their young children. I helped Mr. Sato load the family's luggage onto the bus, and then I backed away so the family could settle themselves before they stepped aboard. Keiko sat in her seat near a window and she waved at me as the bus drove away. At that moment, I saw her bright light dim. When the buses were gone, leaving trails of gray fumes, I felt as though I hadn't done enough. What else could I do, I wondered? I will have more to say about Manzanar another time, my love.

Tonight, before I settled on a bench near the fence to write this to you, I spent some time in the library barracks flipping through the books. If there has been one constant in my life, besides my love for you, it has been the escape of reading. Fortunately for me, we have a library well-stocked with the classics, which you, with your librarian's sensibilities, would appreciate. There is one of my kind, who looks to be about fifty but is twice that age, who was a librarian before she came here. Standing near the bookshelves tonight, I found myself reaching for Persuasion. *Do you remember, Sarah, how I found that book on the end table in your rented brick house? Was it only a year and a half ago when you so nervously invited me inside, and I was so nervous myself, wanting to get to know you and yet so afraid for you to know me? Would you care what I was, I wondered. That book drew you out of your shell and gave us something to talk about. Even now, as I sit here watching the moon reflect against the mountains, I'm struck with the uncanniness, how I have the same surname as the hero, Frederick, who, after some years, won a second chance with the woman he loved. We have won our second chance too, Sarah, we have. Even here I have not lost sight of that. In honor of our first real connection, I checked out* Persuasion, *as well as my comfort classics, my*

Dickens and my Shakespeare, of which I have taken David Copperfield, and for some reason I am drawn to Romeo and Juliet, older copies with loose bindings and yellowed pages. I have passed many lonely hours lost in those words when I had nothing to occupy my time except dwell on missing you. Now I do the same, only tonight you are not a dream. Tonight you wait for me as I wait for you. When the rose-fingered dawn breaks over the Sierra Nevadas, when the barren desert land stutters to life with wind and dust, I will crawl into my army cot with the sinking mattress, pull my thin blanket to my chin, and lose myself dreaming of you. Write again soon, my love. I live for your letters.

JAMES SIGNED his letter to his wife and sighed. When they were together he was reticent about sharing information about his long life with her, afraid of overwhelming her with everything he had done during his paranormal lifetime. He couldn't shake the memory of the horror on Sarah's face when she first understood what he was—unbreathing and undead. And even though she had proven her unconditional love for him many times since then, he was still afraid of crushing her under the weight of his immortality. Now that he was in California trapped within the mountains, he felt like he needed to unburden himself. He needed her to understand. He had begun with Manzanar, making up for the letters he didn't have time to write in those years, and soon she would know it all.

James looked through the silver-coated fence and watched the nighttime gardeners with their hoes and plows in the fields beyond the camp boundaries. There were a few detainees who made their living gardening on the outside, and they wanted to grow things to make Camp Dracula more colorful. The Japanese-Americans were allowed to create Bonsai and other Japanese-style gardens during World War II, they argued. We don't eat fruits or vegetables, but we can grow them for others. We can be useful. Some desert-growing flowers wouldn't hurt to liven things up around here, they said. After several polite discussions with camp authorities, the gardeners were allowed past the gate with guards armed with wooden stakes. They were too far for human eyes to see, but James spotted Timothy working alongside a red-haired, pale-skinned man who looked about twenty but was two hundred and five. He had been a gardener for over seventy-five years, Seamus, the red-haired man, said. When James pointed out Timothy's interest in horticulture, Seamus took the boy on as an apprentice.

"Timothy's going to learn about gardening the old-fashioned way," Seamus said. "By getting his hands dirty."

The workers handed their plows and their hoes to the guards, gathered their bags of seeds, and meandered back to the gate. James stood when Timothy passed, and they walked together toward the barracks.

"I checked the library for gardening books," James said. "Maile, the librarian, said we didn't have any here, but she'll see if she can get a few sent in."

"Thanks, James," Timothy said.

James stopped walking, allowing the others to pass them. Timothy stood near James looking at the slice of waxing crescent moon over-head. "Not a full moon tonight," Timothy said.

"Have you heard from your father?" James asked.

"I got a letter from him last night."

"What did he say?"

"He said yes, he knows Doodlebug. He also said he misses me and he wants me to write more often."

"Anything else?"

"He said he's glad he has Sarah to talk to because they understand each other. They know what the other is going through."

James felt a pinch in his chest where his heart used to be. Now Howard is saying how he's glad he has Sarah to talk to. How much time are they spending together? Again, James shook the uncomfort-able thoughts away. Of course it was nothing, he reasoned. Sarah loved him as he loved her. Of course it was nothing. Of course.

He looked at Timothy, who was saying goodnight to Seamus. They were chatting about the dry desert ground and the harshness of the climate here, but Seamus was certain they could manage to grow some nice watermelons and a vegetable or two. Flowers, Seamus said, maybe not so much, though there were a few varieties that would do well here.

When Seamus disappeared into his barracks, James and Timothy walked into the heart of the camp. "What else did your father say about Sarah?" James struggled to keep his voice steady but failed, at least to his own ears.

"Nothing. It wasn't a very long letter."

James nodded. Of course…

He stopped outside his barracks and stared at the mountains. Always the mountains. Under the dim light of the crescent moon, they were more intimidating than usual, Mount Williamson tallest and most imposing of them all. The sheer bulk demanded James' attention, overpowering everything else, including the camp with the white-cold people. The heights and drops, the precipitous cliffs and lithe peaks cast their shadows wherever James looked. How to get past those mountains, he wondered. He realized, more than ever, that he needed to get home to his wife. He gestured toward the gate Timothy had walked through.

"It's not all that far from the land you're cultivating with Seamus to the fence of the camp," James said. "I bet with your strength you could dig a hole from the garden to the fence without much effort."

He opened the door to his barracks and found it empty. Geoffrey wasn't there. That's good, James thought. He didn't know what he was planning yet and he didn't want to have to explain to Geoffrey.

"Probably," Timothy answered. "Why?"

Even in his windowless barracks, James saw the mountains in his mind, their permanence, the way they threatened to keep you within their boundaries even if you wanted out.

James whispered, always mindful of the ears that heard as well as his, "If you needed to get past those mountains, Timothy, could you?"

Timothy shook his head. "I don't see how. There are too many of them. They're too big."

"What if what was waiting for you on the other side of those mountains was the most important thing in the world to you? What if your father was on the other side? Or that dream job in garden design you've always wanted? Could you find a way around the mountains then?"

Timothy's black eyes brightened, and he nodded. "Not around," he said. "I'd find a way through."

James imagined the sinuous curves in the mountains. He thought of the cactus flowers, the running streams, and the hiking trails. "You're right," he said. "Through would be better."

"Are we going through?" Timothy asked.

James thought of his wife.

"Perhaps," he said.

For the record, please state your full name with your place and date of birth.

I was born on the First of December in the Year of Our Lord 1600 in London, England, United Kingdom. Great Britain, if you prefer.

And your full name?

My name?

Yes, sir, your name.

I am Geoffrey.

Geoffrey...?

Geoffrey.

And your surname?

I haven't bothered with one of those for centuries.

Mr. Geoffrey, you must have a last name.

No last name. You know. Elvis. Oprah. God. Geoffrey.

Very well, Mr. Geoffrey. Marital status?

My Rebecca died on the Second of September in the Year of Our Lord 1666. She was among the few to die in the flames of the Great Fire of London.

I'm sorry to hear that.

It was dreadful. The fire began at one o'clock in the morning, they said in the bakeshop of Thomas Fraynor, baker to none other than His Royal Highness King Charles the Second. Houses in London then were wood and pitch, and it was only moments until the flames spread throughout the city. I was long turned by then, but I kept track of my wife throughout the years. I wasn't in London the night of the fire, and I still live with the guilt. If I were there I might have been able to save her.

Where were you?

Roaming about the countryside. There is nowhere in the world more beautiful than the English countryside.

Did she know you as you are now?

Never. I didn't have the heart for her to see me as I am. They had a penchant for burning witches in those days. I didn't want to find out what they might do to one of our kind or their loved ones. They might have rounded us up and penned us like cattle. Oh no, wait. That's you.

(Cough.) You never remarried?

Never. There will never be anyone like my Becky again.

Any children?

One son.

Where is he?

He died in 1694 or thereabouts. He was a smart boy. Took after his father, of course. Had a great mind for business. Became quite wealthy in his day.

He was human?

Of course.

Any other relatives?

(Pause.) No, no. Not really.

Not really?

If I did have any relatives, I don't think he'd be too thrilled about it.

Because you're a vampire?

Because I haven't been the greatest relative in the world. But there it is. We can only do what we think is best at the time and try to make amends afterward.

It sounds like you have some unfinished business.

Quite.

Have you reached out to him?

What is this, a television chat show? Fix the vampire's relationship with his family?

You looked sad, Mr. Geoffrey. I was only trying to help.

I see.

We're trying to discover where vampires are getting their blood. Where does your blood come from?

From willing donors.

Are you certain they're willing?

Of course. I'm a vampire, not a monster.

Have you ever turned anyone into a vampire?

Why? What have you heard?

What do you think we've heard?

I asked you first.

Let me try that again. Have you ever turned anyone into a vampire?

(Pause.) No. Absolutely not. Never. Nada.

Are you certain?

Of course. I get my blood from willing donors, and I've never turned anyone into a vampire, not even anyone I found out I should have left alone. Not even anyone I might have been related to. Are we through here? I'm finding this conversation rather boring.

(Pen scratching on paper.) I'm sorry to bore you, Mr. Geoffrey. We'll call you back in a night or two.

Why would you need me again?

We need your full name. I'll give you a couple of nights to remember since it's been so long.

I'm not sure I can remember something like my name. I'm rather elderly you see. We old-timers don't have the greatest memory in the world. I'm lucky I remember to put my pants on, and that's pants in the English sense of the word, mind you. When we say pants we're referring to what you Americans call underwear. When you Americans say pants you mean trousers, which is silly.

(Laughs.) I'll keep that in mind, Mr. Geoffrey. I'm sure you'll do your best to remember your last name.

CHAPTER 10

*J*ames walked into his barracks lost in thought. This detainment was a waste of whatever precious time he had with his wife, and it was as pointless as the internments during World War II. He was no longer interested in participating in history repeating itself. On the one hand he was surprised any of his undead neighbors in the camp still put up with this nonsense when they had the superior physical strength that comes with immortality. Many of the undead were still hoping the government would come to its senses, recognize their rights as lawful citizens, and release them. Overtaking the guards and escaping the camp wouldn't do much for vampire public relations, they said, and then it would be all but impossible to return to their much-longed-for lives within society. James understood their rationale, and he agreed with them at first. But it was just as he said during his interrogation—he made a mistake coming here, and he fooled himself into believing anything would be different this time. And he had to get home to Sarah. He couldn't take a chance that she might forget him or decide he wasn't worth the trouble. He thought he heard Geoffrey's voice but didn't pay attention until Geoffrey stepped in front of him.

"What is it, James?"

"How do you know something is wrong?"

"Because you have that creased brow whenever you worry."

"I didn't realize I had a creased brow when I worried."

"You do. Why are you worried? Tell me."

"Why?"

"Because I want to help you."

"Why?"

"Honestly, you're worse than my son when he was a little boy. *Why, Pa? Why?* he asked constantly. No matter what I said, it was always *Why, Pa? Why?* He was a smart boy, too, and he never settled for my simple answers. Always inquisitive, always wondering." Geoffrey became thoughtful. "What's wrong, James?"

James stared at the photographs of Sarah and Grace taped to his wall.

"You asked me before how badly I wanted to go home. I don't want to go home, Geoffrey. I need to go home."

"Understood. Now what are we going to do to get you there?"

"I'm not sure yet. Right now I'm more concerned for Timothy. He let it slip that he thinks you're the one who turned him. He got the interrogator's attention with that, and suddenly the interrogator was interested in whether or not Timothy could point you out, and now they're asking other vampires about the ones who turned them as well."

"That explains why that rude man was so keen on whether or not I've turned anyone."

"What did you say?"

"What do you think I said? No way, José. And who the hell is Timothy?"

James stepped toward Geoffrey, unsure whether to shake or strangle the older vampire. "The dark-haired boy who's been with us since Salem."

"That boy thinks I turned him?"

"He remembers you, or at least he thinks he does. And the vampire who turned him said *You'll thank me later*, and he also abandoned Timothy to fend for himself after he was turned, which reminds me of the way you…"

"Don't start singing that song again. Yes, I left you alone, but I'm here now. I get points for that, don't I?"

"Perhaps. So you didn't turn Timothy?"

"I don't know. I don't think so."

"Do you say *You'll thank me later* to everyone you turn?"

Geoffrey shrugged. "I don't know about everyone."

"So you have said it to others."

"Perhaps a few."

"And you have no recollection of dragging an injured boy from a car accident and turning him?"

Geoffrey shook his head. "None."

"Have you turned many?"

"I wouldn't say many. Occasionally, if there's someone who strikes my fancy or looks like they need help."

"You think this is helpful?"

"I did. Now, not so much."

James needed fresh air. He wanted to breathe in oxygen despite the fact his lungs were dead. In that moment he needed to feel human, and without Sarah's warm hands to soothe him breathing was the only way. He opened the door and stepped outside, but a cold desert wind blew gusts of chalk-like dust across the sky and James didn't like the grime in his eyes.

Geoffrey came outside and stood beside his vampling.

"Could you have turned Timothy?" James asked.

"I reckon I could have. Honestly, James, I don't remember him."

"And yet you kept close track of me for over three hundred years. You know things about me my wife doesn't know. You even remember seeing Elizabeth after she died in the jail, and you knew Sarah was Elizabeth the first time you saw her. I assumed you watched all your vamplings so closely."

Geoffrey shook his head. "I don't keep track of my vamplings at all. I wouldn't recognize another if he tripped me."

"Why me?"

"You're special."

"So I'm special, but now Timothy brought the question of how we became vampires to the minds of the interrogators. They asked Timothy if he would ask you to turn him back, and he said he would."

Geoffrey laughed. "I would love to return the boy, James, like I would love to return you. I know how much you've disliked being what you are, though I can't fathom why. You have everything mortals dream of—perfect health, extraordinary strength, the hyper-senses of the most refined hunters in the wild. And you still look fit though you're how old now?"

"More than three hundred years old."

"You'll never die, James. What could be better?"

"Not being here because of what you turned me into. Being home with my wife and daughter." James' thoughts raced back a few sentences. "What did you mean by returning the boy? You've mentioned returning before. What does that mean?"

"I wonder about you sometimes. How could you be...how old are you again?"

James sighed. "More than three hundred years old."

"How could you be more than three hundred and not know what returned means."

"Just tell me, Geoffrey."

"When I made you into a vampire I turned you. So returned means..."

James' eyes grew wide. "It means to turn the vampire back to human?"

"Correct."

"Can you do that?"

"Of course not. It's a theory no one has ever proven to be true. You see, some of our kind have speculated that if we can be turned then it would make sense that we could be returned. Some have tried with the help of their witchy friends, but it's never worked, at least not to my knowledge. Not only has it never worked, but the results were less than hopeful."

"Why?"

"There's that why again. It depended on how they tried to return

116

the vampire. Sometimes they drank odd concoctions that did nothing but taste bad. Sometimes they tried spells that backfired."

"Backfired?"

"It's only hearsay, but the stories say some of the potions killed the vampires."

"You're so fond of pointing out that we're already dead. What could the spells do to them?"

"Human people can't harm us, but when the witches' magic back-fired the vampires died for good. No more animation. No more talk-ing. No more anything. I've heard stories that the vampires' bodies degenerated into whatever they would have been if they were never turned. So if you were, let's say, three hundred and fifty years old, your body would turn to dust and bones as if your corpse were three hundred and fifty years old."

James covered his eyes with his hand, trying to shut out the image of his skeleton crumpling into a fragmented memory.

"I've never heard of returning before," James said. "How do you know all this?"

"I made it my job to know these things. I was abandoned after I was turned too, you know. I'm not using that as an excuse for what I did to you or Todd…"

"Timothy."

"…or anyone else I might have turned. But when I was alone and unsure what I was, I was determined to find out. I sought out others of our kind and asked every question, learned every legend, every myth, and discovered which were fantasy and which were true. I made it my business to learn everything I could about what I had become so I could understand this life."

"Some of that information would have been useful."

"You're right, James. If I could go back and do things differently I would, but I can't. Now I need you to listen to me. It's better if you forget everything I said about returning. Whatever magic turns us into this can't be harnessed or reversed in any way. How or why we are what we are will always be a mystery, but there's a mystery to all life, isn't there? Perhaps some things aren't meant to be undone."

Geoffrey knelt in front of James. "You have to stay as you are, James, but you can still turn your pretty little human person."

"No."

"You should both be the same."

"Sarah doesn't want to be like us, and you said I can't be returned. We can be happy together the way we are. We still have time. Which is why I need to go home."

James felt the dawn before he saw the rising pink above the rocky horizon. The wind picked up and the dust swirled, a mini twister, whisking toward the wall of mountains in the distance. He couldn't take the grimy air any longer and walked inside his barracks. The brief fantasy of returning to human was gone, leaving him spent with the lack of possibility.

"You look tired, James," Geoffrey said. "Go to bed. We'll talk more tonight."

James nodded, too weary to reply. He slid his makeshift wall to the side and stepped into his quarters, then pulled the wall back into place. He looked at the emptiness, his simple army cot, and the sand-papered wooden box he used as a desk. He pushed the books he checked out of the library from his bed onto the floor, and without undressing he spread out on the cot that was barely long enough for his full length. He slipped his shoes off, letting them drop to the floor with two dull thuds. He closed his eyes and tried to still the worries irking him. Worries from Timothy's inadvertent disclosure to the interrogator. Confusion from the sudden hope brought on by learning about returning and the sadness of learning it could never be. Concerns about this vague idea he had teasing the outskirts of his mind. What if there was no way out of the camp and he was trapped forever? What if it took longer than a year, two years, or a decade for those on the outside to come to their senses? James felt overwhelmed, his head trapped under a cesspool of uncertainties, so instead of dwelling on the negative he tried to focus on his wife. He rolled onto his side and stared at the photos of Sarah. There she was, her long, dark curls, her rose-like lips, the hot pink blush along her jaw, the wondering chocolate-brown eyes. She was smiling in the picture, it was taken in Maine when they first arrived to stay with Olivia's cousins, and those were happy nights. They thought they had escaped the madness by outrunning it, staying ahead of it, and creating a Plan B. But he was here and Sarah was there so they hadn't escaped anything at all.

Suddenly, James heard a noise, something different from the usual conversations and activities at the camp. He sat up, threw his legs over the side of the cot, and looked around. At first he thought Geoffrey was speaking to him, but James heard Geoffrey snoring through the thin wooden board. James walked the seven short steps that made up the length of his quarters looking for an intruder but there was nowhere in the empty space to hide. Perhaps he heard a movement from outside and thought it was inside. Then he felt warm, comforted, as though he were standing in sunlight in the confines of his room, and he remembered when he felt this way before. The first time was when Sarah wanted to adopt a child but he was against it, worrying about how difficult it might be for a child to love him, oddity that he was. Then he heard a voice say it would be all right, and then he and Sarah found their Grace. He heard the voice a second time while he waited to board the train that took him away. The voice said he would be all right, and he was. He wasn't happy, and he could never be content as long as he was separated from his beloved, but he was all right. James strained to hear the voice again, a good, strong, hearty voice that brought him comfort when he needed it most. But all he heard was the dust storm blowing gales in the dawn.

"Are you there?" James asked.

The room was quiet, but the warmth was there and James allowed it to comfort him. Finally, he heard the voice.

"Rest, James. All will be well."

James closed his eyes and allowed himself, for that moment, to believe it.

THE NEXT NIGHT James and Geoffrey walked into the mess hall, grabbed clean tin cups from the tray at the front, and stood in line until the undead attendant slopped the red-brown goop at them. They sat at their usual table at the far end of the barracks, and James watched those seated at the tables around them, drinking from their tin cups, pretending everything was fine. Timothy, Chandresh, and Jocelyn were already there. Chandresh grimaced as he sipped his drink.

Geoffrey puffed out his cheeks as he caught the scent. "Does that taste as hideous as it smells?"

"Worse," Chandresh said. "But it's better than nothing."

"I'm not so sure."

They drank in silence. James thought there was nothing to say, no words to share. It was as though everyone in the mess hall had the same feeling because suddenly no one was speaking and the eeriness of the quiet disturbed him. Why had everyone fallen silent at once? He heard the heavy boot steps approaching from the distance, and everyone turned toward the door, tentative, waiting. The door swung open, and six armed military police walked into the barracks along with a short, stocky man with dark hair graying at the temples and round glasses. James recognized the man and shook his head.

"That's the one who interviewed me," Timothy whispered.

"Me too," said James.

"What do you think he wants?"

The man scanned the mess hall, table by table, studying the white-skinned men and women who were staring back at him just as intently. "That's him," the man said. The military police surrounded James' table and everyone in the mess hall watched in worried silence.

"What do you want here?" James asked.

"It's you we want," the man said, pointing at Geoffrey.

"Whatever for?" Geoffrey asked. "I'm sitting here quietly, not pestering a soul, drinking this hideous slush you call blood without complaint, or much of one anyway."

"Unfortunately, your answers to our questions were met with some concern. We need your information, Mr. Geoffrey."

"What questions didn't I answer?"

"We need your full name."

"I gave you my name. Geoffrey."

"You have a last name," James said. "People born in 1600 had last names."

"I've forgotten it. It was so long ago. You nice gentlemen must have more important things to concern yourselves with."

The interrogator pointed at Geoffrey. "You need to come with us." A military police officer grabbed Geoffrey's arm and tried to make him stand, but Geoffrey was too strong and didn't budge.

Geoffrey balked in annoyance. "I don't think…" He stopped when another military policeman displayed his wooden bayonet.

"You need to give us your full name, Mr. Geoffrey," said the interrogator, "or you need to come with us. If you don't follow orders we'll use whatever means necessary to ensure your cooperation."

"Tell him your name, Geoffrey," Chandresh said.

"Stop being an ass," James said.

"Unless it's Hitler, you can tell him," said Jocelyn.

Geoffrey sighed, his face long and forlorn, James thought, like droopy-faced Eeyore from the Winnie the Pooh stories.

"You leave me no choice," Geoffrey said. "I've been trying to avoid the embarrassment. It's hardly a commonplace name, you see, and Americans only laugh when they hear it though it's quite dignified in my part of the world."

"Say it already," James said.

Geoffrey cleared his throat. "Very well. My name is Geoffrey Ichabod Englebert Tiddlywinks Bumptybottoms." Geoffrey pulled himself upright, casting his eyes around the mess hall like a king surveying his loyal subjects. "There it is."

The interrogator wrote the name onto the file he held in his hand. His voice was incredulous. "Your name is Geoffrey Ichabod Englebert Tiddlywinks Bumptybottoms?"

"The Third."

"The Third?"

"Correct. Geoffrey Ichabod Englebert Tiddlywinks Bumptybottoms the Third. My parents were Mr. and Mrs. Bumptybottoms. It's a fine English name, I assure you."

The interrogator slapped his pen into the file. "If you're not going to tell us, then we'll need to be more forceful. Grab him!"

Two guards tried to grab Geoffrey's arms, but Geoffrey pulled away and the military policemen stumbled to the ground. The other guards stood tensely, waiting for orders, but Geoffrey didn't look concerned. He pointed at James.

"What's his name?" Geoffrey asked.

"That's Doctor Wentworth, Mr. Bumptybottoms," the interrogator answered.

"Wentworth. That'll do."

"That'll do?" the interrogator said.

"Why not? It's a hearty name, a literary name I'm sure the professor appreciates. My name is Geoffrey Wentworth."

"Are you related to James Wentworth here?"

"I told you my name as you requested. Now I bid you farewell. Good night, sir. I said *good night.*"

Geoffrey walked away in a royal manner, as though a colorful procession of lords and ladies waving ribboned fans followed behind while court musicians played Renaissance lute music. He waved at the white-skinned people watching him with expressions caught between apprehension and amusement. An older officer gestured toward Geoffrey with a wooden stake.

"Tell them your name!" James yelled.

James had heard about staking from others of his kind. He had never seen it, he hoped to live forever and a day and never see it, but Geoffrey's immortality was about to vanish into a blood splat. James stepped forward, but Geoffrey held out his hand, stopping his vampling, ready to take his punishment like the preternatural man he was. As the military policeman lowered the stake, Geoffrey ripped his shirt apart, buttons pinging as they hit the floor. He closed his eyes and pushed his chest upward while the wood sliced the air toward his skin. Someone screamed when she realized Geoffrey was about to be staked.

Geoffrey turned his head to avoid seeing the blow. "Goodbye, cruel world."

When the MP struck Geoffrey with the wood, it bounced off his blue-white skin with a thud. Geoffrey was struck again, and again, and he remained tall and strong, his eyes closed, his hands still tugging his shirt from his bare chest. Others in the mess hall murmured with the realization that nothing happened, Geoffrey hadn't dropped puddle-red onto the ground, he hadn't melted like the wicked witch in *The Wizard of Oz*. Everyone applauded.

Geoffrey opened one eye and glanced at his unscathed skin.

"I'm alive!" he said, his smile exuberant. "I'm alive!"

He bowed at his enraptured audience, an actor taking his final bows after an award-winning performance, and he walked with his head high through the mess hall door.

"We're not done here, Mr. Geoffrey!" the interrogator shouted.

Geoffrey winked at the man. "I didn't think we were." The vampire disappeared from view, his footsteps faster and faster while the interrogator and the military police stared at each other, unsure what to do about Mr. Geoffrey Ichabod Englebert Tiddlywinks Bumptybottoms the Third, also known as Wentworth. In front of everyone in the mess hall, their weapon hadn't worked. The wooden stakes they waved at every opportunity were useless. What did that mean to the undead? To the guards? The interrogator and the military police marched out, their faces intent, their eyes avoiding everyone else as they left the internees to speculate.

James shook his head as he left for his barracks. Why didn't Geoffrey want the interviewer to know his name? Something nagged at James, some truth struggling to whisper its knowledge into his ear, but he felt himself spinning, too full of questions to hear any insights then.

CHAPTER 11

I could pretend I don't know why I was compelled to go to Manzanar when of course I do. Thinking of Keiko, her family, and families like hers, thinking of them trapped in a cage, victims of senseless prejudice, I knew I had to do more to help them. It was a month since Keiko and her family were carted away, and I decided I had to go to Manzanar to see for myself what was happening. I read the newspapers, heard the radio, and saw the newsreels, but I only saw what others decided I should see.

The Satos' belongings were safely stored with a fellow professor from UCLA. I left Peppy with the Simons, my neighbors. He was a friendly dog, Peppy, sweet, loving, happy to see me when I arrived home after teaching my classes, and he slept on the bed next to me during the day. He adapted to my schedule, and he was awake at night with me. But I was going to be gone awhile, and the Simons were more than happy to take him. Their twin sons Peter and Mitchell had already fallen in love with the curly-haired dog, and they cared for the little white poodle as much as I had come to care for him. Mrs. Simon said it would be hard to give him back when the Satos returned home.

I drove to Manzanar in the desolate desert, one hundred and seventeen miles from Death Valley. Everything everywhere you look is sand, tumble-weeds, cactus, and mountains. Always the mountains. The tallest peak is

Mount Williamson, the second highest in California at 14,000 feet. Where the mountains rise high, the floor of the valley drops as low as four thousand feet below sea level, making it one of the deepest valleys in the United States. The Sierra Nevadas cast a rain shadow, making Owens Valley a land of little rain, which accounts for the cake-like dust that suffocates everyone. Even as I am I can hardly stand the heaviness.

I found my way along Route 395 to the small town of Lone Pine near the Alabama Hills. When I arrived, it was still winter-like weather in the Owens Valley. The mountains were white with snow and it was cold for the people. I walked from my motel in Lone Pine to Manzanar, nothing of a walk for me, and my first view of the camp was the eight prison-like guard towers. With my hunter's sight, I spotted the two wooden posts on the perimeter of the camp, the four-pronged sign—Manzanar War Relocation Center—as though anyone could have thought this barbed-wired, fenced-in setting was anything other than a jail. I found the military police at their stations, watching the families with impassive gazes. To the army, the people were prisoners, locked inside as though they had broken the law, had the book thrown at them, and now they were suffering their rightful consequences. The families were watched with the same scrutinizing gaze real-life law-breakers received. I saw the flash of submachine guns and thought of the unarmed children within easy range. I scanned the faces for Keiko, but I didn't see her through the gate. Keiko could be anywhere within those barbed wires, I thought.

I had come with a purpose. Two weeks earlier I had read in the Los Angeles Times *how they were arranging schools in the camps for the children. I had already called the camp authorities and told them I had read about the schools in the papers. I said I was a professor of English who would like to offer my services. I taught night classes at UCLA, I explained, and I could teach night classes for students in the camp who work during the day or have other obligations. At first, they weren't sure they needed night classes, and I had to shuffle through several supervisors, bureaucratic nonsense. We don't need university professors, they said. We need a high school English teacher. When I assured them I could teach high school, I was hired. I made my way to the guard tower, explained who I was and why I was there, and showed my identification. The guard, a young man whose hands fumbled with the clipboard, found my name and pushed open the gate to allow me inside. I heard the slam as the gate closed behind me and the rattle as the guard locked me in. For the first time in years I remembered what it was to be the hunted, to feel entrapped and encaged. In those first moments I thought I made a terrible mistake. But I could leave if I wanted to, I reminded myself. I could walk up to the helmeted military police, ask them to open the gate, and they would let me go. And because I could leave, I had to stay.*

I walked into the center of camp, searching for the barracks assigned to me, enveloped by cold wind and dusty air. Cold hadn't bothered me since 1692, yet I felt chilled by the desert winter. I spoke briefly to the butcher, who didn't appear to think it odd that the pale-skinned, blond-haired English teacher asked him to keep aside a container of blood two nights a week. The further into camp I walked the more I saw how the evacuees were doing everything they could to make this harsh environment more comfortable. They added rock-lined pathways to and from their barracks. Some of the residential blocks I passed had large community ponds, along with gardens with waterfall bridges, Japanese tea houses, and pine trees. It was April, and the weather was warming even if it felt winter-bitter in the night. The white powder enveloping the mountains, like Geisha-pale make-up, was melting. As I continued between the barracks I saw people waiting in line for their vaccinations with their shirt sleeves rolled up, tended by nurses in pristine white coats, stockings, and shoes. I passed the laundry barracks with rows of washtubs where everything, including sheets and towels, was washed by hand, and women waited to wash their families' clothing. There was an even longer line where the women waited to use the latrines. Many held long card-board cartons, and from the distance I heard them whispering to newcomers that no doors were separating the toilets and they needed the boxes for privacy.

Inside Manzanar were snapshots of hardworking, honest Americans living in a barbed-wire prison. I saw an elegant-looking woman, Mrs. Naka-mura, and her daughters standing outside their makeshift home, their mouths smiling, their eyes sad. Through their open door I saw how they pasted family photos and magazine cut-outs on the wall. They had a handmade wooden desk like the many handmade items populating the barracks, created from whatever discarded crates, wooden boards, or other throwaway items could be recycled into something useful. People made what they needed from whatever materials they could find. Scrap lumber became chairs, tables, desks, and dressers. Found metal became knives since they weren't allowed to bring sharp objects into camp. For fun, scrap wood was carved into small, painted birds. The Nakamuras had a teapot kettle clock on the wall, books, dolls, and blocks for the daughters. When they saw me pass they scurried inside as though they thought I was there from the administration. In a matter of moments the camp became a ghost town, and all I saw, besides the barracks, were street lights, army trucks, and a car or two parked in the lanes. The people had a curfew and they followed it, not wishing to start problems.

As a volunteer, I had my own barracks, though it was hardly a prize with bare walls, an army cot, thin army blankets, and a feather mattress that sank in the middle—not so different from what I have now. Through my windows, with my heavy black curtains pulled aside, I could see into other barracks where families lived. The families lived separated from each other by stalls like horses in a stable, and there were foot-high spaces between the partitions, privacy now a memory from a time when they had their own homes. I heard every conversation, every argument. I heard them snoring in the nighttime. I heard parents scolding their children. I heard the banging on the doors when teenagers came back past their curfew. I heard the men at their card games where some gambled all night, and I smelled their intoxication from foul homemade liquor. I guessed the people could hear everything within their own barracks as well as I could hear blocks away.

It took two nights of asking around, but I finally found Keiko sitting outside her family's barracks across the camp. She was writing on a scrap of paper with a stubby pencil. I waved when I saw her.

"Professor Wentworth?" she said. "What are you doing here?"

"I thought I could be of some use teaching English," I said. "Don't worry about Peppy. He's being well cared for by my neighbors, and their twin boys are already in love with him."

"Thank you for taking care of him."

I looked over her shoulder at the scrap of paper. "What are you writing?" I asked.

"It's nothing." Keiko glanced at the deserted lanes between the barracks, at her closed door, certain no one else was in hearing distance. "It's a code I've created." She dropped her voice to a whisper. "They watch everything we do

here. I thought it would be nice to be able to communicate freely without everyone knowing what I was saying."

I took the scrap from Keiko and studied it. "It's an anagram code. Like spies use."

"That's exactly what they expect from us, isn't it? They think we're spies for Japan."

"You're not a spy, Keiko. You're a college student studying English literature."

Keiko nodded. "Can you read what I wrote, Doctor Wentworth?"

I rearranged the letters into various words in my mind until I saw their meaning. "I want you to go home soon too, Keiko," I said. "I know you miss Peppy."

She smiled when she realized I understood her secret language. Suddenly, a young woman, perhaps twenty-seven years old, scurried past, her bun-pulled black hair barely visible above the heavy scarf pulled close to her ears, her long coat tight near her chin, her white-socked feet clunking in her geta, the wooden clogs she wore. The young woman looked frantic as she knocked on the door of a nearby barracks. When the middle-aged man answered, he listened to her question, nodded his head, and allowed her inside.

"Mrs. Kawasaki is there to see her son. Marvin was put into a barracks with a different family. He's ten."

"Why?" I asked.

"It was a mistake, Professor."

"A careless mistake," I said. I looked at Keiko's barracks and looked through the window. "How is your family?"

"They're well."

I could see in her far-away glance, her sharp, observant eyes turned from me, that she only said what she thought she should.

"I should say hello," I said.

Keiko shook her head. "I don't think anyone is home." When her father walked past the window, she shrugged.

"Can I say hello to your father?" I asked.

Keiko nodded. We walked up the three steps to her barracks, and, with her hand on the knob, she put her ear to the door. I heard nothing but heavy breathing inside. She knocked, then opened the door.

"Otousan?" she said.

Her father grumbled as he stood from the makeshift sofa comprised of recycled cushions and army-style blankets on the floor. The stink of fermented alcohol burned my nostrils, and Keiko turned away, embarrassed by her father. He was unkempt, unshaven, his hair long from missed trips to the camp barber. His eyes were bloodshot, unable to focus on anything as he looked from here to there and back again the way a blind man tries to see. He was thin-looking and frail, a shadow of the man I had seen before.

"Mr. Sato," I said. Mr. Sato stared at me as though he didn't know what I was. "I'm James Wentworth, Mr. Sato, Keiko's English professor from UCLA. We met the night you left Los Angeles." Mr. Sato blinked, and I saw a flicker of recognition. "I wanted you to know your family's belongings are safe. I stored them with a fellow professor from UCLA, and everything will be ready for you when you're able to go home."

"Home?" Mr. Sato said. "This is home. Will we ever have another?"

"Of course you will," I said. "You can tell Mrs. Sato her family heirlooms are safe. And I found a good home for Peppy."

Mr. Sato nodded, and I saw the alcohol-induced haze lifting. "Thank you, Professor. But why are you here?"

"I thought I might be more use inside the camp than outside," I said.

Keiko stood next to her father, still wary of him, though she kept her voice light. "How can you teach here?" she asked me. "You're a university professor."

"I can be a high school teacher," I said. "The administrators agreed that some older students might need night classes if they work during the day."

"Is that all you teach are night classes?"

I pretended I didn't hear her question. "I'm glad I found you because I thought you could help me, Keiko. I need some help getting the class going, and I could use an assistant who knows the ins and outs of camp. Do you know where Mrs. Morris lives? I was told to speak to her first."

"She teaches English too," Keiko said.

"Good. Maybe she can show me what books you're reading."

"Books?" Keiko shook her head. "I don't think there are any books."

"What does she use to teach?"

"I don't know, Professor."

I said good night to Mr. Sato and Keiko walked me outside and around the barracks, pointing out one a fair distance from hers.

"That's where Mrs. Morris lives," Keiko said.

I looked at Mrs. Morris' barracks, then at Keiko.

"Are you all right?" I asked. "Your father seemed..."

"He's had a hard time, Professor Wentworth. They held him in a separate camp from us for a month and now he's..." She looked into the dark sky, only a handful of stars visible through the dust cloud forming above our heads. "I'm fine, Professor. Thanks for asking."

When Keiko was safely back inside her barracks, I went to Mrs. Morris' door and knocked. When she appeared she looked surprised to see me. I introduced myself, explained who I was, and she nodded. She looked to be about sixty, Mrs. Morris, with her short hair dark where it hadn't grayed and curled around her face in a 1930s style. "Mrs. Blum told me to expect you," she said. "Forgive me. I wasn't expecting someone so young. Come in, Professor Wentworth."

"James, please," I said. I looked around her barracks, as plain as anyone else's. She had a barracks to herself, as I did, and her walls were covered in cut-outs from magazines and photographs of people I guessed were her family. "What are you teaching now?" I asked.

"We're studying poetry."

"Any poet or period in particular?"

"Whatever I can find. We don't have books yet. We don't have pencils, paper, or even crayons for the little ones. The sad thing is, the children want to be in school. They're longing for some normalcy, some sense that their lives aren't so drastically changed. They want back some of the security that was snatched from them for no fault of their own."

"I see we're here for the same reasons," I said.

"If you're here because you abhor the way these families have been treated and you're doing what you can to soften the blow, then yes, we're here for the same reasons."

I nodded my head, a silent yes, we are kindred spirits in that way.

"Where do you find materials?" I asked.

"I have books sent to me. One of the ladies here was a librarian in Los Angeles before she was interned. She contacted some of her librarian friends

who are helping us find book donors. For now," she gestured at a stack of books pressed against the wall, "that's what we have to work with. I'm happy to share what I have with you, Professor."

I sat next to the books and glanced over the titles. I saw one volume of Walt Whitman, one volume of Romantic Poets, and one volume of Shakespearean sonnets. "Which one would you like me to use?" I asked.

"Whatever you like."

I chose the Walt Whitman volume. "I'll take this if that's all right."

"That's fine."

I looked at the single volume in my hand and wondered how I would ever use this to teach a class, even a small one. "Like ancient times," I said. "Socrates didn't have a class set of textbooks. They had to memorize their lessons then. Perhaps I'll have the students write their answers in the sand."

Mrs. Morris laughed. "There's plenty of that around here." She walked me to the door. "Thank you for coming, Professor. I think we'll work well together."

I left Mrs. Morris' barracks and walked into the clear, cold night, watching the stars winking from above. I felt you very strongly then, and I searched the sky for you, trying to feel you in the desert. I wondered if you could see me, since surely you were in heaven, and I wanted you to know what I was doing. I wanted you to understand that I was doing this in your memory. I found my way back to my barracks and spent the rest of the night rereading Whitman and listening to my neighbors snoring in their beds.

Two nights later I was assigned to the high school, teaching English classes for students who were unable to attend the day school because they worked in the camp or had to care for younger brothers or sisters while their parents worked. Keiko signed on as my assistant, the English teacher-to-be, and we set off for a barracks in the center of camp. The barracks looked then like they do now, rows of matchboxes, and everyone we passed was covered in cake-flour dust by the murky wind, as though they had incurred the wrath of the Greek god Aeolus, who shrieked as he released the windstorms. The Ancient Greeks saw the winds as horse-shaped spirits, and in the middle of the Sierra Nevada desert I believed I saw the four-legged animals billowing in the sand clouds.

My students were already there, fifteen of them. I opened the barracks door, flipped on the electricity, and the space was lit by a single light bulb hanging unadorned from the ceiling. The students filed in, stopping short when they realized there were no desks or chairs.

"There's nothing here, Professor Wentworth," Keiko said.

"There must be some mistake," I said. "Perhaps we came to the wrong place."

Keiko shook her head. "This is it, Professor."

The students didn't seem particularly concerned by the empty room. They were used to walking into empty barracks and making do with whatever odds and ends they could find. I sighed and gestured to the bare ground.

"Have a seat on the floor for now," I said. "I'll do what I can to get some furniture in here." I turned to Keiko. "All right, Miss Sato. Class begins."

I introduced myself and Keiko, then opened my book and read:

I celebrate myself, and sing myself,

And what I assume you shall assume,

For every atom belonging to me as good belongs to you.

I loafe and invite my soul,

I lean and loafe at my ease observing a spear of summer grass.

"Does anyone know who wrote this poem?" I asked.

"Walt Whitman," said Keiko. "It's from Leaves of Grass."

"I know you know, Keiko. I was asking the students."

Keiko laughed. "Sorry, Professor."

The students dropped their shoulders from their ears and exhaled for the first time since we walked into the barracks. They sat with their legs pulled to their chins, and I thought they looked more like small children in kindergarten circle time than high schoolers. They brought whatever paper they could scrounge from around camp. Some had scraps, and several had full-length sheets which they split in half and shared with neighbors who had none. They had nothing to write on but the hard ground beneath them. Only four had nubby pencils to write with, and I had nothing to share with them since all I had was the book I borrowed from Mrs. Morris. I repeated the lines from Whitman, and asked, "What do you notice about the narrator of this poem?"

A prim-looking young woman with her hair pulled into a bun, her round spectacles on the tip of her nose, looking much older than the sixteen I guessed her to be, raised her hand.

"Yes?" I said.

"It's an I narrator," she said. "The poem is written from a first-person point of view."

"Very good..."

"Michelle," she said.

"Very good, Michelle." I read more of the poem:

If you want me again look for me under your boot-soles.

You will hardly know who I am or what I mean,

But I shall be good health to you nevertheless,

And filter and fibre your blood.

Failing to fetch me at first keep encouraged,

Missing me one place search another,

I stop somewhere waiting for you.

The students with pencils scratched notes onto their scraps of paper, writing as small as they could.

"Today Walt Whitman is considered one of the greatest American poets, but he faced a lot of criticism when he self-published Leaves of Grass in 1855."

Keiko stood behind me, watching the students with pencils write their notes. She slipped out the door, and before I could ask where she was going she was gone. Another young lady sitting under the window, her dark hair blue in the moonlight, raised her hand and waited for me to acknowledge her.

"Yes?"

"Mariko," she answered. "If Whitman's poetry was self-published, doesn't that mean it wasn't any good? I thought people only self-published if they weren't good enough to get published any other way."

"Whitman's work was controversial in his day," I said. "He needed to find his audience among the people, not among editors or critics who didn't understand his stylistic innovations and the deeper meaning within his work. Leaves of Grass is an affirmation of everything human...nature, friendship, democracy, and love, and he celebrated life in all its sensuality. The book was panned by critics after its release, one going as far as to toss the book into a fire. The sensual imagery made Whitman's work too obscene for polite Victorian tastes. It wasn't until the last decade of his life that he began to find recognition for his work, and even then he was frustrated that his work wasn't more appreciated among literary scholars. He would be pleased that now he's an integral piece within the canon of American literature."

"What makes his work so special, Professor Wentworth?" Mariko asked.

"Whitman created an individual voice, a uniquely American voice, an all-powerful I to narrate this poem. His work is deeply personal and yet it invokes the human experience. Some critics have wondered if Whitman underwent some kind of spiritual transformation before writing Leaves of Grass."

Keiko rushed back into the barracks, the open door sending gusts of chalky dust into our eyes. She carried a stack of notebook paper, magazines to write on, and pencils for everyone. She passed the supplies to the students, who murmured their appreciation.

"Where did you get that from?" I asked.

Keiko smiled. "They had supplies in the newspaper office."

I knew there was more to that story, but with the students waiting I continued the lesson.

"Whitman is considered the Father of Free Verse, though he didn't invent the style. Miss Sato, can you tell the class the definition of Free Verse?"

"Free Verse is unrhymed lines of poetry that have no fixed metrical pattern. In Leaves of Grass, Whitman abandoned regular meter and rhyme patterns and used a Biblical cadence instead."

I waited while the students wrote. I looked at the young people, in class at night for various reasons, squirming on the floor with aching backs and sore bottoms without complaint. I couldn't keep them sitting there any longer, so I dismissed them, saying I would do my best to get copies of the poem for them, as well as desks and chairs. When the students were gone, I turned to Keiko.

"Where did you get the supplies?" I asked again.

"The newspaper office like I said."

"The newspaper office isn't open this time of night."

"I didn't say it was open." Keiko looked pleased with herself.

"Did you break in?" I asked.

Keiko shrugged. "The door wasn't locked, so I opened it like I would open any other door." She flashed her half little girl/half wise woman grin.

"Did anyone see you?"

"I wouldn't have gone in if anyone was there."

I laughed at her matter-of-fact manner. "Thank you, Keiko, but don't break into anywhere again. I don't want you getting into trouble. Next time let me do the breaking-in."

"Whatever you say, Professor."

She stood next to me, her sharp, observant eyes studying me in the moonlight, and I imagined I must have looked even paler than usual. For a moment, I was afraid she might have noticed something odd about me. Finally, she asked, "Why do you teach only night classes?"

"I'm a night owl," I answered.

"I think you are."

I walked her back to her barracks in time for the nightly head count so the authorities could make sure the people were where they were supposed to be when they were supposed to be there. Keiko lingered by the door until she turned to me.

"Are you married?" she asked.

"I was," I said. "My wife died. It was a long time ago."

"That's why you always look so sad. I thought you looked like you missed someone."

"You're right," I said. "I miss her very much."

Keiko nodded. She handed me a note, written in her anagram code. With a cursory glance, I saw the words "Thank you, Professor Wentworth."

"You're welcome, Keiko," I said.

She smiled, pleased with me. She went inside her barracks, leaving me in the dust-prone desert to think of you. I stood there, listening, making sure her father wasn't on a drunken rampage, threatening Keiko, her mother, or anyone else in her family. When I was certain Keiko was safe, I made my way to the newspaper office, checked to be sure no one was around, and went inside to grab more paper, pencils, and a few clipboards. I took enough for my students, but not so much that anyone should notice the missing supplies. I had a lot to do before class the next night if I wanted to handwrite enough copies of Leaves of Grass for everyone. I didn't mind the work. It gave me something to focus on.

· · ·

JAMES WAS SO ENGROSSED in his story for Sarah that he was startled by footsteps heading toward his barracks from across the camp. At first, he thought it must be Geoffrey arriving home, but then he heard Geoffrey humming to himself on the other side of the partition. He listened again and heard the heavy boots growing closer as they crunched the dry desert sand. There was a brisk knock, and James opened his door to two armed guards.

"Yes?" James said.

"You have a visitor, Doctor Wentworth. She's waiting by the west gate."

"I thought we weren't allowed visitors."

"You're not, but you should come with me."

Dawn was still a newborn thought along the mountaintops as they walked through camp. James hoped Sarah was there. He followed the guards, both human, while he scanned for his wife somewhere along the perimeter near the gate. As they headed west, he noticed several detainees lingering outside their barracks whispering amongst each other. When they saw the human guards they continued talking. When they saw James they stopped and waited for him to pass. James tried to hear what they said, but they had gone inside and were whispering too low for even him to decipher their words.

As they drew near the gate, James noticed an elderly woman with white-gray hair and sharp, observant eyes standing a safe distance from the silver-coated fence as though she were afraid it could electrocute her at a touch. One armed guard hovered near her as though she posed a physical threat while another guard stood at attention behind a young man perhaps in his twenties who looked to be her grandson. James knew her the moment he saw her.

"Keiko?" he said.

"I'm surprised you remember me, Professor Wentworth. It's been a long time."

"Forgive me if I seem stunned. I was just writing to my wife about our time in Manzanar. I was telling her about the night you stole the supplies from the newspaper office."

The young man laughed. "You never told me that, Grandma."

Keiko winked at her grandson. "I still have a few secrets, you know." She stepped closer to the gate. "I'm an eighty-nine-year-old great-grandmother now, and you look the same as you ever did, Professor Wentworth. I had quite a crush on you back then."

"Of course you didn't," James said. "And the rest of your family?" James shook his head, wishing he could take back his words when he realized that many of those interned during World War II had passed on from this world.

"We were all very sad when my mother passed," Keiko said. "And my father..."

"Great-grandfather died in Manzanar," Keiko's grandson said.

"Your father was a good man, Keiko," James said.

"He was," said Keiko. "And yet whenever I think of him now, I can't help thinking how he drowned his sorrow in the saki he made from burned rice." Keiko turned to her grandson. "Your great-grandfather dug a hole in the dirt floor of our barracks and buried old rice in a pot and let it ferment. The rice wine smelled foul, but it served its purpose as far as he was concerned." She shook her head. "I'm glad you knew him before he started drinking, Professor. I'm glad there's someone who knew the man he was before the war." She took the young man's hand. "This is my grandson, Arnie Ishigura, Professor Wentworth."

James and Arnie nodded at each other, and he recognized Keiko's sharp, observant eyes in her grandson. "How did they let you so close to the gate?" James asked. "They're not allowing any visitors, even our families."

Keiko smiled the half little girl/half wise woman smile James remembered. "I'm a little old lady now, Professor." She nodded at the guard standing closest to her. "What harm can a little old lady do?"

"I'm happy to see you," James said, "but what are you doing here?"

"The same thing you did in Manzanar. I saw you on the news, and I heard they brought you here. Now I'm here for you the way you were here for me. What can I do to help you, Professor?" She looked at the fence, the guard towers, the barracks. "It looks like Manzanar, doesn't it?"

"They haven't gained any imagination in seventy years, I'm afraid."

"I always wondered what was different about you."

"Did you guess?"

"I knew you were different somehow, but never this. You only taught night classes, you were so pale, you kept your distance from everyone, never let anyone shake your hand. I thought maybe you had tuberculosis or some communicable disease, but you were too strong to be sickly." She giggled like a schoolgirl. "Hence the crush I had on you. But, no, I never guessed you were paranormal, and yet I can't say I was all that surprised when I found out. I'm glad to see you're still a very handsome man, Professor."

"You're still beautiful too, Keiko."

"Please. I'm a wrinkled, gray-haired, old great-grandmother."

James shook his head. "When I look at you, I see the sharp-eyed girl who wanted to be an English teacher because she wanted to teach others to love reading as much as she did. Tell me, Keiko, did you become an English teacher?"

"That's Professor Keiko to you, sir, and yes, I did. I was an English professor at UC Berkeley for thirty years. I met my husband Henry there. We've missed him very much since he's been gone." Keiko dabbed at her watering eyes with her fingers, and Arnie kissed his grandmother's cheek. "You said you were writing to your wife?"

"Yes, my wife, Sarah. She's at home in Massachusetts with our daughter."

"I'm so glad you found someone special. I know how much you missed your first wife."

James smiled. "I'll tell you the story of how I met Sarah one night."

"You always told such wonderful stories," Keiko said.

James looked closely at Keiko, her eyes straight-looking and observant as always. Her hair was white-silver, and perhaps she hunched forward slightly, but otherwise she was the Keiko James knew seventy years before. He was fascinated by her. For over three hundred years James kept his distance from nearly everyone, making few ties anywhere. Yet he knew each successive generation of Miriam's family, and he watched them grow from infants to children to adults to seniors, for those lucky enough to see those advanced years.

"What's it like," he asked Keiko, "growing older?"

"It isn't as bad as some make it out to be. I wouldn't trade the knowledge or the insights I have now for anything. The hardest part about growing older is when those I love pass on, but that happens to all of us, doesn't it? The older I get the more I know to cherish the time I have with those I love most in the world. Time is my most valuable commodity, and I no longer waste it worrying about things that don't matter. Time goes too quickly, Professor, at least for us humans. It seems like yesterday when we were together at Manzanar, and yet it's been seventy years and I'm a great-grandmother now. I'm grateful for the time I've had and for my life experiences, the good and the bad. I'm grateful for my family. I'm grateful I had the opportunity to know you. Growing older is nothing to fear. It can be a beautiful experience if you allow it to be."

The guard stationed near the gate gestured toward Keiko with his hands.

Arnie leaned closer toward the gate, and he whispered as though he knew James could hear. "My grandmother told me what you did for her family by staying with them in Manzanar. We want to return the favor. What can we do for you, Professor? What do you need?"

James looked from Arnie to Keiko with a newfound resolve. If he could trust anyone with the plan he was formulating, it would be Keiko. He realized he would trust Keiko with his life if he had to, and if Keiko chose to help him in his endeavor, he would be doing just that. How to tell her what he was thinking without alerting the authorities? He looked to where the guards stood with their eyes fixed at a forty-five-degree angle on the horizon. He stepped closer to the gate, but he hesitated when he realized he didn't know what to say without causing concern. Arnie's eyes brightened as though he understood.

"Can I write to you here, Professor?" he asked.

"You can," James said. "You wouldn't be surprised to discover that they censor our letters the way they did in Manzanar. It's as if they're searching for hidden messages like they're afraid we're going to try to escape."

140

Keiko laughed. "Escape the camp? Who ever heard of such a thing?"

An older guard appeared out of the shadows and waved his wooden stake in Keiko's direction. "That's enough," he yelled. "There shouldn't be any visitors here. You need to leave."

Keiko looked at James and smiled.

"It was wonderful seeing you again, Professor Wentworth. I'll be in touch."

James moved closer to the gate. He would have moved closer still, but a guard stepped in front of him.

"Do you remember the old language you used in Manzanar?" James asked.

"Always," Keiko said. "I even taught it to Arnie. We need to remember the language of our ancestors."

The guard waved his stake again, leaving no misinterpretation of his meaning. Keiko shrugged as she turned from the gate. "It's time to go anyway, Arnie. This place reminds me too much of when I was in Manzanar." Keiko took her grandson's arm, then nodded at James as she disappeared into the desert night.

CHAPTER 12

*S*arah was behind the cash register in the Witches Lair when Howard rushed in. He looked sidetracked, as though he had walked into the grocery store for milk and walked out fifteen minutes later with everything but milk.

"What's wrong?" Sarah asked.

"Is Olivia here?"

"She's in the storeroom. I can get her if you need her."

Howard looked toward the storeroom and shook his head as though he couldn't decide what to do.

"I'm leaving for California tonight," he said.

"Why so suddenly?"

The more Sarah studied Howard, the more she saw the tightness behind his yellow-hazel eyes. Were his eyes always so yellow, she wondered? She glanced at the calendar at the phases of the moon and saw the full moon more than a week away.

"Everything is fine, Sarah. I just wanted to let someone know I was leaving."

"Is Timothy all right?" Sarah's thoughts turned to James. "It's not James, is it? You would tell me if something was wrong with James."

Howard shook his head, the only mannerism he had that afternoon. "I'm sorry, Sarah. I didn't mean to frighten you. I'm a little distracted today. My mother, brother, and sister are in town, that's all. James is fine."

"Do you need me to go to California? Is there something I can do?"

"You need to stay here now. You'll come to California when it's time."

"When will it be time?"

With a friendly kiss on the cheek, Howard disappeared through the door, the bells jingling behind him. Sarah was certain Howard was hiding something, but what? She wanted to ask him what he meant by this cryptic visit, why he asked for Olivia at first, and she raced through the door, searching both ways down Pickering Wharf, around the florist, the coffee shop, and the Rockmore Drydock. She thought she was being followed so she stopped, watching the tourists snapping pictures of the *Friendship* docked in the bay and the Salem Maritime Historical Site. She felt someone behind her and turned around, but there was no one there, at least no one who seemed to be paying attention to her. She saw mothers out for a walk with their children. She saw tourists browsing in the shops or studying the historical monuments. Suddenly, she felt afraid the way she did when she first moved to Salem and she saw the pock-faced monster following her with his wicked, snake-like chains. She felt paranoid the way she did when she and James fled Salem, fearing what would become of their family if Grace were taken away.

By the time Sarah stepped back into the Witches Lair she was trembling, her mind rattling loose in her skull. She pulled her cell phone from her pocket, thinking to call Howard, but Olivia came out from the storeroom with Grace in her arms.

"What is it, Sarah?"

"Howard is leaving for California tonight. I thought it seemed sudden, but he insisted there's nothing wrong."

"You don't believe him?"

"I don't know. He seemed distracted."

Olivia froze suddenly, her eyes closed. Grace also stilled, as though she sensed Olivia needed the quiet. "It's here," Olivia said. "The presence."

"When I went outside to find Howard I thought I felt someone following me. I looked around and didn't see anyone but I'm sure someone was there. It felt so close I thought it was breathing down my neck." Sarah shivered, and she expected to see a goblin or a ghost waving a haunted greeting in her direction. "What should we do?"

Olivia looked around the cases of trinkets as though she also expected to see someone.

"Come," Olivia said. She led Sarah to the back of the shop where five cubbies were separated from the rest of the store by black velvet curtains. Olivia pulled aside the curtain to the cubby on the end and pointed to a folding chair near the white linen-covered table. Everything, from the black velvet to the folding chairs to the burning candle and spiced incense, was the same as Sarah remembered. "Sit here."

Olivia handed Grace to Sarah and sat on the other side of the table. She took Sarah's hand and smiled at Grace. "I'm giving Mommy a reading like I did when she first arrived in Salem."

"She's the one who told me Daddy was looking for me," Sarah said.

Olivia nodded. "I was right then, so let's see if I'm right now. There's a friendly presence here to communicate with you, Sarah, I'm sure of it."

It was just as Sarah remembered—the way Olivia sat stone-like, the way her eyelids fluttered. But Olivia still appeared conscious, unlike when she drifted to another realm to communicate with spirits.

"You're not in a trance," Sarah said.

"Whatever it is, whoever it is, it's here, in this room with us right now." Olivia closed her eyes. "He's here."

"He?"

Olivia tilted her head to the side, her ear pointed to the ceiling, listening. "I'm not getting a name, Sarah." Olivia gripped Sarah's hands tighter, causing Sarah's blood to warm and her nerves to tingle, but she didn't dare move for fear of disconnecting Olivia from whatever this was. Olivia's eyelids fluttered and Sarah thought she was falling into a trance, but Olivia's eyes flashed open again.

"He's someone who has passed from this life to the next. I'm getting a sound, Sarah. A letter. It's…it's…" Olivia shook her head. "It's the letter J. Who do you know who has passed whose name starts with J?"

"It's not James?"

"Not James, but I feel you're very close. Who do you know who has passed whose name starts with J?"

Sarah shook her head, the space between her ears aching as she struggled to recall someone, anyone who had passed whose name started with J.

"I can't think of anyone besides James."

"Think, Sarah. I feel him poking me, prodding me. We're so close. The letter J…anyone. From this life or your previous one."

"Wait."

Sarah closed her eyes, stilled her breath, and she saw him, his kindly eyes, his warm smile. She saw him reaching out to her on her first wedding day with James in 1691, and she remembered James thinking he saw him at their second wedding. Then she remembered the hearty Shakespearean actor's voice.

"James' father was John," she said.

Olivia nodded. "Yes. John."

Sarah scanned the black velvet-lined cubby, hoping to see him there, wanting to see his smile and hear his voice. She hadn't seen him since 1692. She let go of Olivia's hands and reached tentatively toward the air.

"John?" she said. She couldn't control the sobs in her voice, knowing her beloved father-in-law was so near. "John, are you here?"

And then Sarah heard it, the voice she loved.

"I'm here, Daughter."

John spoke through Olivia. Olivia looked like herself, her face calm, her body relaxed, though she spoke in John's voice, in his English accent with the robust undertones of a man who made his living on the stage.

"Father," Sarah said.

She dropped her head to the doily-covered folding table. Grace patted her mother's hair and kissed her mother's cheek, and Sarah hugged her daughter closer.

"Grandfather John is here, Grace," Sarah said.

In the corner of the cubby, inside the black velvet curtains that separated the room from the rest of the shop, a halo-golden light grew taller and taller and brighter and brighter until it nearly blinded Sarah with its intensity. Within the luminous glow, she saw him, John, his small but kind eyes, his wide smile, his gentleness, his love. He nodded, his hands pressed together as if in prayer.

Sarah stared at Olivia. "Am I imagining this?"

"He's here, Sarah. Speak to him."

Sarah reached toward him, but though she saw his form there was nothing tangible for her to touch. "I see you, Father," was all she could say.

John looked lovingly at the baby on Sarah's lap. Grace was leaning toward John as though she saw him, and her jewel-blue eyes grew wide at the brightness of the golden aura. Even through his transparent form, Sarah saw his watering eyes, and he nodded.

"This is the Grace you were missing," Olivia said in John's voice.

"Did you know?" Sarah asked. John bowed, and Sarah understood. John had guided her and James to their Grace. John looked into Sarah's eyes with the same compassion Sarah remembered, that accepting I'm-so-glad-you're-part-of-my-family love that endeared her father-in-law to her so long ago. "For so many years James missed you," Olivia said for John. "He misses you now. But all will be well. Soon."

John reached toward Sarah. Though she couldn't feel his touch she felt his warmth, his light, surrounding her.

"Have you seen James?" Sarah asked.

Olivia laughed in John's hearty manner. "I have seen him." Another hearty laugh. "He's a stubborn boy, James. He takes after his father, and his grandfather for that matter."

"His grandfather?" Sarah asked.

John's light dimmed and Sarah struggled to see him in the darkened room. He leaned over Sarah and pressed his head toward hers.

"I have always been here, Sarah. Always." He bowed in a courtly manner toward Olivia.

"You're welcome, John," Olivia said.

Her voice was her own again.

AFTER OLIVIA CLOSED THE SHOP, Sarah put Grace in her stroller and walked along Derby Street to Lafayette, turning left at her old route toward Salem State University. She felt an urge to walk the campus and see familiar sights, familiar people. She realized she hadn't seen Jennifer since the Wiccan ceremony and she wanted to visit her friend.

It was the summer term at the college, and Sarah walked across the lightly populated campus, enjoying the warm weather even if it was humid near the shore. Standing on the lawn, she paused outside the U-shaped Meier Hall and pointed out the building to Grace.

"That's where Daddy taught his night classes. Your daddy was a wonderful teacher, Grace. He had such patience for his students. He loved literature so much..." Remembering James in his element, teaching his classes, and helping his students, was too hard. Until she remembered. "He didn't have much patience. He *has* such patience. He's away now, but we'll see him again soon. That's what Grandfather John said, and that's what I believe."

"Daadaa," Grace said.

"Daddy will be back with us where he belongs."

Sarah meandered across the Central Campus, along the bike path, past the buildings as familiar to her as her own home. She stopped at her destination, the library, and she smiled at the memory of her first days in Salem. This job gave her a reason to move across the country, back to her home in Massachusetts, near her hometown Boston, close but not so close. The job brought her here, where she was supposed to be, so she could find her way through the relentless nightmares, so she could find James and Grace. She would always be grateful for this library, even if it was hard to be here now. She thought of taking Grace to the third floor and James' old office, but Sarah didn't think she would like it when she saw another professor in his place. She would expect to see James there, his golden halo hair falling into his eyes, and she would want to walk to him, put her hands on his shoulders, and rub away the tension that living for over three hundred years had brought on. He always loved feeling her hands on him, he said, and how she could press his problems away.

As she walked into the library she looked at the elevator and remembered the nights when she watched the steel doors open hoping to see James come out. How much had changed since then? She saw Jennifer behind the librarians' desk and stopped. "Hi, Jennifer," she said.

Jennifer was startled when she looked up from her work. She came out from behind the desk, hugged Sarah, and kissed Grace's cheek.

"What are you doing here, Sarah?"

"I haven't seen you so I thought I'd come by." Sarah wanted to tell Jennifer about seeing John, about what he said, but she didn't have the words to explain. "It's been some time since I've been here."

"You haven't been back since your last day at work."

"That was the night everything fell apart." Sarah looked at her daughter, dozing off in her stroller, and shook her head. "It's good to see you, Jennifer. Why are you avoiding me?"

"The fact that my mother told you I've been in love with your husband for as long as I can remember might have something to do with it."

Jennifer looked at the stacks, at the books piled on her desk, at the students punching words into the computer keyboards, at the industrial-style lights hanging from the ceiling. Finally, she looked at Sarah.

"From the first time he told me about you when you first came back to Salem, I saw his connection to you. He didn't know you were Elizabeth then. He only knew you looked like her. But even if you weren't Elizabeth reincarnated he would have loved you forever from that night forward. He moved past loving Elizabeth to loving Sarah." Jennifer's smile was stunted. "I understood for a long time that James could never be mine, and when you were reunited with him it only solidified what I already knew. But I love Chandresh now, and it's not because he's a vampire, and it's not because he's James' vampling like my mother thinks. I love Chandresh because he's Chandresh."

Jennifer sat on the edge of her desk and smiled at Grace. "I told you the truth before, Sarah. Nothing happened between James and me even though I tried. When I turned eighteen I got him alone in my mother's house while she was out and..." Jennifer turned away, a guilty shrug on her shoulders. "He wasn't having any of it. *I love my wife*, he said.

"*Elizabeth is long gone, James*, I told him. He shook his head and smiled sadly. *Not to me*, he said. And my mother was right. I did marry two tall, blond ex-husbands because they reminded me of James, but they weren't James. I never could find another man like him. And then I met Chandresh, and Chandresh became enough in himself. Are you mad at me, Sarah?"

Sarah embraced her friend. "I'm not mad, Jennifer. I'm not even that surprised to be honest. I asked you when I first met James if you liked him."

"I said he was an *old* family friend."

"I had no idea how old at the time. But even then I suspected you felt more for him." Sarah took Jennifer's hand. "I'm so glad you found Chandresh. He's a wonderful man in his own right. You deserve to be happy."

"I think the reason you're not upset is because you know James has never had eyes for anyone but you."

"That helps." Sarah looked into Jennifer's hazel eyes, her long auburn hair tucked behind her ears. There was a sadness in Jennifer that Sarah understood. "I don't want anything to come between us, Jennifer. You mean too much to me."

"You are my dearest friend in the world, Sarah. If something from the past came between us, I don't know what I would do."

"I'm glad we got that out of the way. Now I have to ask you, do you know why Howard is rushing to California?"

Jennifer sat in her chair and resumed typing into the database. "Is he?"

"He said he was leaving tonight. He seemed distracted, like something was wrong. Do you know why he's leaving so suddenly? I haven't heard from James in over a week, and he didn't mention anything worrying in his last letter."

Jennifer leaned closer to the computer screen as though she couldn't see the words on the monitor. "I'm sure it's nothing, Sarah."

A line of students appeared and Jennifer stood to help them.

"I remember lines like that," Sarah said. "I'll let you get back to work."

Jennifer hugged Sarah from behind the desk. "I'm glad you came, Sarah."

Sarah pushed Grace past the metal detectors, back across campus, around students finding their way to their classes. She headed down Lafayette Street back to Derby, past Pickering Wharf and the Witches Lair, past the House of the Seven Gables where tourists waited on the manicured lawn for the red trolley that would take them across town, to home where she sat on the sofa near the diamond-paned casement window with her daughter on her lap, her tailless black cat asleep beside her, looking out at the dwindling daylight struggling to understand everything that was happening then.

CHAPTER 13

I have been communicating with Keiko. Yes, that Keiko, the one I have been telling you about, the one I knew in Manzanar. She is still such a bright light. She will be visiting you soon, and I am glad you will meet her. I trust Keiko with my very life, which means I trust her with you.

Sharing letters with Keiko brings back my nights in Manzanar even more strongly than before. Part of my frustration being there was I didn't see what good I could do but teach class, and I felt useless beyond my job description. It took all my self-restraint to not scream. I remember the night I saw Keiko while she stood outside our classroom staring into the mountains. I heard people scampering to their barracks, and while their feet hurried, their faces remained calm. Some smiled, some bowed to their elders according to custom, the younger ones shouting their greetings. Mainly, they were subdued. I couldn't understand the lack of anger, the absence of hostility. Where was their righteous indignation, I wondered?

"They look like they're fine," I said to Keiko. "How can this be fine?"

Keiko shook her head. "They're not fine on the inside, Professor Wentworth. You have to understand Japanese culture. There are six main cultural values: gaman, which is endurance; gambaru, which is perseverance; giri, which is duty; oyakoko, which is loyalty; on, which is filial piety; and *kodomo no tame ni, which is sacrifice. This is how they endure the shame. They have to go with the flow."*

"You're being imprisoned without cause," I said, my righteous indignation rising as hot spots on my white cheeks.

"You saw the propaganda after Pearl Harbor was bombed. We're probably safer in here than we would be out there. Out there we're portrayed as animals, vampires."

"You're definitely not a vampire," I said.

"At least I'm not that." Keiko's sharp eyes clouded and she looked away. She scanned the area to see if anyone, internee or guard, was near. Her voice dropped to a whisper a human would strain to hear. "Don't you see, Professor? The country we love has turned on us. You've never experienced anything like this. I don't think you can understand."

How could I explain to this young girl that I knew what it was to be unjustly accused, that I had lost you to such madness? Keiko watched me, sensing I wanted to say something, but she couldn't know what I was, how long I had lived, the circumstances that took your life. Instead, I said, "It's natural when you're being unfairly judged to feel fear, apprehension, even rage."

"I'm not saying we don't feel those things, Doctor Wentworth, but in Japanese culture you don't express your feelings and you never complain. It's called saving face. People go to great lengths to avoid loss of face. They don't openly criticize or insult anyone. That's why you see what looks like acceptance. This is how we have to cope. This is what happens when you have something to be angry about but you're conditioned not to show anger."

"When you have something to be angry about and you don't express it, you turn it in toward yourself, or onto others like you. I know too well how it goes. You feel anger toward everyone except the ones you should be angry with." Keiko nodded. "Come on," I said. "You should get back to your barracks before head count. We don't want them looking for you."

We walked toward the residential block where she lived, and we passed the mess hall where there were still people in line waiting for their dinner while those at the tables ate army surplus off tin pie plates. My nose shriveled from the foul-smelling slop the weather-hardened Army cooks fed their charges, oblivious to the fact that they were feeding families with young children and older grandparents.

"What are they feeding you?" I asked.

"Hot dogs," Keiko said. "And hot dogs. And ketchup, kidneys, butterless bread, Spam, and potatoes. And hot dogs. After enough people protested, we started getting rice, but they don't know how to cook it and it's burnt most of the time. We make hot dog sushi and Spam sushi. We've been eating weenie royale—onions, soy sauce, hot dogs, eggs, and rice." Keiko shrugged at my horrified expression. "You get used to it." On the surface, it seemed as simple as feeding ten thousand people with government surplus, but they were denied their culture, their comfort foods, and therefore their identity. Through the open mess hall door I saw an elderly woman I recognized alone at a corner table. "There's my grandmother," Keiko said.

"Why is she in there alone?" I asked.

"I ate earlier," she said, "and my mother is working at the orphanage. My brother and sister are off with their friends somewhere, and my father..." Keiko closed her eyes. "My father is busy." I knew she meant drunk. "My grandmother has no one else to eat with. I hardly see my family all at once anymore. Everyone is off doing their own thing."

Life in Manzanar blurred night by night, one into the next and the next after that until weeks, then months passed. I taught my classes, helped internees around camp where I could, and asked people on the outside to send supplies where I saw scarcity. Spring, summer, and autumn passed, and then it was snow again, the beginning of December. A buzzing, first faint and unrecognizable, grew louder until every person throughout camp showed signs of restlessness. Some people turned upon each other, finger-pointing, shouting, I'm right you're wrong, my way or the highway. It was exactly as I predicted—they didn't turn their anger toward those who caused the incarceration, but the resentment had to be directed somewhere so they turned on each other. The tension was mainly between members of the Japanese American Citizens League and the first-generation Japanese. Although the JACL leaders acted as representatives of the administration, the elders didn't share their views and had little respect for them. Men were accused of being spies for the administration, of working for the very people who were incarcerating them, while others wanted the two sides to work together. Neither group made *headway in negotiations, and the buzzing became overwhelming. Meetings turned into shouting matches, beatings, and death threats against the pro-administration group. People were snapping under the strain.*

When I awoke on December 5, 1942, there was an uneasy stillness throughout the camp. No usual sounds of people out and about, coming to and from the mess halls, the gardens, the sports complexes, the latrines. I had no class that night, so I stayed in my barracks, flipping through the twenty copies of Shakespearean sonnets sent by a fellow professor from UCLA. Deep into the darkness I heard heavy footsteps slapping against the cold sand. I heard screams, threats, and thumping that sounded like bricks against human flesh. I raced from my barracks and found hundreds of people converging outside, shouting about the six masked men who had disappeared. As I drew nearer to the commotion I saw Keiko and her mother huddled to the side.

"What happened?" I asked.

"They say six masked men beat Fred Tayama while he was sleeping."

"The JACL leader? Why?"

"For working with the administrators."

The people were disparate in their reactions. Some sided with those who perpetrated the crime, saying no one should cooperate with those who put us here. Some sided with Fred and the JACL, believing the best way through this situation was for everyone to work together. Most people stared, unbelieving that violence had broken out at Manzanar.

The leader of the Kitchen Workers Union, Harry Ueno, was arrested for Tayama's beating, removed from Manzanar, and jailed in the nearby town of Independence, California. While I slept the next day, thousands of internees gathered in support of Ueno, demanding his return to Manzanar, and several of Ueno's supporters negotiated his release. The center director agreed, and Ueno was to be jailed in the Manzanar detention center. Evacuees gathered again, this time to demand Ueno's unconditional release. The director requested military police presence because the agitated protestors began arming themselves with knives, hatchets, stones, and any other weapons they could find. A small group forced their way into the hospital looking for Tayama, and hundreds of protestors surrounded the police station demanding Ueno's release. While the Ueno crowds were in full force, others appeared in support of the beaten Fred Tayama. I heard the roar and thunder of the protests, ebbing and rolling like the high tide waves along the Salem shore during a thunderstorm, a dangerous squall of human irascibility. When the crowds surged forward, military police threw tear gas. People ran to avoid the fumes, and some pushed a driverless truck toward the jail. The MPs fired their guns into the crowd, killing a seventeen-year-old boy. A twenty-one-year-old man died later of his gunshot wounds. Nine others were wounded.

By the time I left my barracks that night it was silent in the camp. Not a sound from anywhere. Everyone stayed inside. No one spoke to others in their stalls. It was as though they needed space within their heads to make sense of what happened, though nothing could help them understand the madness that consumed their lives since Pearl Harbor was bombed.

Thinking of the violence in Manzanar, I realize now that the Japanese-Americans had to stay within the confines of the camp. They were fully human, too susceptible to the injuries of beatings and gunshot wounds. All they could do was steep in their bitterness until the inevitable explosion. After the hysteria of the riots, there was calm after the storm. In time, at the end of the war, the camps were closed and the law-abiding Japanese-Americans were released. This too shall pass, and then we return.

What does it mean to return? Return home? Return to those you love the most? Could the Japanese-Americans return to their lives after they were freed from Manzanar? Is it true what they say, you can never go home again? Can I return to you, truly return, in all that the word means?

When I come home when this madness is done, will everything be the same? Can you and I ever be the same? It's all I want now—for us to be the same. Return means to go back, to appear again. That is what I want, my love, to appear again. Remember that no matter what happens, whatever the future holds, I will always love you. My love has not wavered in over three hundred years. It will not waver in another three hundred years or a millennia after that. You are my life, Sarah. I will do anything for you.

CHAPTER 14

Sarah didn't know what to make of James' latest letter. Was he expecting something to happen? Something bad? Was he saying goodbye? He seemed confused, she thought, disjointed, as though he didn't know himself what he was trying to say. Nothing was edited out, no heavy black marker deleted his words, no scissor cuttings. There was nothing the censors didn't like. But Sarah couldn't shake the feeling that something was about to happen. How odd, she thought, that James had been telling her about Keiko, and then suddenly he began communicating with her. Sarah opened the bottom right drawer of James' seventeenth-century desk and, while there were no letters from the 1940s, she did find several black and white photographs of Manzanar—snapshots of the people living in the camp and the scenic desert landscape—and she saw Ansel Adams' name printed across the bottom. Through the etching of the gray-scale pictures, Sarah understood how the camp was both beautiful and ugly—beautiful in the perfect postcard mountains, ugly in its purpose. There was one photograph of a lovely young woman with sharp, observant eyes smiling at the camera. On the back James had written, "Keiko outside our classroom barracks."

Two nights later Sarah answered the knock at her door. Even

without James' letters she would have recognized Keiko immediately from the photograph. She was older, grayer, but still lovely, her round face smooth, her eyes as sharp and observant as they were seventy years ago. Keiko extended her hand in a warm greeting.

"Hello, Mrs. Wentworth. I'm Keiko Sato Ishigura, and this is my grandson, Arnie. I knew your husband a long time ago." Sarah folded her arms around Keiko in welcome. Keiko returned the greeting.

"Please come in," Sarah said. "James told me you would be visiting."

"This house is amazing," Arnie said. "How old is it?"

"It's from the seventeenth century," Sarah answered. "Most of it is original, though we had the kitchen remodeled last summer."

Arnie pulled out his cell phone and started taking pictures.

"You should ask permission, Arnold," Keiko said.

"People take pictures of the house all the time," Sarah said. "We don't mind."

Keiko grasped her grandson's shoulder. "Arnie is a history teacher," she said proudly.

"I was always fascinated by the stories Grandma told about World War II. She's the only one in our family who will talk about it." Arnie snapped a photo of the attic and James' seventeenth-century desk. "I'll show these to my students when we study colonial times."

Sarah gestured to the sofa, and Keiko sat facing the diamond-paned casement window, looking into the Salem night. It was later August now, the beginning of the end of summer, the beginning of longer nights, meaner tides, and cooler air along the coast. Sarah made some tea for her guests, and when she brought out the tea service, Keiko and Arnie were deep in conversation. Sarah poured the tea from the wooden table a few steps away, leaving them their privacy.

"Excuse us, Mrs. Wentworth," Keiko said. "We didn't mean to seem as though we were in a private conversation."

"Sarah, please."

Sarah sat next to Keiko, immediately warming to the grandmotherly woman, seeing what James meant when he said she was a bright light. There was such intelligence, even cunning about her. Keiko held Sarah's hand.

"I saw James about a month ago," Keiko said. "He looks well, Sarah. As strong and handsome as ever. Since then we've been exchanging letters."

"How did you see him?" Sarah asked. "I've been trying to get permission to go to Camp Dracula, but they said no visitors allowed."

"Grandma is a little old lady now," Arnie said. "What harm can she do?"

"What harm indeed?" Keiko said, a naughty grin on her face. "I'm a retired English professor. English professors are meek, aren't they?" Keiko winked at Sarah.

"James has been telling me about his time in Manzanar," Sarah said. "I'm sorry you and your family were incarcerated."

"And I'm sorry it's happening now to the professor," Keiko said.

"James said he'd be home soon," Sarah said. "I don't know how. Our lawyer says the Supreme Court isn't even hearing the internment case for a few months, and then it could take time to come to a decision." Keiko looked at Arnie and shook her head, a movement so slight Sarah thought she imagined it. "I'm afraid of how all of this will affect James," Sarah said. "It couldn't have been easy for you and your family once you were out of the camp."

"It wasn't," Keiko said. "My family left Manzanar as soon as we were able while others stayed behind as long as they could since they had nowhere else to go—no homes, no jobs, and now their families were scattered across the country. We stayed with family in Ohio, and it took years to get ourselves back on track. My father became too lost in alcohol while he was in camp, unable to deal with what happened. He struggled for years to get his grocery store off the ground, and he was finally seeing a profit from his hard work. Then everything was taken away. For what?"

Sarah shook her head. "For nothing."

"But you got the money," Arnie said. "That must have counted for something."

"People bow to the god of money," Keiko said, "but I can tell you it does very little to heal emotional scars." Keiko sat straight, her back against the sofa, her bearing firm, and Sarah saw the college-age girl who snuck into the journalism office to steal supplies for the high school students. "When I was younger I was taught to respect authority." Keiko smirked. "I have a different opinion now. I know what it is to be treated unfairly without cause, and I feel obligated to do whatever I can for your husband, which is why I have this odd request for you, Sarah. I'd like you and your daughter to come to California with Arnie and me. I would like to show you where Manzanar was, very close to where Professor Wentworth is now."

"I've thought of going," Sarah said. "I know I can't see him, but just to be closer. I want him to know I'm there for him the way he's always been there for me."

Keiko brushed her hands together as though she were shaking away the dust that eighty-plus years had brought on, though Sarah thought there was nothing dusty about Keiko. Arnie whispered something into his grandmother's ear, and she nodded. "In one of the professor's letters he asked about a friend of yours, a doctor, Thomas Masters I believe his name is."

"Thomas moved with his family to San Francisco."

"That's near where I live in Berkeley. Do you have his address? The professor mentioned wanting to write to Thomas but he wasn't sure where he was."

Sarah pulled up Thomas' new contact information on her cell phone and wrote it onto a post-it note for Keiko. "James never mentioned anything about Thomas in his letters," she said.

"I'm not surprised," said Keiko. "He wouldn't want to write anything that could be suspicious."

"What's suspicious about wanting someone's address?"

"It's probably better if we don't find out. You will come to California with us, won't you?"

In her heart, Sarah felt herself already on the plane, flying across the North American continent to where she wouldn't be able to see James himself but she could write to him and let him know she was near. Sarah thought of everything she learned about her husband, the way he helped Olivia's grandparents during the Depression, the way he helped Olivia's cousins in Germany, and she pictured James grabbing a guard's uniform at Camp Dracula and walking through the front gate before anyone thought to look for him.

"Is James up to something?" Sarah asked.

Keiko laughed. "What makes you say that?"

"I know my husband. In some ways I know him better now than I did before he left."

"Some things are clearer from a distance," Keiko said. "I didn't realize the impact Manzanar had on my family until I could examine it later. For years I thought since we were out of the camp we were free. I didn't know true freedom until I could face the tragedy head-on, feel the pain I never allowed myself to feel while I was there, and accept that it happened. For a long time I wouldn't even allow myself to think about Manzanar. If I pushed it out of my mind then it wasn't real. At least that's what I wanted to believe."

"Then you started talking about it, Grandma," Arnie said.

"When I started talking about it, when I acknowledged the effect the experience had on my family, and me, the ache lessened. As hard as it was in Manzanar and after we were released, we survived." She brushed Arnie's cheek with the back of her hand, her love for her grandson evident in the sweetness of her gesture. "We prospered. And we're here to tell the tale so future generations will learn." Keiko grasped Sarah's hand. "Come with us to California, Sarah. I want to take you to Manzanar. I want you to see. And remember, when this foolishness is over, as happy as the professor will be at seeing you and your daughter again, being released back into the world after you've been locked away is hard. I don't think your husband will suffer physical ailments like we did, but the mental impacts are hard too. There are Japanese Americans still suffering from the trauma. It's the trauma of being incarcerated like a criminal when you haven't committed any crime. It's the distress of the betrayal. We lulled ourselves into believing the propaganda directed against us. We believed Doctor Seuss when he made fun of us in his comic strips. We must be bad enough to warrant the caricatures and the meanness, we thought. If we believed the propaganda against us then we could still believe in the goodness of the United States government. Uncle Sam was good to us, there for us, protecting us by putting us behind a barbed wire fence. We were told we were being kept under watch and key for our safety, but we were put away to appease other people's prejudices.

"You have to help Professor Wentworth talk about this experience," Keiko continued. "I know his quietness, not unlike my father's. My father was a man of few words, and he never expressed his anger though he had plenty to be angry about. He never complained, but the pain seethed until it created the disease of alcoholism within him. Others in the camp also repressed the trauma, and later they suffered depression, relationship problems, ulcers, and addictions. As I said, I'm sure the professor won't suffer physical ailments, but he needs to be aware of his emotional health. Help him get closure, Sarah. If he's immortal then he'll have these memories for a long time. We don't want them haunting him forever."

Sarah nodded. "He holds onto his grief a long time."

"Your husband did a brave thing then," Keiko said, "living among us when he was in danger of being discovered for what he truly is. I never realized the extent of the sacrifice he made until I learned how special he is."

"He is very special," Sarah said.

Later that night, when Olivia came home after Keiko and Arnie left, Sarah told her Wiccan friend what happened.

"At first I thought I would go to California, but now I'm not so sure," Sarah said. "Maybe I should stay here."

"What does your heart tell you?" Olivia asked.

Sarah closed her eyes and listened. "I feel like I should go with Keiko and Arnie," she answered. "My heart needs to be as close to James as possible right now."

"Then go," said Olivia.

Sarah called Jennifer and asked if she wanted to go as well, but Jennifer chose to stay behind. She was overseeing the move into the new library building, she said, which was a lot of work, and besides, she had only received one letter from Chandresh since he had been gone. Maybe Chandresh had forgotten her. Maybe Chandresh didn't think she was so special after all.

"If he wants to hear from me he knows where to find me," Jennifer said.

Sarah threw some clothing for herself and Grace into her luggage, and she realized she was worried about what would happen when she arrived in California. To be closer to James—would that be easier or harder than being in Massachusetts? To be within distance of him, but unable to see him or brush his gold hair from his eyes, hold his hand, or feel his strong arms around her? The thought of being so close yet so far was unbearable, yet she felt compelled to go. She felt the tug of her eternal union with James, as though the invisible fairy-like thread she felt connecting them was pulling her toward the Sierra Nevadas.

Two days later, Sarah, with Keiko and Arnie, boarded a plane at Boston's Logan Airport with Grace in her arms.

IN CALIFORNIA, Arnie drove the white Ford Escape his grandmother rented down U.S. Route 395 to the small town of Independence, the seat of Inyo County. Sarah saw the green rectangle sign in front of the white auto repair shop noting the town's population at six hundred and sixty-nine. To Sarah, the town was both Old West and Art Deco, and in the one-hundred-degree August heat there was a ghost town feel. Independence was quiet and quaint with manicured lawns, shrubbery, and trees from less desert-like locales growing along the sidewalks. They drove by old storefronts, corner markets, and a smattering of tourists on their way to a day of hiking, fishing, or sight-seeing around the Sierra Nevada or the Pacific Crest Trail, gathering supplies, stopping for a meal at a diner, or filling their cars at the gas stations. They passed the 1920s-style Inyo County Court House, a sand-beige building with Doric columns and steep steps. Arnie pulled into the parking lot alongside the Winnedumah Hotel, established in 1927 according to the sign. The hotel was nestled at the base of the mountains, the rocks nearly close enough to touch. Arnie disappeared into the lobby to check into the quaint Spanish-style bed and breakfast with the red-tile roof. When Sarah got out of the car to help him, Keiko asked Sarah to wait beside her.

"Arnie will handle everything," Keiko said.

Sarah found her rose-patterned room with two single beds clean and comfortable, and as she fell asleep that night, she thought of James, calling to him in the silence of her mind, letting him know she had come to California. She was so close to him that she could feel him there beside her. When she awoke in the night she smiled when she saw Grace sleeping peacefully. She kissed her daughter and fell back to sleep.

In the morning, after they shared a continental breakfast of coffee and pastries, Keiko and Arnie took Sarah and Grace to the Manzanar National Historic Site maintained by the National Park Service. Arnie drove the rental car along the dusty desert road until they saw the sign proclaiming the 'Manzanar Relocation Center' in the distance. They parked near the stone sentry post, a guard shack with the pagoda-style roof James described in his letter. Sarah felt as though she knew this place because the preserved pieces looked exactly as James described them. Inside the Manzanar Interpretive Center, in the Layers of History room with its photographs and audiovisual aids, Keiko saw without seeing, heard without hearing the stories she already knew because she lived them. This had been her life, not a chapter in a U.S. History text-book. She had been interrupted for three years, Keiko, and the pain of it, seventy years later, was strong. Sarah felt her own eyes watering in compassion for this woman who flew across the country to visit her though they had been strangers. Keiko could have been an angry, bitter woman, Sarah knew. She had every right to be. But instead of wallowing in self-pity she had become a university professor. She raised a beautiful family, which Sarah knew from her grandson's obvious devotion to her. And now Keiko was there to support James the way James had been there to support her and her family, and Sarah loved the older woman dearly for it. When Sarah wondered why anyone would go to such extremes for James, she remembered Olivia's words—because James gave help wherever he could, and he found it whenever he needed it.

Keiko reached for Grace, who reached for Keiko, instinctively feeling her parents' trust in the grandmotherly woman. Keiko carried Grace as she led Arnie and Sarah to the rock gardens, the orchards, and the foundation remains from some of the camp buildings. When they came to the cemetery, Keiko wept.

"My father was buried here," she said.

Arnie put his arm around his grandmother's shoulders, and Grace patted Keiko's hair, making the grandmotherly woman smile through her tears.

"Thank you, Grace," she said, kissing the baby's cherub-pink cheeks. "Your parents named you well."

They stood outside the wooden fence as they studied the white obelisk created in memorial for over one hundred and thirty-five internees who died at Manzanar, the black Japanese words a stark contrast to the pristine white cement. The three steps of the pillar were strewn with flowers, and the point of the column directed their gazes toward the cobalt-blue sky dotted with billow-white clouds at the peak of Mount Williamson, which watched the mourners from ten miles away.

"The obelisk says I REI TO," Keiko said.

"What does it mean?" Sarah asked.

"Literally, it means soul consoling tower," Arnie answered. "We'd translate it more like monument to console the souls."

"That's beautiful," Sarah said.

They walked on the sand a few more steps to the memorial graves where the desert brush overtook the landscape as far as the mountains. There were ten graves surrounded by stone circles, three of them with stone markers.

"Is your father there?" Sarah asked.

"We moved him to a cemetery closer to Los Angeles after we left the camp. We couldn't stand to think of him here alone after Manzanar was deserted. Nearly everyone who was buried here was moved to other graves by their families. There are still a few buried here, though. Three middle-aged men who had no family in the

United States, two babies whose parents were moved to other camps, and one unnamed stillborn infant."

Keiko bowed her head and closed her eyes, lost in a place where those who hadn't been interned in Manzanar couldn't follow. After several moments of silence, she pressed her hands together in front of her chest and bowed deeply toward the graves. Sarah and Arnie followed her lead. As they walked back toward the car, Sarah felt a sense of déjà vu, as though she had been here before. The mountains were just as James described—omniscient and all-encompassing. They could set you free or keep you enclosed. They had a mystical, magical quality, Sarah thought, imbued with secrets from the ages. Those were the mountains James saw when he was in Manzanar with Keiko and her family, and they were the same mountains he saw now.

"Where is Camp Dracula?" Sarah asked.

"Not far," said Arnie.

"I'd like to see it," Sarah said. "At least I'd like to get as close as I can."

Arnie glanced at his grandmother, who was sitting in the backseat of their white rental car. "We'll drive there tomorrow," Keiko said.

Sarah nodded. She could wait one more day, she thought. It wasn't like she could see James when they went anyway. She strapped Grace into her safety seat, and they headed back down U.S. Route 395 to Independence, the silence in the car allowing Sarah space to wonder what other similarities she would find between Manzanar and the camp where her husband was now.

Later that night, after it grew dark, Keiko asked her grandson if he would take her for a drive. She wanted to see the desert by night again. It had so many memories for her, she said. When Sarah offered to go along, Keiko insisted she stay.

"Grace is sleepy, Sarah. Let her rest. You need your rest too."

Sarah waved at her new friends as they drove away. She took a hot bath, stretched out on the bed next to Grace until the baby fell asleep, then crawled into her bed. She fell asleep dreaming of James.

CHAPTER 15

*J*ames stood outside his barracks that late August night staring at the cloudless sky and the full Grain moon pointing its heavenly spotlight onto the camp, the mountains casting their peak-and-valley shadows, the vast barrier more imposing in the obscurity. He felt fidgety, James, his nerve endings sparking like Independence Day firecrackers because he knew Sarah was close. He had to settle the raw giddiness he felt knowing his sweet, beautiful girl was there. He had to stay calm. He had to see this through.

Outside James' barracks was deserted while other internees stayed inside. No one walked about or chatted, and those who worked past the gates had already come in, leaving an eerie quiet behind. James closed his eyes, praying as he had done so little since he was turned long ago, but tonight he needed all the help he could get. He thought of the voice, so hearty, so warming, the voice that had given him strength when he needed it most.

"Are you there?" James asked. "Can you help me now?" When James heard the voice, he wanted to weep.

"All will be well, James." And then, "You will return."

"Let it be so," James said.

Geoffrey opened the door of their barracks and joined James outside. Geoffrey looked up to the sky, nodding at the full moon as though he had to see the round glowing orb for himself to know it was there and not a figment of the lunar calendar's imagination.

James dropped his voice, hoping only Geoffrey was listening. "You know what to do?"

Geoffrey nodded. "I have one card up my sleeve even you won't be expecting."

James grasped Geoffrey's shoulder. "Geoffrey…"

"Have faith in me, James. I know how important this is to you." Geoffrey looked around, but they were still alone, no one peeking around their door to see, no one obviously eavesdropping on their conversation. "Did Thaddeus do his part?"

James sighed. "Yes, Timothy did his part."

"Let the games begin."

On cue, Timothy walked past James and Geoffrey as though he didn't see them. He continued past the neat row of barracks, past another neat row, and another, and another, until he was past the living quarters, the mess hall, the recreation hall, near the silver-coated gate where MPs stood guard. Timothy sat on a bench where he could see through the gate he was allowed past as part of the gardening detail. He didn't say anything. He merely looked at the mountains in the distance with a wistful gaze. He sat straight when Geoffrey meandered past.

"You still don't remember me?" Timothy said.

Geoffrey looked at the silver-coated gate, the sand beneath his feet, and the barracks behind him as though one of them had spoken. He shook his head, he must have imagined the voice his shrug said, and he staggered forward as though he had been drinking something more potent than blood.

Timothy pointed at Geoffrey. "You!"

Geoffrey turned, surprised. "Me?"

"Yes, you. I'm tired of you getting my name wrong. My name is Timothy. Not Taylor, or Travis, or Trenton, or any other T names. My name is Timothy Bryston-Wolfe, and you need to get it right, especially since you're the one who turned me. You remember James so well. You know everything about him from the night you turned him. You watched him and now you're helping him here in camp. What about me? Why can't you remember me?"

The guards stationed nearest the gate watched with a mild interest. They were too far for human ears to hear, and as far as they could tell these were simply two undeads in a passing conversation.

"You must have me confused with someone else, Telemachus. I'm not the one who turned you."

A few internees came outside to see what was happening, though Timothy and Geoffrey didn't seem to notice.

"My name is Timothy!" The boy sprang forward, his fists like a boxer's at the ready. "Why can't you call me Timothy, you...you..."

"Me, me what you runt. Don't you see what the problem is? You're not that interesting. You have no distinguishing characteristics, absolutely nothing to recommend you to my memory. And you are too bloody young. How old are you, anyway?"

More internees gathered around, then more. Suddenly, there was a crowd of undead and ten human armed guards at the periphery of the scene. The crowd watched the stand-off, a reality television show unfolding before their eyes, vampire against vampire, ready to cut each other to death with the sharp slice of their words.

"I'll be nineteen next month," Timothy said.

"You look like you're ten. And you talk like a spoiled five-year-old." Geoffrey's fists went to his eyes as though he were rubbing tears from his face. "Wah wah wah. The dapper, charming vampire man doesn't remember me because I'm nothing and no one. Boo hoo." Geoffrey looked at the white-blue faces staring at him. "Anyone here remember little Tangerine? Anyone?"

"It's Timothy! Timothy!"

James stopped at the edge of the crowd near Jocelyn and Chandresh, watching with wary eyes, waiting like the others to see if this was going to break into violence or fade away as stupid arguments should.

Geoffrey squared his shoulders. "Now you listen here, Testic..."

"Geoffrey!"

James stepped in, arms out, a referee parting the boxers in the ring. Geoffrey pointed at Timothy. "He started it."

With his hands on his knees, James leaned close to Timothy's face. The boy's dark hair fell into his eyes, and he was panting with frustration, his white-blue face pink from the heat brought on by Geoffrey's insufferable attitude. While James allowed Timothy to settle himself, more undead came from the mess hall and the barracks to see about the commotion.

"What's happening, Timothy?" James asked.

Timothy pointed at Geoffrey. "It's him! He pretends he doesn't know me, but he turned me. He's the one who dragged me from the car the night my family was killed. He bit me. He told me I'd thank him later. It's him, James, and he can't even remember my name. Why does he know everything about you but he can't remember me? He keeps calling me Turtle or Tricycle or whatever stupid T words he can think of though I've told him my name a hundred times."

"I'm sure Geoffrey doesn't mean anything by it," James said. "He can be annoying sometimes, but..."

"I beg your pardon," Geoffrey said. "I'm acknowledging the boy's wish by calling him by his name. Isn't that right, Tarantula?"

Timothy charged toward Geoffrey and the crowd surged. Whether they were there to agitate things further or calm things down, James couldn't tell from their impassive faces. Their hands reached for their pockets for the cell phones they didn't have, and James imagined them filming the fight between the mismatched vampires, the older, seasoned one with almond-shaped black eyes and spikes of gray in his red-brown hair and the younger, smaller one with his dark hair falling over his brows. What would happen if the uber-strong vampires fought? Would Geoffrey have the edge since he was older when he was turned? Would Timothy have an advantage since he was younger? The crowd, several hundred strong, leaned forward, eager to find out. There were twenty armed guards now, the crunching of heavy boots pounding the sand as more approached from the distance. The newly arrived guards stood on the periphery of the scene, close enough for their meager ears to hear but far enough that they weren't involved, though their tentative balance on their toe-tips said they were ready to jump in should the need arise. James scanned the throng and saw everyone pressing forward, an impending mosh pit of undead head-banging. He turned toward the ridiculous older vampire and stood to his full height, eye to eye with Geoffrey.

"Leave him alone," James said. "And for God's sake, his name is Timothy. What is so difficult about remembering the name Timothy?"

"Don't tell me what to do, vampling." Geoffrey smirked at a white-skinned woman who looked like all she needed was a bucket of blood-flavored popcorn to complete her viewing pleasure. He nodded toward James. "Thinks he can tell me what to do because I left him alone when I turned him over three hundred years ago. He can't let it go, poor boy." Geoffrey paced toward the gate, and the swarm of bystanders and guards followed him with their eyes. "I've tried and tried, over and over again, for nearly two years now I've tried to make it up to him. I've been nice. I've been helpful. I've been entertaining." He turned to another white-skinned woman, this one middle-aged-looking, watching from the side. "Haven't I been entertaining?" The woman nodded and Geoffrey smiled. "I've been quite wonderful, actually, and that one," he pointed at James, "hasn't shown any grati-tude, any understanding. He groans and whinges, and it's getting rather old, I assure you. I show up at his house after three hundred years, offering friendship and guidance, and all I get is stroppiness in return."

James stood before Geoffrey, the frustration boiling the blood in his brain. "You left me alone! You turned me and then you left me like I wasn't worth your time. Like I didn't matter. Didn't you realize I was terrified?"

"You're immortal, James. You had nothing to fear."

"But I didn't know that. Why didn't you tell me? Why didn't you stay? I had nowhere to go. My wife was dead. I couldn't stay with my father without endangering him. I lived in the forest with the animals, because that's what you made me, a bloodsucking animal without a home. I didn't know what I was until Miriam told me. Do you know how lonely I was?"

Geoffrey dropped his eyes. He lost his challenging stance when his shoulders slumped. He stepped back from James, allowing the silence to fall like a burial shroud over everyone. The full moon was overhead now, its white-glow beam a spotlight over the actors in the scene and the spectators in the audience. The nighttime breeze touched the tufts of brush here and whisked someone's hair there. Geoffrey scanned the faces of those closest to him, and he drew strength from them. He stood tall and looked James in the eye. He sounded contrite.

"I wanted to come to you sooner, James, I did. All those years I watched you grow into the being you are tonight. The man who loved his wife and father with all his heart."

"I don't have a heart thanks to you," James said.

"But you do. You have the largest heart I've ever known. The way you've never loved any woman but Sarah. The way you protected your father after you were turned. The way you helped that witchy woman in the woods. The way you walked that hideous trail with the native human people though you hardly had to. The way you stayed in the camp down the way because you hoped your being there might bring some solace. What you did in Germany..."

"I still don't know how you know what I did in Germany."

"I told you, James. I've been keeping track."

Timothy pushed his way back into the center of the fray, standing behind James, his arms crossed over his chest, his black-night eyes drilling holes into Geoffrey. James held his hand toward Timothy.

"Why did you keep track of me when you don't even remember Timothy's name? Why?"

Geoffrey's voice was a whisper. "You're so like your father. *Why, Pa. Why?* All the time. *Why, Pa. Why?* Johnny never did get answers that suited him, not from me anyway."

When James shook his head, Geoffrey stepped toward him.

"How did you know my father's name was John?" James asked.

"I knew your father from the day he was born, James. In case you haven't guessed, my name isn't Geoffrey Ichabod Englebert Tiddly-winks Bumptybottoms the Third. My name is Geoffrey Wentworth."

James backed away, as far from the ridiculous vampire as the onlookers would allow, the rows of undead acting as a buffer between James and sanity. A sudden stillness lingered over their heads as the fullness of the moon grew brighter in contrast to the deepening skyline. James felt all eyes on him, the spotlight in the sky illuminating his soliloquy where he examines life and death, meaning and purpose, and what was the use of anything anyway? Geoffrey turned, his body forward, his hands and feet ready to sprint, but he stopped mid-rush and dropped to his knees. He reached his hands towards his frozen vampling, pleading for understanding.

"I'm your grandfather, James. I should have told you sooner. I'm so sorry."

James backed further away, bumping into those behind him, his footing unsure. For a moment, he thought he was home in Salem with Sarah by his side, his life ordered and perfect as he thought it would be when he found his beloved wife again. It was painful to come back to himself, caught within the pressing crowd and the curious faces, the bland desert landscape in the background, and the eyesore barracks surrounding them. When his loose, muddled mind snapped back into place, James remembered what they were doing and why they were there. Geoffrey's confession was preposterous but perfect, James realized, the performance award-worthy. And then, as if on cue, her scream pierced the man on the moon, slicing the silence in her agony.

"You killed him! My father died here! And you killed him!"

The crowd rushed to the gate. As James followed, he saw her, Keiko, her eyes wide with fright, grasping the silver-coated fence, pushing it, pulling it, trying to shake the desert into consciousness, wanting the sand, the brush, the cold-blooded lizards, the impassive mountains from their fearful heights to hear her cry. The horde of onlookers and guards stood back a respectful distance, no one daring to get too close to the distraught grandmotherly woman and push her further over the edge.

"What did we do to deserve this?" Keiko cried. "We were good people! Honest people! We never broke a law, never hurt anyone, never even raised our voices! We trusted you! We believed in you! And you locked us here like penned cattle ready for the slaughter. How could we fight you? Where could we go for help? So we suffered in silence, wondering all along what we had done, what was so terrible about us that our government had to portray us as monsters and lock us away where no one would have to look at us. We thought we were that bad." Keiko shook the fence vigorously. "Don't you see how we suffered? My father drank, and he drank, and he died in camp because he drank. All because he needed to forget the pain! Otousan!" She called the attention of the heavens to her long-standing sorrow. Finally, she vented the grief she had carried for seventy years, and everyone who heard her understood.

Suddenly, out of the darkness, Arnie appeared by Keiko's side, grabbing his grandmother's hands and gently prying her fingers from their fierce hold on the fence.

"She's here!" he shouted into the shadows. "I knew she'd be here."

Thomas Masters raced toward them, his worry illuminated by the glimmering moon. Three guards stepped toward the fence, and Thomas held up his hand.

"Please," he said, "let me take care of this. My name is Thomas Masters, and I'm a doctor at Saint Francis Memorial Hospital in San Francisco." He held up his hospital identification, and one of the guards stepped forward to examine it, nodding toward the others when the credentials passed inspection. "Professor Ishigura is a patient of mine. She was incarcerated at Manzanar as a young woman, and she's been suffering from a relapse of the post-traumatic stress syndrome she developed during the war." Thomas tilted Keiko's chin up and she looked into his eyes. "Everything is all right, Keiko," he said gently. "Come with me. Arnold and I will take care of you."

"But my father," Keiko said. "I can't leave him here. Otousan!" Her scream for her father caused the crowd to bow its collective head in sadness for this suffering old woman.

"Great-grandfather isn't here, Grandmother," Arnie said. "Your family moved his grave, remember? Please, Grandmother, come away."

As the crowd strained to see over and around those in front of them, the guards stood to the side, tapping their wooden stakes on the ground, their heads tilted, unsure what to do about the harmless grandmotherly woman haunted by a similar camp from seven decades before.

And, then, there were the wolves.

They stood back to back, four of them, their howls, like the white obelisk meant to console the souls, pointed at the full moon. They were husky, powerful, their fur ranging from sable-black to ice-white, their eyes fierce, their fangs bared and not to be deterred. Two sang their desolate howls to the sky while the other two growled at the onlookers, spittle dripping from their eyeteeth. When a guard stepped toward them, the wire-silver wolf flattened his back, ready to tear the offending human into manageable bites. The onlookers encircled the wolves, fascinated rather than frightened by the animals. Four guards charged forward, their wooden stakes useless against the wolves, and chaos erupted. Hundreds of feet, undead and human, trampled the dry desert ground. Hands pushed bodies out of the way. One guard screamed when the ice-white wolf snapped at his bottom. When undead hands pushed the human people in their haste to escape the pandemonium, the humans crashed to the ground, bumped and bruised. There were more screams, some from fear, some from entertainment, some merely to join in, and above the din, loudest of all were Keiko's cries for her lost years and her dead father. Dante's stages of hell were alive and well in the vast Sierra Nevadas, echoing the unholy chorus to the mountains and back. It was a communal catharsis, and, caught up in the release of frustration and grief, no one noticed when five undead disappeared through the hole under the fence.

Before James flashed into the desert night, Keiko smiled at him.

CHAPTER 16

*R*un. Now. Run. One leg in front of the other, rightleftrightleft, straight ahead toward the nooks and crannies of the mountains, the ones that have followed your every step from the moment you arrived, then and now, concentrating your tiniest fibers faster, faster, faster. Even at your preternatural speed, too quick for human eyes to see, flash here, flash there, flash faster and faster until you're hidden from their view. There are no moments to waste. Your very existence, whether you will find freedom or be dragged back to the camp, depends on your special speed. Run faster still, pressing forward, forward, pressing yourself to your limits though your strength is brisk and your abilities strong. Run faster still, knowing Sarah is there, only miles away, and you will see her soon, so soon. In a matter of time you will have her in your arms where she belongs and you shall never leave her ever. Madness will not touch you again. You have decided. This nightmare will end and you will be with your wife again.

James ignored the circular spotlight of the now-waning moon as he raced alongside the four other vampires pushing themselves as fast as James. For those moments, perhaps for the first time, James was grateful for his preternatural abilities. For more than three hundred years he pretended away and explained away everything that made him different from the humans he lived alongside. He had a human job. He lived a human lifestyle as much as possible. If he was pale, or cold, or didn't eat and drink what those around him ate and drank, he downplayed those differences, ignoring them when he could. And yet, as he ran from Camp Dracula, escaping into the mountains until the search party passed, he was glad to be paranormal, preternatural, supernatural, whatever you wanted to call it. He was thankful for his extrasensory perception, for his hunter's abilities, for his quicker-than-human reflexes. But when he was most thankful for his extraordinary abilities he realized he no longer wanted them. Running for the hills, his body pushing its capacity in its need for speed, his mind was left to wander, and it meandered toward a new idea, a vague plan he couldn't articulate yet.

The vampires traipsed the flat desert terrain twenty human steps at a time, and in a matter of moments they were at the base of the mountains. Behind them, they heard the quick-time scamper of wolves, who escaped the chaos through the same hole under the fence the vampires had used, and behind them was the bark of search dogs and the shouts of confused men. James stopped while the others camouflaged themselves within the brush. He scanned the flat desert terrain until the wolves began to scale the mountain. He waved, and the silver-gray wolf with yellow eyes snapped, too softly for human ears to hear. Timothy sat beside James, and the silver-gray wolf with yellow eyes sat next to his son, murmuring softly. When the ice-white wolf appeared behind the others, Timothy nodded.

"Hi, Grandma," Timothy said. The ice-white wolf licked his hand.

The silver-gray wolf murmured again, and Timothy shrugged. "I'm fine, Dad. I didn't get caught on the gate. James pulled me through." Timothy nodded at the black-brown wolf. "Hi, Uncle Devon."

A black-haired wolf with green eyes, cat-like in its sleekness, pointed its nose toward the gate of Camp Dracula. "I hear them, Aunt Emma," Timothy said. He looked at James. "What do we do?"

Geoffrey peered around the black-haired wolf, who barked. "I beg your pardon, Miss. I am not checking out your bottom half. I'm merely looking to see the location of the search party."

"Do they have any of our kind with them?" Chandresh asked. "It would make sense for them to have some in the search party. Other undead would be able to track us when humans wouldn't."

Geoffrey squinted into the deeper darkness, the moon falling into the other side of night. "They're all human, I reckon. Except for the dogs, though why they bothered with the fleabags I shouldn't know. Horrid, drooling creatures." The ice-white wolf barked in an annoyed response. "I beg your pardon, Grandmother." Geoffrey looked into the white wolf's face. "My, Grandma, what big teeth you have."

"Can the dogs smell us?" Jocelyn asked.

"I shouldn't think so," Geoffrey said. "Stupid dogs who spend their time sniffing their own arseholes." When Grandmother snapped, Geoffrey shrugged. "I meant that in the most complimentary way possible."

"Won't they come up here looking for us?" Timothy asked.

"They have a lot of ground to cover, Timothy," Geoffrey said. "We can keep ahead of them."

"You know my name?"

"Of course. I'm not a moron." Geoffrey pointed at James. "No comments from you."

"I'm not staying," James said. "A few more moments, and then I'm headed to Independence and Sarah."

"It will be Independence for all of us," Chandresh said.

They sat in silence, vampires and werewolves, each looking into the sky as the moon continued its downward arc into daylight. The night was broken by dog barks and human shouts in the distance, growing closer and closer. Military jeep tires skidded across the sand, but the desert was vast, the mountains numerous. The brush, the ridges, the ravines, the sinuous bulks rising and falling, high into spires and buttresses, low around the lakes and hills, everything more imposing when faced by humans hunting unnatural beings. The humans had a limited force and a lot of territory to cover, and the hidden vampires were deep enough into the ridges that they weren't in any danger of immediate discovery. They breathed in deeply though they didn't need the air so they could exhale with the relief. At that moment, James understood perspective. From the camp, the mountains were a barrier, vast, impenetrable, overwhelming. But once you were nestled within the rocks and boulders the view was scenic in a picturesque way. A problem from the distance became safe, even beautiful with proximity.

Geoffrey looked at the wolves. "You may need to dig some holes," he said. "If the human people don't disperse soon, we'll have to hide here during the day."

"In the dirt?" Jocelyn said.

"I've seen vampires do it on television," Timothy said. "It can't be that bad."

"I'm not staying," James said. "I'll run along the perimeter of the mountains if I have to, but I'm getting to Sarah before daybreak." He looked at Timothy, Jocelyn, Chandresh, the wolves. "You all know where you're headed?" Everyone, vampire and wolf-people, nodded.

"We'll be fine, James," Geoffrey said. "We know you need to go. Go. Be safe."

James looked at Geoffrey, and there was sadness behind the almond-shaped eyes James had never seen before. "I've been meaning to ask you," James said, "that night at the mess hall when you were attacked with the stake. You knew the stake wouldn't hurt you?"

"Of course. Do you think I'd let them near me with that woody thing if I thought it would hurt me? I can't believe vampires ever believed that superstitious nonsense. What can a piece of wood do to someone already dead? Give us a splinter? What can any of their so-called weapons do to us, for that matter? Garlic? We might get bad breath like anyone else but otherwise nothing. Silver? If it's crap silver it might turn us green but otherwise nothing. Religious symbols? Crosses and holy water? Rubbish, all of it."

"What about daylight?" James asked. "I've been outside in the sunshine twice since you turned me, and both times I felt like my eyes were burning."

"Sunlight is different," Geoffrey said. "What happens to a dead body left outside on a hot day?" James shook his head at the thought. "Exactly. Decomposition isn't the loveliest thing in the world. So, yes, I would stay away from sunlight, but the rest of it is nonsense. It's just as I've told you, there's...," Geoffrey paused, his lips pinched, "very little that can be done to us that's damaging in any way. And why is that, Professor?"

"Because we're already dead," James answered. "You didn't have to be so dramatic about sharing that fact with everyone at the mess hall. All you had to do was give them your name."

"I did."

"Sure you did, Bumptybottoms," Jocelyn said.

James grew serious when he saw how the sadness remained behind Geoffrey's eyes. "I appreciate everything you've done tonight," James said. "You almost had me going at the camp. For a minute I thought you really were my grandfather. You certainly got everyone's attention with that line."

Geoffrey took James' face between his hands. He leaned so close their foreheads touched.

"My name is Geoffrey Wentworth, James. I am your grandfather."

Timothy held his hands over his mouth and pressed air between his fingers. He spoke in a deep voice.

"Luke, I am your father."

Timothy laughed, Chandresh and Jocelyn laughed, the wolves nickered. James almost laughed. He wanted to joke off the tension brought on by Geoffrey's zeal, but the sound was caught somewhere inside. James tried to look away, but Geoffrey held him firm. Suddenly, the recognition struck James somewhere in his dormant DNA.

"No." James pulled away with such force Geoffrey stumbled back. "It's not true." When Geoffrey offered his hands in a gesture of surrender, James froze. "Oh my God." He wished he could disappear down the deep gorge five feet away. "How?" Geoffrey, never short of words, could only shake his head. "How could you turn your own grandson into this?"

James wanted to weep but his blood was dry. He sat on a boulder, away from everyone else, unable to look at the ridiculous vampire, forgetting even Sarah at that moment.

Geoffrey knelt behind James and spoke softly, trying to make it all right. It was one of the few times James could recall when Geoffrey didn't sound sarcastic or irreverent.

"I didn't know you were my grandson when I turned you, James, I swear I didn't. When I saw you sitting outside the jail that night you looked so sad, and there was something about you, something familiar, but I never guessed you were my Johnny's son. I was only trying to help. I knew what they were doing to the accused witches." Geoffrey paced through the brush, running his hands through his gray-streaked red-brown hair. He glanced at James, then looked away. "In my defense I hadn't seen your father since he was six years old. I was turned suddenly one night on the docks where I had come home from sea. I was a sailor, and I was gone for long stretches of time. One night I came off the ship, ready to see your grandmother Rebecca and my Johnny, and some mean old vampire man grabbed me, bit me, turned me, and left me alone."

James scoffed.

"That sounds familiar to you, I know. We do what we know." Geoffrey glanced toward his grandson and saw blank indifference in James' turned back. "I stayed around England for many years, but then I decided to give the colonies a try. One night I walked the Boston streets and saw this handsome young man weeping outside the jail. I had seen you before that night, you know. I had been near your house in Salem Town several times, trying to place where I might know you from. When I saw you outside the jail I guessed you were upset over your wife because I couldn't imagine you being that upset over anyone else. I had seen you and your wife together, and I knew you were very much in love. I couldn't shake the thought that there was something familiar about you, and it drew me to you. I kept looking at your face, and something was tugging at the back of my mind, as if I should recognize you but I didn't. That night outside the jail I wanted to help you, James. I wanted to help your wife. When I turned you I gave you extraordinary strength and agility. I turned you into the greatest natural hunter in the world. I gave you eternal life. I made sure you were all right, and then I went back to turn your wife. It was just as I told you. By the time I got there she was gone. When I read over the list of deceased prisoners I saw her name, Elizabeth Wentworth, and I knew. I knew you were my Johnny's son, my grandson. I should have recognized you as soon as I saw you. You look so much like your grandmother."

James sat up straighter. He wanted answers yet he was afraid.

Geoffrey nodded at James' back. "You have the same straight nose, the same heavy gold hair. Your grandmother had the bluest eyes I've ever seen, so big they took up half her face, like yours. Yours aren't blue any longer, I reckon. You're so like her, James. Did you know she loved to read?"

James turned to Geoffrey. Taking courage, Geoffrey sat next to James on the boulder.

"She read anything she could get her hands on, and it wasn't common for sailors' wives to read much of anything then. Working-class women weren't usually literate in the 1600s, but your grandmother wasn't any common woman. She was strong, smart, and determined. Like you. Did you know her at all?"

"I remember her a little. She died in the Great Fire of London when I was a child."

"I wish you could have known her better. I do not doubt that she adored you." Geoffrey sighed. "I should have gone to see your grandmother and father, even as I am. I regret it now. I didn't want to put them in danger. I didn't want them to despise me or fear me because of what I had become. I left them behind, thinking I was doing the right thing."

"Father accepted me as I am," James said.

"I know. Johnny always had a big heart, and you did well to take after him in that way. Once I learned you were my grandson, I was always there, watching you, checking on you, making sure you were all right. I know you struggled at first, but you grew strong and made your way in the world. I am so proud of you, James. I always have been."

James paced to the edge of the ravine, looking into the bottomless gorge, unsure whether he wanted to jump himself or push Geoffrey down.

"Why did it take Kenneth Hempel for you to come see me?"

"How could I explain that I was your grandfather, and oopsie, I turned you into a vampire by mistake one night? Once I decided to stay away, I thought it was too late to change my mind. I made my decision, so I kept in the distance. The more the years passed, the more I felt the need to see you in person. The Hempel fiasco gave me the excuse I was looking for." He brushed James' hair from his eyes, a fatherly gesture. "Always in your face, like your grandmother."

James smiled.

"It's good to see you smile, James."

"It's not easy when you have such an annoying grandfather."

"Sarah thinks I'm funny."

"She has more patience than I do."

Geoffrey shook his head. "You think I'm funny too, James, though you're loathe to admit it. I think you've always known there was something that drew us together. You invited me to your wedding when you weren't even sure you liked me. Deep down, you knew, maybe not that we were related, but something was connecting us. We're two peas in a pod, you see. I annoy you because I say the things you're thinking but are too polite to say. You're very much your father's son in that respect. Johnny was a good-natured boy, and so are you."

Suddenly, a halo light appeared, the same one James had seen in his barracks. It started small, egg-sized, but it grew larger until it was as tall as a middle-height man. When James recognized the figure before him and heard the voice he loved so, he bowed his head in reverence.

"All will be well, James."

"Father," James said.

Geoffrey examined the apparition. "Johnny, is that you? You're bald."

Geoffrey was tall, and he still had most of his gray-splattered red-brown hair. He looked to be about forty-eight, Geoffrey, and his son, John, still looked the sixty-eight he was when he died. The son looked older than the father, but James knew that was the supernatural way. The father was a vampire, the son a ghost, and this was merely one more oddity James had to deal with since joining the paranormal world. His father was shorter than Geoffrey, five-foot-seven to Geoffrey's six-foot-two, James' height, and yet his father was so much more calm and steady. Seeing them there, next to each other, gazing at each other as though no time had passed since the last time they met, James saw the resemblance between them. His father's eyes weren't wide like Geoffrey's, but they had the same strength that challenged you to tell the truth. And the truth was, though James had trouble admitting it, Geoffrey had been caring—in his way. He had kept track of James from the distance. He went out of his way to get to Maine. He made sure he got on the same train and into the same barracks as James so they could stay together. John was more obvious in his loving, gentle nature, but Geoffrey did care. It was a revelation to James, and yet he was still angry, still wounded that his grandfather would abandon him.

When John disappeared, his light diminished, James felt his absence the way he did when he ran away from his father all those years before, finding refuge in the Massachusetts forest. He thought he would never see his father again, but John had been at James and Sarah's second wedding, James was sure of it now, and John had just been beside them there in the Sierra Nevadas. Suddenly, James felt like an abandoned waif, an orphan, all alone in a world that didn't understand him. He wanted his father's light back. He wanted something to make sense again.

"You may call me Grandfather if you wish," Geoffrey said.

"I'll stick to Geoffrey for now," said James.

"As you like it." Geoffrey smiled. "I made a Billy Shakespeare joke. See, I'm down with the literature professors."

The moon was nearly gone, the blackness on the eastern horizon revealing a layer of white-pink light within the layers of the ridges and ravines, casting a heavenly radiance, leaving the rest of the mountain in night-like shadow. Howard barked, and Geoffrey nodded.

"Go," Geoffrey said. "I don't need to see naked people because you were still here when the moon disappeared."

"I'm going with my family," Timothy said. "Jocelyn and Chandresh are coming with us. You can come too, James. It'll be daylight soon."

"I'm going to Sarah," James said. "I can make it before the sun is too high."

The ice-white wolf yapped.

"That's kind of you, Grandmother Wolfe," Geoffrey said, "but it's better if we split up."

"Where will you go?" James asked. As angry, or upset, or whatever it was he felt for Geoffrey in that moment, James didn't want him to decompose in the sun. But by the time James turned around Geoffrey was gone. James sighed, exasperated as always by the ridiculous vampire. He nodded at his friends, and then, with the barking dogs, churning trucks, and aggravated humans shouting in the distance, he flashed into the breaking daylight toward Independence.

CHAPTER 17

*I*n her dream, James was home. They were in Salem, in their wooden gabled house, in their bed. She was asleep, and James was beside her, reading, writing, or simply watching her sleep as he would at times. Grace slept in her room, the night passing peacefully into daylight as the white-pink sunlight pierced the dimness. In Sarah's dream, when she awoke the blackout curtains were drawn, it was cave-black inside the room, and though she couldn't see James in the darkness she felt him beside her. She rested her head against his chest, safe near her dear and loving husband. It was the same dream she had every night since James was gone. In her dream, sometimes she spoke to him. Sometimes, she told him about Grace and what new firsts their baby girl accomplished that day. James always knew he would miss a lot of Grace's firsts since he slept during the day, and Sarah took pictures of everything so she could show him later. Sometimes, she told him about her day, the type of ordinary conversations they had before he left. In her dream, she felt closest to James when she felt his muscles beneath his t-shirt, his strong arms around her. But then, when she awoke in the morning and saw the daylight, no blackout curtains, she realized her dream was over and she moaned.

That night Sarah slept fitfully. The spotlight beam of the full moon pierced the lace-sheer rose-patterned curtains and poked her awake. She thought of James, so close and so far, and she wondered what her beloved was doing then since these were his waking hours. Through the window Sarah saw the deserted roads, the street lights, the looming mountains in the distance. She peeked at Grace, asleep in the other bed, unconcerned by the moonlight, very much her father's daughter in her ability to sleep through anything. Sarah pulled the flimsy curtains closer together, trying to darken the room so she could get some sleep.

She crawled back into bed and pulled the blankets to her chin. She closed her eyes and turned away from the moonlight, now fainter but still pointing at her. She felt like the heavenly spotlight was directed at her, though she couldn't guess why. Finally, near dawn, she dozed off, dreaming of James once more. She rolled onto her side, and she thought she heard a crack as the door opened and someone stepped into the room. She must be dreaming, she decided. She felt too disconnected from herself, from her body, from the bed beneath her. She thought she was floating upward, but where? Maybe if she flapped her arms she could fly over the camp and see James. Maybe if she squinted she could spot him on the ground. She could let him know she was close by, she was there, she had come for him and they would be all right again.

The footsteps grew closer, and Sarah imagined someone pausing by Grace's bed. She tried to open her eyelids, but her body wouldn't obey her brain's commands. The steps slowed as they grew closer to her, and then she felt a weight on the bed, first light as hands pressed down beside her, then heavier as the bed sank under the weight of another body.

"Hello," she heard.

It was James' voice, a simple greeting, the same one he used when he saw her each night. In Salem, the wait for her husband's hello helped her through the long daylight hours. Now, after their three months apart, it was her reason for living—the hope that one night soon she would hear it again.

Sarah, her eyes still closed, decided she must be imagining James' voice because she wanted to hear it. She needed to hear it. She felt strong arms around her, but even then she lingered on the cusp of consciousness, in that limbo where you're not sure which is which and what is what and whether you're awake or sleeping. James couldn't be in the room with her. He was in Camp Dracula, within the gates, watched by the guards. Suddenly, she felt strong hands slip down her arms, her back, under the sky-blue t-shirt, the one she wore to bed to keep him close. She gasped aloud at the shock of cold hands against her sweating skin and she knew it was true, he was there. She opened her eyes, threw her arms around his neck, and pulled his lips to hers. She turned on the lamp and saw him, James, his dark-night eyes overcome with gratitude. He kissed her lips, softly at first, as though he wanted to savor his first touch after too many lonely nights in an ugly army-style barracks.

James was gentle with her, as though he were still afraid she was injured from the car accident. His hands were slow as he lifted his t-shirt over her head, and his lips were slow as they started on her fore-head and worked their way over her eyelids, pausing for long moments over her mouth. They were connecting the way they were always meant to be. The two pressed close in the thin twin bed, his arms clutching her as though he were trying to meld her to him so they would never be separated again. To Sarah it seemed like no time had passed and they had always been together, there was never any painful separation. It could be 1692, it could be now, but James and Sarah were together again.

Sarah crawled out of bed and looked at James, who was stretched out on his side on the thin twin bed, and she threw some long terrycloth towels over the curtain rod to block out the brightening dawn. In the darkness, without the aid of moonlight or street lamps, Sarah couldn't make out the room around her. She felt unreal, detached from herself, as though she were once again caught between dreams and reality. For a moment, she thought she had imagined James' return that night, and she thought of Romeo's words as he speaks to his beloved as she stands on her balcony, "Being in night, all this is but a dream/Too flattering-sweet to be substantial." Was this too flattering-sweet to be substantial, Sarah wondered? But then she heard his voice, and she knew he was there, he was real, and he loved her.

"Come back to bed, Sarah."

She crawled into bed beside him and slept safely in her husband's arms. When the sun was high, it wasn't as dark in the room as it was with the blackout curtains at home, but it was dark enough and James slept peacefully. Sarah and Grace stayed close to James in the darkened room, Grace clapping and laughing at the sight of her father. The noise didn't disturb him, so they stayed in their room, leaving only once to see Keiko and Arnie. Sarah was disappointed because her friends had checked out in the night, leaving an envelope behind. The envelope was addressed to James, so Sarah didn't open it, but she wondered at the heavy contents inside. Back in their room, Sarah left the envelope on the nightstand by the bed and turned on the television, the volume mute, wanting to see and yet afraid of the twenty-four-seven cable newscasts. She had been so overwhelmed the night before that she hadn't had a chance to ask how or why he was there. She only knew he shouldn't be. Camp Dracula was still very much in operation. But he was there. Her beautiful, brave husband was there. Sarah guessed he must have broken out somehow, the way he broke Olivia's cousins out of a concentration camp and out of Germany. She watched the news headlines and the ticker as it rolled across the bottom of the screen, but there was nothing about the vampires, not even about the impending Supreme Court decision that would determine whether or not they could hold the undead in internment camps.

Sarah carried Grace from their room to the corner store and bought a newspaper. She stood near the curb and watched the scattered groups of people walking the town as they restocked for their camping or hiking excursions on the scenic mountain paths. The people looked relaxed, happy, ready to enjoy their day beneath the true-blue sky. Then Sarah brought Grace to the garden at the Winnedumah Hotel. She sat on one of the white-lace lawn chairs, enjoying the dry heat of the desert sun while flipping through the newspaper, her hot fingers smudging the ink. There was nothing about any escaped vampires, even in the local Independence newspaper. There didn't seem to be any panic in the area as residents or tourists fled for their lives for fear of an impending bloodsucking attack. Sarah exhaled fully for the first time that morning. Could he have escaped and no one noticed? It didn't seem possible.

The afternoon passed slowly, but Grace enjoyed the garden. She crawled on the grass and pointed at the butterflies fluttering above the yellow, orange, and red blooms rupturing within the green grass. Sarah helped Grace stand upright, and Grace took a few tentative steps toward the lawn chairs. Sarah pulled out her cell phone and snapped some photos for James.

"Wait until Daddy sees you walk," Sarah said.

When the sun dipped behind the mountains to the west, Sarah carried Grace back to their room. She unlocked the door as softly as she could, unsure if James was awake yet. James was still in bed, his eyes closed, his arm over his face, the way he had slept for over three hundred years. Grace reached toward her father, and Sarah sat Grace on the bed beside James. He opened his eyes and pulled his daughter into his arms.

"Daddy," Grace said.

James squeezed Grace closer and kissed the top of her gold curls. "Hi, Gracie," he said. "I missed you so much when I was gone. Look how big you are."

"She was taking some steps this afternoon in the garden," Sarah said. "I took pictures to show you."

James kissed both of Grace's cheeks, and Grace squealed with delight. He got out of bed and pulled his t-shirt over his head and his jeans over his boxer shorts. He looked out the window, over the tops of the Art Deco buildings at the mountains in the distance. James nodded at them, thanking them for their cover. I'll never look at you as a prison again, he thought. You helped me to Independence.

Sarah ordered room service for herself and Grace, and James explained his great escape while they ate.

"I knew Keiko and Arnie had to be involved," Sarah said. "The timing was too coincidental. But your letters were being censored. How did you communicate the plan to Keiko?"

"Using an anagram code she created while she was in Manzanar."

"Olivia will be thrilled to learn that you used an anagram code. She and I were always looking for hidden messages in your letters. After Olivia told me what you did in Germany, I knew you would be up for anything."

"Are you mad I didn't tell you?"

"I'm so glad you're here right now I'm willing to let that slide." Sarah looked out the window, her eyes fixed on the mountains, now barely visible in the darkness. "I wish Keiko and Arnie hadn't left so soon. I would have liked to have thanked them."

"Thomas thought it was better if they left after their performances. Keiko was amazing, Sarah."

"I think her screams came from a real place. It was hard for her to be here again. I saw it in her eyes when we visited the Manzanar remains."

James nodded. "She's an amazing woman, still such a bright light." He sat beside Sarah on the floor, taking her hands, and pulling her into his lap. Sarah left her dinner forgotten on the coffee table and rested her head on his chest. She found her sustenance from the closeness of her husband. "There's more to the story," James said. "It's Geoffrey."

"Is he all right?"

"He's fine, I think."

James fell silent. Sarah looked into his face while he stared at the door as though he expected to see Geoffrey walk in. James was a beautiful-looking man, but Sarah had always known that. From the first time she saw him over the supper table in 1691, she knew he was the most beautiful man she had ever seen. His eyes were so blue then, she remembered, like topaz.

"James? What about Geoffrey?"

"He's my grandfather."

Sarah laughed. "Of course he isn't."

When James fell silent again, Sarah sat on the floor beside him, taking his face between her hands.

"Oh, James," she said. "It's true."

James stretched out on the carpeted floor, reaching his arms toward the wall behind him. He closed his eyes, and for a moment Sarah thought he had fallen asleep. When he opened his eyes, she was startled at how dark they were when she had just been thinking how blue they used to be. For a moment, Sarah missed the blue, though the feeling didn't last. She and James had been separated for three months —too long for them—and she wouldn't waste time wishing for something that could never be again.

James told her how he learned about Geoffrey. "My father was there too," James said, "briefly, but I saw him. I've heard his voice for some time now."

"I saw him too." Sarah told James about the reading with Olivia, and about John, and they laughed together. "He's always been here, James. We were finally open enough to hear him."

"And see him."

"Where is Geoffrey now?" Sarah asked.

"I don't know."

Sarah had a million questions about Geoffrey, but James fell into a thoughtful mood and she decided it was better to ask another time. She hoped Geoffrey was safe, wherever he was. She always liked Geoffrey, as much as it annoyed her husband that she did. Hoping to shake James back into the moment with her, she handed him the envelope Keiko left behind. James turned it over in his hands as though he knew there was a fortune inside and he kissed it.

"Bless you again, Keiko," James said.

"What is it?" Sarah asked.

James tore open the envelope and pulled out two Nebraska drivers' licenses, one for James and one for Sarah, with the names Justin and Stephanie Wilkins. There were social security cards with the same names, including one for Grace Wilkins, as well as two platinum credit cards, one for Justin and one for Stephanie, passports, and fifty thousand dollars in cash.

"Where did she get this?" Sarah asked.

"You can buy anything over the Internet these days, and the cash is ours. I cashed out one of our bonds. Howard took care of it for us in Salem."

"That's why he was so nervous when I saw him outside the bank. How did he know what to do?"

"Timothy told him. Howard and I have had a code between us for years in case one or the other of us was in trouble and needed cash. He knew what to do, and I know what to do for him if he needs me to return the favor."

"What's the code?"

"Doodlebug."

"That's silly."

"Precisely. That's how it made it through in Timothy's letter."

Sarah studied the drivers' licenses, which were realistic as far as she could tell. They were recent photographs, and James' had been photoshopped to make his skin tone more human-like.

"Nebraska?" she asked.

"It was all Keiko could get."

"James?"

"What, honey?"

"I was right about your trying to pass secret codes, only they were to Keiko and not to me. Why didn't you want me to know what was going on? Why didn't Keiko and Arnie tell me you were escaping last night? I've told you a million times that you need to tell me what's going on. I think I've proven I can handle whatever I have to handle."

"You've proven how strong you are a dozen times over," James said. "I couldn't have written to you about the escape in a letter since our letters were being censored and I didn't think you'd understand the anagram code. Perhaps I should have had Keiko tell you."

"Perhaps."

"I didn't want to worry you, and I needed to know you were safe while I was making my move. Don't you see? I couldn't stay away from you any longer. I had to be sure you still loved me."

Sarah pressed her palms to James', like Juliet to her Romeo: *For saints have hands that pilgrims' hands do touch, And palm to palm is holy palmers' kiss.*

"Were you ever afraid I didn't love you?" Sarah asked.

James sighed. "When you said you were keeping company with Howard, and then Timothy said Howard mentioned you two were spending time together…" He shrugged at his foolishness. "You know how your imagination sometimes gets the best of you."

"I know all too well how imagination can run wild. I'm so happy you're here, James. I'm glad you couldn't stay away any longer. We need to be together." She grinned at her husband. "You were jealous of Howard? Really?"

James pulled Sarah into his arms. "Call it temporary insanity."

"Didn't you talk to him about it at the camp?"

"I was too busy escaping. I didn't get a chance."

Suddenly, the realization that James escaped the camp and that her husband was a fugitive, struck Sarah vividly. Her hands raced, her mind shook, and she feared he would be discovered there in the hotel, this time to be carted away somewhere he could never escape from. James pulled her onto his lap, squeezing her to him as tightly as he could without hurting her, though for Sarah it wasn't close enough and she pressed even closer.

"I don't care how far and how fast we have to run. Don't you ever leave me again, James Wentworth."

He kissed the top of her dark curls. "I shall never leave you ever," he whispered.

"And I promise you the same."

She looked into his face while he stared through the window, far away, she thought, like he was remembering the camp, or somewhere worse. She felt his tenseness in his worried muscles. She wanted to know what he was thinking, but she found herself treating him with kid gloves, as though he were an antique porcelain heirloom too fragile to handle without damaging beyond repair.

"What do we do now?" she asked.

"Whatever we want. We can drive the Pacific Crest Trail down to

Mexico or up to Canada. We can go anywhere in the country you want."

"But aren't they looking for you? You're still nocturnal. Even if you have a different name on a fake ID, if anyone takes your pulse..."

"We need to stay hidden enough so no one will pay much attention to me. I know how to do this, Sarah. I've had to stay hidden for a long time now. We couldn't run the first time because you weren't well enough." James cringed with the memory. "Now, we can run like the wind."

"We can't go home to Salem."

"Not for a while, honey. That's the first place they'll look for me."

Whatever was worrying James had disappeared. Now he was level-eyed, confident, and ready for this new adventure. Sarah was ready too. She was ready for anything that allowed them to stay together. Suddenly, she remembered the ring she wore around her neck. She pulled back her dark curls, James unclasped the gold chain, and his wedding ring fell into his palm.

"Let me," Sarah said. She slipped the gold band onto his finger, the symbol of their eternal love. They kissed, passionately. When Grace laughed and clapped her hands, James lifted his daughter and kissed her cheek.

"That's enough from you," he said.

Sarah was on her way to check out of the hotel when James grabbed her hand.

"You don't need to go into the lobby," he said. "Keiko and Arnie paid the bill through tomorrow. We can leave whenever we're ready."

Sarah packed the two bags she had taken for herself and Grace. She looked outside and saw the hotel parking lot deserted, so James carried the luggage to the rented white Ford Escape Keiko left behind.

"How did Keiko and Arnie get to the airport?" Sarah asked.

"They took a cab."

"She thought of everything."

James beamed, proud of his student. "Yes, she did."

As they drove away from the Winnedumah Hotel, Sarah stared at the steep steps of the Inyo County Court House, watching for anyone standing near the doors, worried that someone would see James behind the wheel. It was late now, after ten p.m., and the offices in the courthouse were long closed. Sarah exhaled as James drove toward U.S. 395. They passed the white box-looking U.S. Post Office, the feather-green shrubbery of the trees a sharp contrast to the jagged skyline of the mountains. They saw the sign for scenic Onion Valley, fifteen miles away, and the lonely road was a long stretch alongside sprouts of brown-green desert brush. The bulk of the mountains grew smaller with every mile put between the car and the Sierra Nevadas.

"The mountains look like they're waving goodbye," Sarah said.

"Hopefully for good this time," James said. "I've been here twice, and however long I live I hope I'll never see them again." He watched the mountains grow even smaller in the rearview mirror. "They're more beautiful from the distance."

"I agree," Sarah said.

CHAPTER 18

*A*s they drove away from Inyo County, James realized he hadn't felt so awkward around Sarah since their first moments together two years before. His first nights around her—seeing her in the library, walking her around Salem, discovering her frights from the nightmares that haunted her, learning her interest in the Salem Witch Trials—those were strange times since he wanted to be close to her but he was afraid of what would happen if she discovered his truth. But then she learned his truth, and she didn't care. With his silly concerns about Howard behind him, he trusted that her love for him was unconditional. She loved him no matter what. Even when her world was turned upside down, even when he was taken away from her because of what he was, she loved him as much as he loved her, and the truth of it humbled him.

Driving away from Camp Dracula in the darkness, they were alone, their little family perfect in their togetherness. For those moments, James pressed his worries aside and focused on his beautiful wife, who was there beside him, smiling at him. He reached for her, and she reached for him. She clutched his hand, then his knee, then his arm, then his hand again, unable to stop looking at him as though if she looked away he would disappear back into the mountains. James smiled at Sarah, thankful for these moments with her, thankful for the sweet scent of strawberries and cream and the warm cinnamon of his daughter. They didn't turn the radio on. Sarah was content watching James and letting the hum of the accelerator fill the air. James was content listening to his wife and daughter breathe.

James pressed the gas pedal closer to the floor, wanting to fly past the California state line as quickly as possible. He saw that Sarah had drifted off to sleep, so he let go of her hand and brushed a dark curl from her cheek. Every rush of love he ever felt for her flooded his long-dormant veins. Then Geoffrey's voice rattled his memory. Talking about returning. About how it had never been done so it doesn't pay to waste time worrying about it. About how other vampires had tried the spells and failed. About how James would always be what he was. But why didn't the spells work, James wondered. What were the others doing wrong that they disintegrated into rotten corpses? If the magic existed to turn us into these supernatural creatures, he reasoned, it must exist to turn us back. He wanted to talk to Sarah about it, but not yet. He remembered how upset she became when he told her about his plan to beat Kenneth Hempel at his own game by meeting the persistent reporter at the library at Salem State at noon. Did James nearly die from the sunlight that day? Geoffrey had pointed out that sunlight on dead flesh wasn't pleasant. But would it kill him? They were already dead, as Geoffrey liked to say. How do you kill something already dead?

Take away its reason for living.

At that moment, James lived to keep his family together and his wife and daughter safe. While no police sirens were blaring behind him, he was keenly aware that he had escaped a prison camp. But what if he were human again? Driving under the darkness of night, aware that they might be chased at any moment, James fixated on the idea of returning. How could he go about that? He remembered Miriam's prophecy, and she had said he would return. Surely, he had already returned in other ways. He returned from the monster he had become after he was first turned, when he had lost touch with his humanity. He returned to his true love when Sarah appeared in his life. He was returning now from an unfair imprisonment. Could Miriam have also meant that he would return to human? After all, she did use the word return. Was it possible? James realized he would give anything to be like his wife, breathing, warm, alive. Suddenly, more than anything in the world, he wanted to be human again. He nearly woke Sarah to talk to her about it, and he wondered…would she be supportive? Would she hate the idea? He decided he wouldn't mention it to her until he knew if it could be attempted. It didn't pay to worry her about something that may prove to be as impossible as Geoffrey said.

James exhaled loudly. If he were human again, this escape wouldn't be necessary. He wouldn't have been locked away if he were human. He could shake someone's hand without worry. He could submit himself to any doctor's test and he would breathe, he would have a pulse, he would have a heartbeat. He could touch his wife without worrying about sending a chill down her spine. He would be on her schedule, and he wouldn't miss all of Grace's daytime firsts. He would sleep at night when it was dark like other people. He remembered the night, over a year before, when Sarah said she was going to stay up later into the night and sleep later into the morning, but that decision didn't last one night as she fell asleep sitting on his lap.

If he were human again…

It was what he wanted all along. The thought of returning had never occurred to him, but when Geoffrey mentioned it in the camp it sounded so logical. Geoffrey was sorry he had even mentioned it, and well he should have been. Where it had never occurred to James that he could be human again, knowing that the possibility had been considered and others before him had tried made him hungry for the chance. Which spells might work? James knew who could find out. He would ask her when they arrived home. Even if it was a long shot, he felt better, like there was a way out of this mess. When he was the same as Sarah, everything would be all right.

· · ·

SARAH HAD ALWAYS WANTED to see the Grand Canyon, so that was their first destination. James headed south for the ten-hour drive, traveling down U.S. 95 toward U.S. 93. When the dawn began peeking into the skyline, James crawled into the backseat with Grace, pinning thick terrycloth black towels, conveniently left behind by Keiko and Arnie, around the four sides. As Sarah continued the drive through the southern Nevada desert, James sighed. The sight of the darkened backseat reminded him of the time Jennifer and Olivia hid him from the sunlight when he went to confront Kenneth Hempel. But he shook that thought away, too much had happened since then, and he watched his daughter sleep in her safety seat. He fell asleep with the steady rumble of the car beneath him, Sarah's smooth steering allowing him to feel safe. When the thought of returning occurred to him as he drifted into undead oblivion, he pressed it aside. Another time, he said to himself. I will worry about returning another time.

They passed south from US 93 into Arizona and the I-40 East toward Flagstaff/Phoenix. From there they took the AZ 64 North to Village Loop and Grand Canyon National Park. When James awoke, the car was slowing. Grace was sitting up, watching her father, eager as though she knew they were somewhere special. It was dusk, and the thin layer of clouds cleared away leaving the dwindling sunlight to brighten the nature-made gorge in the Arizona desert. They passed the sign stating they had arrived in Grand Canyon National Park, and there was nothing much to speak of at first, the trees, the signs, the nighttime tourists walking the dirt roads which seemed to lead nowhere until there it was, the vast hole in the middle of the desert floor, the ridges and ravines, visible now in the moonlit night. Sarah parked the car, and James carried Grace outside.

James stood beside Sarah looking over the expanse of natural beauty. Most of the tourists were gone, though a few lingered near the railings at the edge of the canyon, making out the rust-red ridges as the gorges faded with the sun. James and Sarah walked in silence to the edge of the precipice, looking out over the striking scene. The colors were muted in the dwindling light, but even in the impending darkness Sarah saw the russets and golds. She looked over the railing as far as she dared while James held onto her waist to prevent her from slipping.

"It makes you feel insignificant, seeing how vast the canyon is," Sarah said. "I feel so small in comparison. Being here puts you in your place."

James nodded. "I know what you mean."

Sarah couldn't take her eyes from the cascading gorges now fully covered in darkness. She seemed lost in thought, far away.

"What are you thinking?" he asked.

"About everything we've been through the last two years. Knowing what I know now, that you're paranormal, that I'm a reincarnated soul, it gives me a larger vision of the world than I ever dreamed of. I know the world is more than my five senses tell me. Olivia told me I have good instincts, and right now my instincts are telling me there's something wrong with you. With us."

James clutched Grace closer with one arm and slid his other arm around Sarah's shoulders. "What do you mean, Sarah? What's wrong?"

"I've been feeling some distance between us since you escaped. You were worried if I still loved you. But do you still love me?"

"Sarah."

"I thought maybe this separation finally broke the tie that held us together for over three hundred years." She dropped her face into her hands. James pressed his wife's head to his chest and kissed the top of her dark curls.

"Good God, Sarah, I escaped from camp because I couldn't be separated from you any longer. Do you have such little faith in my love for you that you think I could forget about you in three months when I haven't forgotten you in over three hundred years?"

Sarah shook her head. "I know you love me. I have all those letters you wrote to me over the years, so full of your heart, like the letters you wrote to me while you were in camp. I don't know what came over me just now. I don't even know what I'm saying. I thought you seemed distant in the car and I was worried about what it meant." She stood on her toes and lifted her chin, waiting for James to kiss her, which he did, gladly. "I don't want to be a nagging wife, but I don't want to be left in the dark if something is bothering you. You've always been quiet, James, I know that's your way. And I know you like to keep secrets from me." James shook his head, but Sarah held out her hand. "It's true. Eventually, you come clean, but you do like to hide things you think might hurt me." Sarah looked back over the canyons, barely visible now except for the ridges lit here and there by gleaming moonbeams. "When Keiko came to Salem to bring me to California, she said I should help you talk about your experience in the camp. She said you need to find closure."

"I'm all right," James said. "It's a lot to take in, being in the camp, and now being back with you and Grace. I want to believe everything is going to be fine, but I'm afraid something else is going to happen, like being reunited with you is only temporary and we're going to be separated again. I don't think I can take being apart from you anymore. And it sickens me to think you and Grace have to suffer because of what I am."

"The worst is over," Sarah said.

James nodded, though he saw in the flatness behind his wife's eyes that she was still struggling with some unasked question, and he was afraid of where her thoughts were headed.

"You're not leaving me, are you?" Sarah asked. She could hardly say the words.

"Is that what you think? I want to leave?"

"I don't know what to think."

James pressed Sarah even more tightly to his chest. He couldn't get close enough to her at that moment. He needed her to understand.

"I'm not going anywhere, Sarah. No matter how difficult things may get. No matter the obstacles. No matter if we have to keep running for the next twenty years. You are my only reason for living. You have been for a very, very long time. This internment has proven beyond a shadow of a doubt that I can't live without you."

Grace had been silent the whole time, watching her parents with curious eyes. She saw a graceful hawk glide over the canyon and she pointed and laughed.

"Daddy!" she said.

"That's a beautiful bird, Grace," James said.

Sarah scanned the ridges that spread toward the horizon. "I still can't get over the canyons. They're like sculptures from God. How else can you explain them?"

"When water levels dropped..."

"Stop being logical, James, and enjoy the scenery."

James leaned his forehead against Sarah's and smiled. "I am."

He saw the flecks of green on the red-brown ridges, trees perched precariously near the edges of ravines, the gulches stretching down to the river flowing on the bottom. It was a master design, the way the spires at the top stripped down to the rocks, the gradients of red earth suited to the desert landscape. Each sliver of natural architecture was a shrine to a higher power James no longer understood, though he wanted to. He wanted to admire the red-pink-gold sunrise over the nooks and crannies of the canyons with his wife and daughter in the daylight. He wanted to be in awe of the beauty surrounding them, not just in Inyo County or here on the edge of the Grand Canyon. He wanted to be at peace with himself and his place in the world, something he hadn't felt in over three hundred years, since the night Geoffrey, his grandfather, had turned him.

James pressed Sarah to his side and buried his nose in her hair, savoring the strawberries and cream scent he loved. Sarah was right. He did keep things from her that he thought might hurt her. Though he knew she didn't like his secrets, James felt a duty to protect her. How could he explain? He couldn't live as he was any longer. They could run together now, and as far as he was concerned, they could run for years. But everything changes. Nothing stays the same. And then? That was why he needed to return. Even with the risk, he was willing to take his chances. After all, he risked everything when he met Hempel in the daylight and he survived. He risked everything when he escaped the camp. He would survive the return too. He could sense it. He would return and they would be the same, and they would live their lives happier and fuller for it. Again, James decided he wouldn't worry about it now. He would stay with his wife and daughter, remembering why they loved each other all over again. When they were able to go home, James would see Olivia, and they would work it out from there. For now, he was with Sarah again, and at that moment that was all he wanted.

THE LAST DAYS of summer faded into autumn while James and Sarah traveled the country. From Arizona they drove through majestic New Mexico where the landscape was spiritual in its serenity. They drove through Texas, visiting the Alamo, and from there they drove through Oklahoma and Missouri to Chicago, Illinois. They spent time in Indiana, Kentucky, Martha's home state of Alabama, and Georgia. From there they passed into Florida, thinking of visiting Orlando and wondering if Grace was old enough to appreciate SeaWorld and Disney. Grace was aware of her surroundings, and she knew her favorite characters when they came on television. Her vocabulary was growing, and she was able to sing most of the ABC song by herself. She was growing so fast, James thought. They decided they would go to Orlando, the October Florida weather a perfect eighty-five degrees. If nothing else, James and Sarah would enjoy the time at the amusement parks. They could use the entertainment.

They discovered from a newspaper that the Supreme Court verdict about the internment camps was expected at any time. That night they sat on the floor of their motel room in front of the television waiting for the announcement.

"What do you think will happen?" Sarah asked.

James shook his head. "It could go either way. In 1944, in the case *Korematsu v. United States*, the Supreme Court decided in a 6-3 decision that the wartime internment of Japanese Americans was constitutional. The six judges defended internment on the basis of national security, threat to the country Keiko and her family were."

"That doesn't sound good," Sarah said.

"It doesn't. But then in the case *Ex Parte Endo*, the Supreme Court decided Mitsuye Endo, a woman confirmed to be a loyal American citizen, should be allowed to go home. Days earlier the U.S. Army rescinded the mass evacuation order and they told loyal citizens they could go home, for those who had homes to return to. Their lives were destroyed when they were forced into the camps. Their jobs, their businesses, their homes, their livelihoods were gone."

"But they survived," Sarah said. "Keiko survived."

"Yes, she did."

And then, in the white words flickering ticker-tape style across the bottom of the screen, they saw the headline before the talking head announced it. Because of the 5-4 decision in favor of releasing the vampires, James and Sarah could go home.

CHAPTER 19

The Supreme Court decision was a victory of sorts. While the undead were released on their recognizance—no one had been able to pin any violent crimes on any of the interned, and no one knew what to do about how or why some vampires turned others —they were ordered to add their names to a watch list so the government would know where they were at all times. Concerned citizens could check the registry to see if any undead lived in their neighborhoods. Employers could check the registry before they chose to hire someone. Anyone out of curiosity could see where the vampires lived.

"It's like a sex offender registry," James said, unable to hide his disgust.

"But you're free," Sarah said. "We don't have to run anymore."

James heard the relief in Sarah's voice, and he nodded. His need to return struck him acutely, and he knew he had no choice now. He wouldn't sign his name to that list. He wouldn't have his wife and daughter stained by their contact with him. What good could it do for Sarah to be known as the vampire's wife? Grace as the vampire's daughter? Would people point them out, mock them, or worse, threaten them with violence because their husband and father was one of *them*? He thought of telling Sarah about the possibility of returning, right there, right then, but he couldn't upset her that way. Geoffrey had been insistent that no witch had ever successfully completed the spell. But James was determined. He had one piece of the puzzle no one else had—Olivia. If anyone could cast a spell no one else could, it was her. James was sure of it, so sure he was willing to put his immortality in her hands. He promised himself that if this went according to plan, it would be the last time he kept anything from Sarah.

They weren't in any rush to get home. Their wooden gabled house had been there for over three hundred years, and three hundred years from now it would be there still. They drove south to Orlando as planned and spent a few days roaming the amusement parks, taking Grace on some of the children's rides, and she loved them all. She loved the crowds and the chatter and the laughter and the salty smell of popcorn, pointing and saying, "That! That!" as though she couldn't get enough of everything. When Sarah pressed him, James admitted that he loved the amusement parks as much as Grace. They were simply fun. He couldn't remember a time in his life, ever, when he did something simply fun. This is what humans do, he thought, and I like it.

From Orlando they headed north, back through Florida, Georgia, South Carolina, and North Carolina, making a bee-line through the Eastern Seaboard states home to Massachusetts. It was November now, the red-yellow-orange leaves on the trees dropping to the ground, houses celebrating the autumn holidays with scarecrows and pumpkins on their lawns. The summer heat had passed, Halloween a memory, the tourists gone with them, leaving behind a nighttime cool of thirty-five degrees. James drove Highway 114 past the Salem Superior Court to Washington Street, and he marveled at the sights that had gradually evolved over the last three hundred years. From Washington Street, he turned right onto Essex Street near the three historical homes of the Salem Inn, the red brick four-story Captain West House, the happy yellow Federal period Curwen House, and the smaller, pale yellow Dutch Colonial Peabody House. He was driving in the opposite direction of their wooden gabled home, but James needed to remember. He wanted to see where he and Sarah were reunited.

Sarah pointed out the red brick house to Grace. "That's where Mommy lived when she first moved to Salem. That was before I knew who Daddy was, or who I was." Sarah touched James' cheek and smiled. "Are we going on the James and Sarah tour?"

James nodded. "I needed to remind myself I'm really home. I thought it would be a lot longer before I was able to come back again."

He drove from Summer Street to Norman where he turned left back onto Washington Street and right onto Essex past the Pedestrian Mall toward home. From there they passed the Peabody-Essex Museum and the Hawthorne Hotel until he swung left around Washington Square North to the Salem Witch Museum. James stopped the car in front of the red brick church-like building with Gothic arches. It was night, fully dark, and people were in their homes, near their fireplaces, fighting off the chill that late autumn brought near the shore. Sarah pulled her jacket closer around her neck, and James turned the heat on in the car, reminded how quickly humans felt cold.

"We walked here the first night we left the library together," Sarah said. When her eyes welled, James reached across the front seat and pulled her closer. "Do you want to go home?"

"These are happy tears. This reminds me of when we found each other again."

"And we'll keep finding each other, over and over again. I'm sure of it. No matter what happens."

Sarah pulled away from James, her eyes wide. "What's going to happen?"

James pulled Sarah back into his arms, whispering his words into her ear. "Nothing, Sarah, nothing. We're going to be fine. We always are."

He held her until her breathing settled. When she was calm she looked at the museum.

"You know, I've never been in there," she said.

"You don't have to go in. You saw the horror yourself."

James turned right down Washington Square East, around the

green lawn of Salem Common. He turned right down Essex Street, down Orange Street to Derby Street, near the bay, and home. He parked near the curb of their wooden gabled house and sighed. The crooked wooden oak was looking better than it had before he left, standing a bit taller, perhaps less left of center. He left in May, and now it was November, only six months. He had been gone years at a time, decades at a time, yet he had never been so happy to be back. In the past, he came home because he wanted to be near Elizabeth and he always felt her most strongly in their house. But now, he arrived home with his wife and his daughter beside him. And this time he was determined to stay with them as long as humanly possible.

Yes, he thought. As long as humanly possible.

"We're home, Grace," Sarah said. But Grace had dozed off in her safety seat, her head tilted to the side, her eyes closed, a smile on her lips.

"We can wake her up in time to put her back to bed," James said. As he stepped out of the car, the electric lights in the great room flipped on. Sarah froze, staring at the diamond-paned casement window. James closed his eyes as he listened. The musk of sandalwood floated toward him, and when he heard her humming and the jangles of coin jewelry, he smiled.

Olivia peered out the great room window and waved. She rushed outside, taking a sleeping Grace from James' arms. She kissed Sarah's cheek, and James gave her a gentle hug around his sleeping baby.

"When Sarah called to tell me you were coming home I wanted to make sure everything was ready for you," Olivia said. "I've had the cat with me, and I brought her back. I went grocery shopping for you and the baby, Sarah, and I have a fresh supply of bags for you, James."

"Where did you get the bags from?" James asked.

Olivia smiled. "I have sources."

"Not the hospital?"

"No," Olivia said. "Not the hospital. I wasn't sure it was safe to get it from there now."

James kissed Olivia's cheek. "Thank you, Olivia."

"It's what you need, dear. A sort of grocery shopping."

James nodded. He stopped short near the crooked oak tree and he realized how much he missed the old house while he was gone.

"I hired a tree doctor to fix the tree," Sarah said. "It was looking a little sad and I wasn't ready to see it go. It's been here as long as the house."

James patted the tree. "I'm glad you had it fixed. It wouldn't look the same around here without it." He walked toward the house, pausing by the green front door. "You know, I used to leave this place because I thought I needed to move on. And for a while I'd go on with my life. I'd teach. I'd explore. I'd read and I'd learn. I dreamed of you every day. Then after a time I'd wake up in a panic thinking about this house, about how there was nowhere in the world I felt closer to you, and I'd come home as quickly as I could because I couldn't relax until I was here. I kept thinking that one night I'd walk into the house and you'd be here waiting for me. And then one night here you were, looking at that tree. That night is the most important night of my life, Sarah. I will do everything I can to keep you safe so we can have many more happy days together."

"You mean happy nights."

James nodded. He saw Olivia dragging two bags of luggage through the door.

"You don't have to leave now, Olivia," Sarah said.

"You and James need time to reconnect."

"We did that on the drive home," James said.

"You need your privacy," Olivia said.

Sarah hugged her friend. "Thank you for everything you did while James was gone."

"Heaven knows, James has helped us so much over the years. Consider this a small repayment for all he's done for my family." She hugged James again. "Welcome home, James."

"Maybe you could repay me by helping me stay home for good."

While his words were simple enough, his deeper meaning was suggested in his tone. Olivia raised an eyebrow but said nothing. James took Olivia's luggage and walked her outside. Olivia took one last look around the wooden gabled house and she smiled.

"It's a grand old place," she said. "You're very lucky to have this house. It's a record of your history with Sarah." She pulled her scarf closer around her neck and shivered in the cold autumn air. She opened the back door of her silver Prius and James lifted her luggage into the trunk.

"Geoffrey told me some interesting stories in camp," James said.

"Geoffrey always has interesting stories." Olivia opened the driver's door. "What did he say?"

"He's my grandfather."

Olivia stared at James. "He isn't."

"He is."

Olivia walked to James, her detective seeking clues look scanning everything about his expression, his eyes, his mouth, the shrug of his shoulders as he considered his long-lost relative.

"What do you think of that, James?"

"I'm still processing it, to be honest. I have to reconcile the fact that the vampire who turned me and left me alone to fend for myself for over three hundred years is my father's father. I have to deal with the fact that my own grandfather abandoned me to fate." James felt the muscles in his shoulders tense at the thought of Geoffrey and his disappearing act. "Geoffrey left shortly after we escaped the camp, and I've been too busy being with my wife to think much about him."

"He's been very attentive to you since he's come back," Olivia said.

"After the fact."

"Better late than never."

"That's what Geoffrey said."

"Geoffrey isn't always wrong."

Olivia got into her Prius and turned the key in the ignition.

"Geoffrey also told me about vampires trying to return to human."

"Did he tell you it's never been done?"

"Why?"

"No one ever found the right spell."

"Geoffrey said that when some of the vampires tried to turn back to humans, for those for whom the spell worked even that much, it turned them into a corpse the age they would be if they were never turned. So if someone tried the spell on me and it failed I would turn into a three centuries old corpse."

"Assuming you were to find a witch irresponsible enough to try that ridiculous spell, then yes, you might turn into dust and bones." Olivia eyed James, her suspicion darkening her steel-gray eyes. "I think Sarah likes the way you look now."

"Can you find out why those spells didn't work?"

"Why are you asking, James?"

"I keep thinking about Miriam's prophecy. She said *You will return, James. You will.*"

"You have returned, dear. You're home from that dreadful camp. You're safe here with your wife and daughter."

"Are they safe with me the way I am? The vampires have been released, but now what? I haven't signed my name to the watch list, but they'll catch up to me eventually and everyone is going to know what I am. And they may still come for me. I broke out of camp, after all. We may need to keep moving."

"I hate to be the one to break it to you, but everyone already knows what you are. And I haven't heard a word about anyone looking for you. You haven't been on the news. None of you jail-breakers have been on the news. No one has come sniffing around."

"How could they not come looking for me? I broke out of camp, which is essentially the same as breaking out of jail."

"They probably don't want to be embarrassed. How sad for them, they couldn't even hold you inside the camp. They must have realized how powerless they were against your strength. And besides, you would have been released by now. I don't think you need to worry about them coming after you here, James. I haven't felt any disturbance in the energy as far as that's concerned. As for your worries about what will become of Sarah and Grace, the only thing that will happen now is they'll be happy because you're home. Everything else, you'll overcome it. You three are meant to be together. It's your destiny."

"This is our destiny? For me to have to put my name on a government watch list while my innocent wife and daughter are caught in the crossfire?"

"What crossfire, James?"

"Is it our destiny for me to be immortal and Sarah human? If things stay the way they are…"

Olivia stroked James' cheek with her motherly touch, her ungloved hand cold even to James' skin. "You're tired, dear. You've been through a terrible ordeal, and it's going to take time for you to understand the impact it's had on you. I know you would never do anything to put yourself in jeopardy now that you're home with Sarah. You know what that would do to her, and to Grace." She looked at the beginning traces of light on the horizon. "It's nearly dawn. Have something warm to drink. Get some sleep. Things will look better tonight."

"Olivia…"

"Welcome home, James."

She got into her car and drove away.

THE NEXT NIGHT they were reunited with Chandresh, Jennifer, Timothy, and Howard, though they missed Jocelyn, who had gone to Canada to be with her husband and son. It felt like old times for them to be there again, gathered in the wooden gabled house as though no madness had happened, no time had passed, and James and Sarah were together with the people who meant the most to them. Olivia busied herself in the kitchen, checking everything on the stove and in the oven. James and Sarah sat next to the fireplace, his arm around her shoulders, Grace on her father's lap watching the flickering red-orange flames. While Jennifer and Chandresh arrived together, there was a distance, a coldness between them. When Chandresh spoke, Jennifer hardly answered and she rarely looked in his direction, such a contrast to the nights before the internment when she couldn't take her eyes off her tall, muscled, raven-haired man. When Martha arrived her loud southern-style laughter filled the space with joy, and she scurried to Sarah and Grace. Grace held her hands out to Martha, and Martha scooped the baby into her arms.

"I've missed you," Martha said. "How is my little Gracie? Look what a big girl you are."

While Sarah and Grace huddled near Martha, Timothy and Howard sat near Chandresh, and James stayed in his seat before the fire, watching Olivia, willing her to look his way. Olivia stayed stubborn, engrossed in what appeared to be an all-important conversation with Jennifer, who turned her chair aside so she wouldn't have to see Chandresh. It was as though Olivia knew what he wanted, James thought, and she wasn't humoring him.

"Olivia," James said.

"Dinner is nearly ready, everyone, or," Olivia laughed, "at least for the humans among us. Let me warm some drink for you boys."

"I don't want anything to drink," James said. "I want to talk to you." He looked at Sarah, who was still chatting with Martha. Sarah smiled at him, and he knew he had to keep pressing.

"I made fried eggplant lasagna especially for you, Sarah," said Olivia. "I know how much you love my fried eggplant lasagna."

James stepped in front of Olivia. "Listen to me," he said. "I know you don't want to talk about returning, but I have to know what you know. If there's any chance I can be returned I have to know."

"I've told you, James. You don't need to worry any longer. No one is looking for you. You're fine where you are as you are. Sarah and Grace are safe here."

"They're not pursuing the escaped vampires," Chandresh said. "It turns out we weren't as resourceful as we thought planning a fancy escape. Many of our kind escaped camps across the country, most by simply jumping the fence. That's why the government decided to shut the camps down. It had nothing to do with the Supreme Court decision. They realized they couldn't keep us inside if we wanted out." Chandresh nodded at James. "I think Olivia is right. You don't need to worry that they're coming after us, though they may insist you sign their watch list." He looked at Jennifer, whose head was tilted toward him like she was listening though her eyes were fixed on the woven rug beneath her feet. Chandresh watched Jennifer, and when she didn't look in his direction, he sighed, walked into the kitchen, and removed one of James' red-filled bags from the refrigerator. "Do you mind?" he asked. James shook his head without looking away from Olivia.

"Allow me," said Olivia. She sliced the top of the bag with a knife, poured the heavy liquid into a coffee mug, put the mug into the microwave, and set the timer.

Chandresh sat next to James. "It's all right, James."

James shook his head. There was an agitation in his voice that caused everyone in the house to watch him. "No," he said. "I can't relax as long as I'm like this. What if they come knocking on our door in the middle of the night, frightening my wife again? She's been through that twice before, and she's not going through it again because of me. We have to be together."

Sarah knelt before James, taking his hands in hers, her chocolate-brown eyes small with worry.

"We needed to run when you first escaped the camp," she said, her voice soothing, "but that's over. The camps are closed. They're not looking for you though you escaped. We're home now. We don't have to run anymore."

"We'd never have to worry again, Sarah. We'd never have to flee again if I were returned."

"You've already returned," Sarah said. "You're home."

Olivia shook her head. "James..."

"It can't be done," Howard said. "I've looked into it for Timothy."

"You knew about returning too?" James asked.

"Howard is right," Olivia said. "This is a pointless conversation. Grandfather Geoffrey did you yet another disservice by even mentioning it to you."

James pointed at Olivia. "Just because a spell has never been cast before doesn't mean it can't be done. You know that better than anyone. You've cast spells no one else has."

Olivia walked to the end of the kitchen, as far from James as the house would allow.

"No, James."

"I remember now. When I saw Miriam in the forest she said I'd need to find a magic as powerful as the magic that turned me. You're one of the most powerful witches, I know you are. If anyone can cast the returning spell it's you. You can do this."

Olivia turned toward the sink. "How can you ask me to do this? You have been part of my family for generations. We owe you beyond anything we can ever repay."

"Do this and we'll call it even," James said.

"You know what the consequences could be if the spell doesn't work. We're only allowed to use our spells for good."

"This is good," James said. "For me, there's nothing better."

Sarah stood next to her husband, her eyes wide as the conversation began to make sense. "What spell are you asking Olivia to cast?" she asked.

James stared at Olivia as though he didn't hear Sarah. Sarah grabbed his hand, and when he didn't seem to feel her she shook his arm until he looked at her.

"Geoffrey said there are vampires who tried to return," he said.

"Return to what?"

"Human."

"Is that possible?" Sarah asked.

"It's not possible," Olivia said, "which is why this conversation needs to end."

"What happens when the spell doesn't work?"

Sarah looked around the kitchen, the great room, from person to person at the faces she loved above all others in the world. No one offered an answer, looking away with downcast frowns that didn't want to acknowledge the answer she already knew in her heart.

Finally, Olivia said, "He'll die. For real this time."

Sarah stepped into the hallway, putting some distance between her and everyone else, the panic causing an unnatural stilt in her voice. "No, James. No!"

James stood, his hands in the air, his voice a plea. "Don't you see, Sarah? I want to do this for you. I'm dead, and I can't live with whatever I have that keeps me animated like this any longer. I can't risk the madness again. I need to live a normal life, eat normal food, and drink normal drinks that didn't need to be drained from another living creature. I need to be human again, to live alongside my human wife and daughter on their schedule. I've never been comfortable with this life. Now I know there's a way out. And Olivia is going to help me."

"No," Sarah said. "You can't do this. I can't risk that anything will happen to you. Why would you want to do this now? We're finally together again." Her tears fell unrestrained down her cheeks. When Grace saw her father's apprehension and her mother crying she became agitated and looked as though she would cry herself. Martha carried the baby into her bedroom, singing a soothing melody, away from the tense scene, and closed the door behind her.

Olivia stepped close to James, her hands out, a gesture of surrender. "I know you've been through a difficult time. It's not fair what happened to you and the others. Prejudice has never been fair. You know as well as I do that sometimes bad things happen to good people for no reason we can discern, at least not with our earthly senses. But giving into the paranoia, allowing yourself to be swayed by fear, that's not going to help you, or Sarah, or Grace. They need you here. We all love you exactly as you are. You don't need to pretend to be something you aren't, and you aren't human. You haven't been human for a long time. Accept yourself the way you are. You don't have to be human to deserve our love. You deserve our love because you are one of the strongest, bravest, most caring beings I've ever known. I will not be responsible for casting a spell that could take the wonder that is James Wentworth from this world."

James shook his head, his lips pulled, his eyes tight. He wouldn't be swayed. "Geoffrey said you can't kill something already dead."

"He is so very wrong about that," Olivia said. "He told you so himself. If I tried to return you and the spell didn't work, you could become a corpse. You'd be lost to Sarah and Grace forever."

The silence in the great room was overwhelming, echoing the emptiness in James' mind. How could he explain what this meant to him? How could he explain he wasn't afraid of the consequences because he knew, in his dormant heart, that this would work because it was their turn to be free from the madness? It was their turn to find some happiness that wasn't contingent on secrets or escapes.

All he could say was, "This is what I want, Olivia."

"What about Sarah?" Jennifer asked.

Sarah dropped her head into her hands. She wept with such force that her lungs coughed for lack of air. James stood before her, taking her into his arms. She tried to push him away, but he was too strong.

"Don't worry, Sarah. I'll be all right."

"James," Jennifer said.

James pointed at Jennifer. "At the Witches Lair that Halloween you promised me three wishes. Do you remember? I used my first wish when you cast a spell to help me recover after meeting Hempel at the library at noon. I used my second wish at the train station when I asked you to keep Sarah safe and strong. So this is it. I'm calling in my third wish. I want to be returned. And I want Olivia to do it."

Olivia shook her head. "I can't do it."

"Yes, you can," James said. "If I believed I would lose all animation forever I wouldn't do it. But I know you can do it, Olivia. I believe in you."

"Witches have been searching for the returning spell for centuries and no one has found it."

"But you will," James said.

Sarah shook her head. "It's too dangerous," she said, her voice a hoarse whisper. James reached for her, but she pulled away. "Every time we're together again you come up with some dangerous stunt that could separate us. How long will we be separated next time? Three months? Three years? Three hundred years? What if it's forever? I need you here, and I won't let you do this."

"I'll be returning to you, Sarah, not leaving. I'll be back to the way I was always meant to be. This is the one thing I've gone back to, again and again…if only I were human. All these years I didn't think it was possible, but it is, Sarah, and Olivia can make it happen."

Sarah was overcome by another wave of tear-soaked misery. "Olivia says it can't be done," she said. "Why are you so insistent about this? I've already told you, James, I love you exactly the way you are with your cold skin, silent chest, and your blood bags. If we need to run again we'll run. I'll follow wherever you go. I'll follow you to the ends of the earth and back again if that's what I need to do to stay with you."

"But if I'm human again we can have our life back. A quiet, normal life like the one we started the first time."

"It's not 1692 anymore. I knew when I married you the second time our lives would be different. I'm all right with that, but I'm not all right with knowing you might die from a spell Olivia doesn't think she can cast."

James took her into his arms, and this time Sarah didn't fight him. She pressed her head into his chest, and he whispered into her ear. "Wouldn't it be wonderful if we were both human? We would be awake at the same time, sleep at the same time, eat the same food. I wouldn't have to worry about finding blood to drink."

"I've told you before you can drink from me."

"No!" James couldn't hide his frustration. "I won't drink from my wife! I don't want anyone's blood. I want to drink water like everyone else. I don't want to miss Grace while she grows every day. I need this, Sarah. I need it for you, I need it for Grace, and I need it for me so I can live with myself."

"But you'll live forever," Sarah sobbed. "Why would you give that up?"

"Forever doesn't mean anything if you're not there."

Sarah pulled away from James. She tossed her dark curls behind her shoulder and bared her neck, leaning toward him. "Turn me!" she yelled. "Do it!"

James stroked the tears from her cheeks. "No, Sarah. You said no after the car accident, and that was your truth. You don't want to be like me, and you're right. I want to be like you. I want to breathe again. I want to be able to take you into my arms and warm you when you're cold at night. I want you to hear my heartbeat when you rest your head against my chest."

"I liked knowing you'd go on after I was gone," Sarah said. "You'd be there for Grace, and her children, and her children's children. And you'd be there when I come around again." Martha came out of Grace's room, closing the door gently behind her, and Sarah took Martha's hand. "What will happen if James and I are both human?" she asked.

"You'll both be reborn when the time is right. You'll find your way back to each other again, and again, and again."

"James wants to…"

"I know," Martha said. "Remember that your destiny doesn't change because of your bodily form, Sarah. Your destiny is just that, fate, and whether you're human and James is supernatural or you're both human nothing can change your destiny."

Sarah looked at Olivia. "Are you sure it's impossible?"

Olivia's shoulders slumped and she shook her head, defeated by the debate. "It's never been done, but maybe there are witches with some ideas about where to begin casting a returning spell."

"I'll do whatever I can to help," Martha said.

"Me too," said Jennifer. She looked at Chandresh for the first time that night, and he smiled at her, his love for her everywhere in his soulful eyes. Jennifer's cheeks flushed.

"Miriam," James said. "She knew all those years ago I needed to find strong magic to be returned. When I stayed with her in her cabin in the forest she spent hours scratching words onto paper, often working herself into a manic frenzy while she wrote. It was like her hand couldn't move fast enough for all the words she needed to say and it was painful for her to keep them bottled inside. The language looked like gibberish to me, and I could never read what she wrote."

Olivia nodded. "Miriam left behind books of magic spells. I have those very same pages you saw her writing since they've been passed down through the generations. And you're right about the language. I don't understand it any more than you do. I'll need to decode her writing to make any sense of it."

"Do you think there could be a returning spell in there?" Jennifer asked.

"Perhaps," said Olivia.

"Then you'll do it?" James asked.

"I'll try, James. But if it doesn't go well…"

James looked at Sarah. He kissed her gently on top of her hair as he did in the days when he was afraid for her to feel his lips on her skin.

"It will go well," James said. He smiled for the first time that night. "I trust you with my life, Olivia."

Olivia sighed.

"You don't know how true that is."

CHAPTER 20

Double, double toil and trouble;
Fire burn, and cauldron bubble
Fillet of a fenny snake,
In the caldron boil and bake;
Eye of newt, and toe of frog,
Wool of bat, and tongue of dog...

FOR SHAKESPEARE'S witch sisters in *Macbeth*, magic was as simple as boiling animal parts in a cauldron. But when you're a witch looking for a spell, a special spell that has never been cast successfully, who do you turn to? Where do you look? Do you go to the witchcraft store and spend hours into the night after the shop has closed and the customers are gone and study every book on the shelves? Do you pull out old scrolls from your ancestor and try to make sense of the squiggles and scratches though it looks like gobbledygook to you?

Olivia held true to her promise. She did her research. She called in favors from fellow Wiccans all over the world who combined their knowledge to scour the globe for the returning spell. Mainly, Olivia, Jennifer, and Martha spent hours hunched over Olivia's desk in her office in the Witches Lair studying timeworn copies of Miriam's spells that nearly disintegrated in their hands as they turned the three-hundred-year-old pages. They discovered that some of the spells were written in Gaelic, some were written in seventeenth-century English, some in Latin, and others in Hebrew. Sometimes Miriam switched languages within the same spell, giving her pages the gibberishness James noted. With help, the three Wiccans translated Miriam's meanderings into present-day English, and for the first time, Olivia could read her ancestor's words. When she read the translations aloud to Martha and Jennifer, they nodded and knew they found what they were looking for. They had searched the wide world for what was in front of them all along.

In December, two weeks before Christmas, it was cold in Salem. The naked branches of the spindly trees trembled in the spiky air. Snow flurried to the ground, covering the lawns of Salem Common. People bundled up more than usual when they went outside, protecting themselves from the sharp slap of winter. The sea was flat and foggy, reflecting the flat and foggy sky. Olivia and Martha braved the frigid weather to visit the wooden gabled house and they knocked at the green front door. They were hardly recognizable under their hats, scarves pulled high around their noses, heavy coats, and gloves, but Sarah was expecting them and welcomed them inside. While they warmed themselves near the fireplace, Sarah made them coffee. After a few sips and casual conversation, Martha pulled one of Miriam's frayed scrolls from her oversized quilted bag. Sarah leaned over Martha's shoulder to see.

"That looks like Hebrew," Sarah said. "Where is your family from, Olivia?"

"We're of Jewish origin, and we had ancestors who migrated to England and Germany over time. Miriam was born in England."

Olivia fell silent. Martha sat on the floor beside Grace, who was watching her favorite puppet show and clapping and singing along. Sarah waited, worried about what Olivia wanted to say. Olivia wouldn't look at Sarah or Grace, her eyes focused on the fire.

"Is James awake?" Martha asked.

"Not yet," Sarah said.

"I am," he said. James walked out of the bedroom tucking his button-down shirt into his jeans. He tapped the screen of his cell phone and slid it into his pocket.

"Who were you talking to?" Sarah asked.

"Goodwin Enwright, head of the English department at Salem State. He said he didn't care what I was and he offered me my old job back. He even offered me my old office in the library."

"Did you say yes?" Sarah asked.

"I said I'd think about it." James looked at Olivia. "You have a spell." It wasn't a question. He knew.

"Yes," Martha said. "We think we've come upon a spell that will work. If it's done correctly."

Olivia shook her head. "I'm not sure about this, James."

"You have to do this," James said.

"I don't have to do anything. I love you like a son. I can't take a chance I might hurt you."

"Like a son? I'm more than three hundred years old."

"I look like your mother and that's all I need to know. How could I be responsible for something that could kill you?"

"I'm already dead, Olivia."

"How can you say that? You have Sarah here beside you. Your daughter. You just got a call from the head of the English department at Salem State University wanting to hire you back. Would he rehire a dead person? How dead are you, James, when you have so much to live for? Everyone in this room loves you the way you are. Sarah loves you unconditionally. All those years you wrote letters to her to feel connected to her. You never stopped talking about her. Even through the centuries our ancestors knew how you loved your wife and how you were devoted to keeping her memory alive by helping others. Here she is, James, that wife you missed so much, standing beside you, heartbroken at the thought that anything might happen to you because of my misguided spells."

James pulled Sarah close to him and pressed his lips into the dark curls near her temple. He lingered there, holding her tightly, his eyes closed, lost in strawberries and cream.

"Nothing bad is going to happen to me," James whispered. "I have Olivia, and she's going to protect me. She's going to be the first witch to make this spell happen."

Martha put her arm around Olivia. "As soon as Olivia believes in her powers, she'll make this happen. Miriam predicted it in her prophecy."

"You will help me," Olivia said.

"I can't be there during the casting of the spell," Martha said, "but I'll help you prepare however I can."

"When do you want to do this?" Olivia asked.

"Now," James said. "Tonight."

"Tonight is too soon," Olivia said. "I need time."

"Then tomorrow, or the next night."

"How about New Year's Eve?" Martha said. "It's the perfect time for such a transformation."

James nodded. "All right."

"That will give me time," Olivia said. "Yes, that works for me."

When Sarah shuddered James pulled her closer. "What better way to start the new year than for me to be human again? It's what I've wanted for oh so very long."

"I love you the way you are," Sarah said.

"I know you do, and I love you even more for it. But it's better this way."

"Better for who?"

"For all of us. You trust me, don't you?"

"Of course I do."

"And you trust Olivia?"

Olivia stood tall and level-eyed. The worry that left her steel-gray eyes sunken only moments before dissipated, leaving behind her motherly strength. This was the Olivia Sarah loved from the moment she met her, the Olivia of confidence, kindness, and wisdom. The Olivia who always knew what to say. The Olivia who rearranged her life to help Sarah when she needed it most. The Olivia who was one of the most powerful witches in the world.

"Are you sure you want to do this?" Sarah asked.

"I didn't ask for this, but I was chosen by fate, it seems," Olivia said. "If it's James' destiny to be human again, then it's my destiny to return him. Miriam said as much."

"What do you mean?" Sarah asked.

"When we were reading Miriam's spells, we found a reference to the returning of the vampires, that it would take stronger magic than she had. It would take one in her future generations to make it happen. And it would happen for the vampire who helped her survive the forest men."

"That's me," James said. "I protected her from the men in the forest."

Martha nodded. "Your returning was foretold by Miriam over three hundred years ago."

James brushed his lips against Sarah's cheek. "See, honey. It's Miriam's prophecy."

While Sarah's mind followed James' logic, her heart still struggled against the knowledge that if things went wrong she would lose him again, for good this time. But he needed to try. She understood that. He needed it the way he needed to go into the sun to meet Kenneth Hempel. She didn't like his idea then like she didn't like his plan now, but she knew how stubborn her husband could be so she nodded her consent. James waited for her to say something, but there was nothing to say.

Olivia walked to the door. "I have to prepare. I'll see you here on New Year's Eve at midnight."

She left without another word, and Martha disappeared behind her, leaving James and Sarah to stare after them and wonder.

SARAH STRUGGLED to make December 30 an ordinary day. While James slept in their darkened bedroom, she went around the house taking down the Christmas decorations, the pine wreaths, the Santa plates, the glass ornaments, and the rainbow lights, putting everything into the plastic containers James would store in the attic when he awoke. When Christmas was gone and the house was its normal eclectic self again, Sarah played with Grace with her stuffed animals, and Grace was able to name a few of them—the doggie, the cat, the cow. This is what James doesn't want to miss, Sarah thought.

While Grace took her afternoon nap, Sarah went into her bedroom, opening and closing the door quickly so the light wouldn't bother James. It was cave-dark, but Sarah found her way to where James slept. She crawled into bed beside him, slid her arms around his waist, and pressed herself against his back, spooning him. Whenever a thought popped into her brain, any thought, she pressed it away. She didn't want to think about anything then. She wanted to concentrate on James. On the strength in his muscles. On his cool skin. On the stillness of his body. No breath, no heartbeat, no pulse. She pulled him closer and she nuzzled into his hair, the same golden halo hair she loved since the first time she saw him. She breathed in deeply, wanting to remember. She couldn't put a name to his scent the way he did to her strawberries and cream, though she enjoyed trying. Was it musk, she wondered? She was comforted being this close to him and it soothed her unsettled mind. She was having trouble silencing the noise. She couldn't worry about James, not now. She had to believe it was their turn to be free of the madness. It was their turn to live a quiet, normal life. She pressed even closer to him, her face and arms cool against his skin. Outside it was northeastern winter raw, but inside was warm with the heat on, and James' coolness felt comforting. In forty-eight hours, he could be warm again, she thought. She might be able to hear his heartbeat again. Would that feel strange to her, she wondered? And how would it feel for James?

Suddenly, the worries struck Sarah one by one and she couldn't avoid them any longer. What if James changed when he returned to human? What if he forgot himself, who he is, who he's always been? Sarah had fallen in love with James the second time, without even knowing their first connection, because preternatural James was wonderful. As she learned the truth about herself, that she was Elizabeth, she realized that preternatural James was the same in so many ways as the human James she had first fallen for. But what if the magic of the returning spell was so strong he forgot her, their lives together, their eternal love? And then, worst of all, the thought she had been most avoiding. What if it didn't work?

Sarah shuddered. She opened her eyes and looked at James' sinewy back. When they were married the first time, when he was human, he couldn't run as fast or hear or see as far, but even then he was strong-looking. She dozed off imagining life with a human James. She was startled when she felt herself shaken, and she opened her eyes to see James looking into her face.

"Sarah? Are you all right? What's wrong?"

Sarah shook her head. "I'm fine. I wanted to be close to you so I came in here." She sat up and threw her legs over the side of the bed. "I should get Grace."

"She's fine. She's playing in her crib." James sat beside Sarah on the bed and took her into his arms. He held her to his chest for a long time, saying nothing, his nose in her hair, expressing their love through the silence. Sarah knew she was put on the earth to love this man, in whatever form his physical presence took. She loved his kindness, his intelligence, his stubbornness—all of him, even when he made her crazy with worry. "Everything is going to be all right," he whispered. "This is the way it's supposed to be. We should be the same."

When James' arms tightened around her, Sarah exhaled.

"I love you, James," she said. "I loved you from the first moment I saw you over the supper table at my father's house, and I loved you from the first moment I saw you outside this house two years ago. Even before I met you the first time I imagined the man I would fall in love with. I knew he'd be beautiful beyond measure in every way. I knew he'd be kind, and caring, and gentle in his love for me. I knew his ability to love would be limitless. From the moment I saw you, both times, I knew you were that man, even if it took time for me to understand the depth of my feelings for you. You have proven your love for me, and for Grace, again and again. I have been the luckiest woman in the world to have the devotion of a man like you for so long. I don't know what I did to deserve you, but whatever it is, I'm thankful for it." Sarah stopped, the words she wanted to say escaping her. What could she say to make him understand? "You are my everything," she said.

James kissed her lips, softly at first, then with more intensity, more passion. When he pulled his lips from hers he smiled.

"I could talk from now until next year and never explain how much I love you," he said. "Your external beauty makes perfect sense to me, Sarah, because your external beauty is merely a reflection of the beautiful person you are inside. You have been my whole life for more than three hundred years. Even when you were gone, you were my reason for living. You were my reason for waking up every night when I would have rather died for real. I didn't like what I was. I never made peace with it the way I never made peace with losing you. But thinking of you, writing to you, helping others in your memory gave me a reason to go on." He kissed her cheek and leaned his forehead against hers. "But what we're saying now sounds like goodbye, and I'm not leaving. Not this time. I'm returning, for good. We should be celebrating our love, not mourning it. Once we're the same, our love with grow even more with time. It's our turn to be free of the madness."

Sarah nodded. "Yes, it is."

NEW YEAR'S Eve was sepulcher-silent in the wooden gabled house, as though the old place waited for something either wonderful or terrible to happen—it wasn't sure which. The house had seen so much since it was built by a wealthy merchant for his son's wedding, a monument to Father Time. It had seen centuries fade, fashions come and go, and marvels of science and technology appear and disappear as new marvels were discovered. Stagecoaches were traded for trains, and horses for automobiles. Yet, through the years, human nature hadn't changed, the good and the bad of it. The quiet Salem neighborhood by the shore felt largely the same as it always had. Buildings had been built and others torn away, maybe less so in history-loving Salem than in other places, but still the neighborhood changed. Those who lived there wanted to do better and be better, yet they were held back by human follies and foibles, some more than others, and certainly no more and no less than people everywhere else in the world. What was socially acceptable had evolved, who was socially acceptable had evolved, and yet some were held back by beliefs and ideas from hundreds of years before. But that night, something new was going to happen, and the house creaked its knowledge, sharing its hope that now everything would be as it was always meant to be. Flipping through its memories, a slideshow of moments, the house had seen many extraordinary occurrences when the pale-cold man was home. Now, tonight, a great wrong could be righted, and the house shivered its hope in the wintry wind.

James followed Olivia's directions exactly. He drank no blood for seventy-two hours—not so very long for him at his age, he assured Sarah when she worried about his strength. He bathed in the lavender-infused water prescribed to cleanse him of external impurities. He even tried to meditate, hard for him with over three hundred years of thoughts pestering him. He did his best to settle himself, and he remembered Martha's suggestion whenever useless words and phrases disturbed him—they're only thoughts, and thoughts only have the power you give them. If you give the thoughts no power, Martha said, then they have none. Whenever his thoughts turned to what might go wrong when Olivia cast the spell, he thought of Sarah, right now in their bedroom, and he pictured her wondering chocolate-brown eyes, her dark curls, the full lips he needed to kiss whenever he saw them. He remembered the baby was with Jennifer and Martha that night, and he sighed. This would not be the last time he saw his wife or his daughter. He had decided. Geoffrey's words came back to him—you can't kill something already dead. But if the magic that kept him supernaturally alive was taken away, what would be left? No. No. He was meditating. He had to clear his mind again. These are just thoughts, he reminded himself, flights of a fanciful imagination.

He knew Olivia arrived before she knocked on the door. He heard her Prius sputter as she parked by the curb. The ignition shut down, she stepped out of the car and grabbed something, perhaps a bag, from the trunk. She walked with plodding steps and knocked. Sarah opened the door

"How are you this evening, dear?" Olivia asked. To a casual observer Olivia's voice would have sounded ordinary, like this was any other night under any other circumstances. James heard the heavy undertone beneath her words.

Sarah exhaled. "I'm all right, I think. Come in, Olivia."

"Where is James?"

"I'm here." James kissed Sarah's cheek. "I was meditating like you said, Olivia."

"How did that go?" Sarah asked.

"Not well. Quieting my mind isn't something I've ever been able to do."

"Are you ready, James?" Olivia asked.

"I've been ready since 1692. The more important question is are you ready?"

"I've been fasting and meditating myself, and I'm ready. Let me cleanse the room." Olivia took two white candles from her bag, lit them, and waved them around, up and down, back and forth, side to side, whispering Wiccan prayers. It reminded James of the night when Sarah went through the past-life regression, proving who she had been all along. James remembered how frightened she was and yet she went through with it, determined to face her fear. James found strength in the memory. That night had been scary for Sarah, but she survived and grew stronger on the other side. It would be the same for him, he thought.

Olivia put the candles on the wooden table in the kitchen and lit some sage incense. She gestured to the sofa.

"Lie here, James. Close your eyes. Everything will be fine."

"I know," he said.

"You have to trust me," Olivia said. "If you have even the slightest doubt of my ability to do this, it won't work." She shook her head. "You have to believe this will work."

"I believe it will work. I trust you, Olivia."

Olivia nodded. "Sarah, perhaps you should go to Jennifer's since she and Martha have Grace."

"No," Sarah said. "I'm not leaving."

"Maybe Olivia is right," James said. "It might be easier for you if you're not here."

"You sat outside the jail in Boston for me. You stayed with me during the past-life regression. I'm staying with you now."

James looked at Olivia. "She can stay if it's all right with you."

Olivia nodded. "All right, Sarah."

Sarah kissed James' lips. "I'll be right here. The whole time. Right here."

"That's what I said to you before the past-life regression." James stretched out on the sofa, his head against the pillow, and he grasped Sarah's hands. "I said I'd never leave you ever. Then I had to leave you because of what I am. After tonight, we'll be a normal family, with a normal life, a regular daylight schedule, and sleeping when it's dark. Grace won't have to explain to her friends why her father can only come out at night."

"But none of those things matter," Sarah said. "We can find a way around them. You've always said you didn't have a heart. You said it stopped beating when you stopped breathing after Geoffrey turned you. And I've always said you do have a heart. I know you do. I see it in your eyes every time you look at Grace and me."

"I can feel it too, for the first time in centuries. It's getting ready to beat again. Don't be afraid, Sarah. I'm not afraid. Olivia will help make this right."

Sarah smiled, doing her best to be brave, though James saw the straining worry behind her eyes. He looked at Olivia, who was concentrating on the page of Miriam's spell in her hand.

"I'm ready, Olivia," James said.

Olivia nodded. She dropped the page onto the wooden table, then stood over James, her wand pointed over him. James laughed when he saw it.

"I thought they only used wands in boy wizard movies," he said.

"The wand directs the energy where I want it to go, that's all. Stop making fun." Olivia winked at Sarah. "All right, be serious now, James. Close your eyes. Concentrate. Don't pay attention to my words. They won't make sense to you. Follow the tone of my voice. Allow yourself to drift away, backward, forward, to the end of time, to the beginning of time, and back again, wherever you're led. Free yourself to follow. Picture yourself in 1692 before you were turned, before Elizabeth was accused of witchcraft, imagine your human self, with your human wife in your arms, how content you were, how happy. Imagine yourself in the future when you're human again, your warm blood flowing through your pulsing veins, your heartbeat in synchronicity with Sarah's, your breath flowing up through your nose, down into your lungs. You are the same as everyone else. The same as Sarah. As Grace. You are yourself. Stay focused on your return. No matter what you hear from me, no matter what I say, whether you understand me or not, whether you can hear my voice or not, stay focused on your return. Do you understand?"

James nodded. "Yes," he said.

"All right, dear." Olivia looked at Sarah. "Are you sure you want to stay?"

"Yes," Sarah said. "I need to be here."

"Why don't you sit there." Olivia pointed to the dining room chair near the sofa. "Why don't you hold James' hand? That will help him stay focused on his goal, which is to return. But you can't say anything, Sarah. Not a word. You can't do anything to disturb the spell."

"I understand."

Sarah started at the feel of James' colder hand against her flesh, and she wondered if she felt any sadness because this might be the last time she felt him colder, harder against her softer skin. This might be the last time he looked white with a blue undertone, his eyes black as night, the last time he could hear Geoffrey's arrival from miles away, the last time he was faster, stronger, better able than the strongest human man. Would she miss that, she wondered?

Olivia stood over James, unmoving, unbreathing, all her energy concentrated onto James, her wand pointed where his heart should beat again. She chanted in what sounded first like Latin, then Gaelic, then Hebrew, then some combination of the languages. The chanting was ceaseless, encircling James in its repetition, over and over, sounds, syllables, phrases without rhyme or poetry. Without punctuation or grammar. The words and the words, and the repeating of the words, Olivia's voice louder, softer, harsh, or baby-like. The words, and the words, and the words never stopped and never made sense. James was caught in the vortex of the chanting echoes. Was it a prayer, he wondered? An invocation? He didn't know, but he felt the magic under him, around him in the words, and the words, and the words. The room grew lighter, smaller, and James thought he was levitating though he wouldn't open his eyes to see. He felt Sarah's smaller, warmer hand in his, which brought him back to himself and he remembered his task to stay focused on his return. He imagined himself as he was in 1692, before the madness stole his wife, his life, from him. He shook away that thought, it was only a thought, he remembered, and he focused on the good times, the happy times, the times before the Salem Witch Trials set them off on a trajectory they were only now able to recover from. When he was returned, they could press that madness aside forever. Olivia's chanting grew louder, and louder, the words, and the words, and the words filling the wooden house to the peaks of the high-pointing gables, filling the space between James' ears, and again he felt himself floating above them all.

James reached out his hand.

"Father!" he called.

Sarah squeezed his other hand tightly, and James tried to squeeze back. He remembered her. He remembered his task. He was ready to return. But he was certain his father was there, he felt his father's presence, and he wanted to see him.

"Father!" he called again. He turned his head, waiting. Olivia's chanting boomed from her throat as though she spoke with the voice of one hundred men. James strained to hear his father's beloved voice, but all he heard was Olivia's chanting. Then, in a flash, he lifted his head, pulled his hand free from the grasp Sarah struggled to keep on him, and he saw the face he longed for. "Father! I see you!"

He saw his father's outline within the bright-white halo. John Wentworth smiled, his hands pressed together in front of his heart as though in prayer, and he bent over his son. Like the wind god consuming bales of air, John breathed in deeply and pressed the air into his son's mouth. James struggled to keep the air inside, but it was too hard. His lungs didn't want the oxygen. They were so used to doing without. John breathed into his son again, and again, but James felt himself drifting.

When the bright light flashed, James screamed and he fell, fell, fell into the void.

SARAH WAS BLINDED by the flash, and Olivia was knocked to the ground. James' scream was awful, painful, a yelp that brought bitter tears to Sarah's eyes. She saw the outline of her father-in-law breathing into James' mouth as though he were giving CPR, then kissing his son's cheek. James' head fell to the side. His eyes were closed, and his essence was gone. His energy was gone. Sarah grabbed James' hand and she knew she was touching a corpse. She looked wide-eyed at Olivia.

"What happened?" Sarah asked.

Olivia stood over James, listening for breath, a heartbeat, feeling his wrist for a pulse.

"Olivia?"

"Oh, Sarah. I'm so sorry." Olivia fell at Sarah's knees while Sarah stayed stubbornly in her place, grabbing onto James' hand, determined to will it warm, thinking if she concentrated enough he would open his eyes, smile at her, greet her with his usual "Hello" and they would traipse into the sunlight together. But he was cold and unmoving.

"No!" Sarah screamed. She knelt by him, kissing his cheeks, his forehead, his lips. "James!" she cried. "James!" The horror of the realization that he was gone from her, for good this time, wracked her in every nerve fiber. She felt knives poking her arms, her legs, her heart. She screamed again, but it was a sound with no meaning. Maybe this isn't happening, she thought. Maybe this is another nightmare like the ones that used to plague her. Maybe she's still in bed with James, her arms around him, pressing her chest into his back. Maybe.

She opened her eyes, saw Olivia a weeping heap on the floor near James' feet, saw James so still, too still even for his deepest daylight sleep, and she knew it was true. James was gone.

Olivia clasped Sarah's hands, her head bowed. She could hardly say the words. "Can you ever forgive me?"

"It's what he wanted," Sarah said. "He wouldn't leave you alone until you did this for him. He would rather die trying to be human again than live as he was."

Sarah didn't know what to do with her grief. It was worse than anything she had ever known. Worse than being an accused witch. Worse than dying in a putrid dungeon cell feeling her baby's life ebb away with hers. Worse than the gnawing unhappiness that comes from wasting away in a bad marriage. Worse than night terrors that woke her up in heartbeats of cold sweat. Worse than losing James to the internment camp. She understood this was a sadness she might never recover from. She crawled on top of James, his lifeless body beneath hers. She put her arms around him and held him tight, as though if she held him closely enough she could share her body heat with him and he would recover. When she kissed his lips and there was nothing, she gave in to her anguish and wept.

"You should be careful, Sarah," Olivia said. "I don't know what's going to happen now that he's…" Olivia considered her words. "He's more than three hundred and fifty years old. If he doesn't have preternatural magic keeping him animated, I don't know what will become of him."

Sarah didn't care if he turned to dust and bones in her arms. She wasn't ready to let him go. She tightened her arms around him and wept herself to sleep. Sarah slept fitfully that night.

Olivia slept, equally fitfully, in the wing chair near James' seventeenth-century desk until the depressing daylight pinched her awake.

She sighed as she looked around, the overwhelming sadness creeping through her at the sight of Sarah asleep on James' corpse. Olivia walked to them, and leaned over them, checking that Sarah was all right, or as all right as she could be. Sarah, her eyes red and swollen even in her sleep, appeared to be resting. Olivia shuddered at James' death-still body, but at least he hadn't crumbled to dust. He still looked like himself, handsome, golden-haired, strong. Olivia wept silently. She didn't want to wake Sarah, not yet. She wanted to give Sarah these last moments with James, this last time holding him close. Olivia went into the kitchen to make herself some tea, wondering how they would ever explain this to Grace.

WHAT DOES it mean to return? Can you ever go back to where you were? How you were? Is returning a homecoming? An arrival? A departure? Perhaps returning is simply when you reconsider, or put something back where it belongs. Or perhaps it's a reflection, or a chance to repay something you owe. But no matter when, or how, or where you return, time has passed, situations have changed, and life has gone on with or without you. So is it true then, you can never go home again? You can go back to your hometown, your old house, see your friends and your family, but are you the same after time has passed and life has happened with everything good and everything bad and your experiences have moved you along? Returning is such a simple word, yet its meaning is so complex. Even a witch's spell cannot guarantee return. Even one of the most powerful witches in the world. And yet, beneath the storm clouds, beneath the obstacles and the forces that would push you away from your dreams, there is always another chance, an opportunity to begin anew. Spring always appears after winter, and there, in the renaissance, is the return.

SUNSHINE. Daylight. The darkness lifted somewhere up there, too far to touch. Suddenly, as though God spoke, there was light. And it was good. Here, even in the softer January morning, was the incredible brilliance of life and new beginnings, a spring of sorts in the Massachusetts winter. The brightness poked but didn't burn. It was warm, affirming, soothing even. Warm rays spread over him, first his face, then his arms, then his legs. He opened his eyes, one at a time, squinting in the brightness. He didn't feel odd. He was awake, that was all. At that moment, he wasn't sure why he was there. He felt Sarah's weight on top of him before he saw her. Sarah. Sweet Sarah. Beautiful Sarah. The girl who was his Lizzie Sarah. She was sleeping on him, her head on his chest, her arms around him. He brushed a few dark curls from her face and saw her swollen eyes and he guessed she had been crying. He sat up, pulling her into his arms, kissing her forehead, gently waking her.

"Sarah? Are you all right?" When she didn't open her eyes, he worried. He rocked her the way he would rock Grace, holding her head to his chest, kissing her forehead. "Sarah?"

When she opened her eyes she gasped. "Am I dreaming?" she said. She closed her eyes and shook her head as though she were afraid of the answer.

"Dreaming about what? Speak to me, honey."

When she heard his sweet, strong voice, and saw the words come from his mouth, she touched his face, allowing her fingers to trace his lips, his nose, his eyelids as though she were blind and needed to know him.

"James?" she said.

"What's wrong, Sarah?"

Sarah touched him more, his cheeks, his gold hair, the purple veins in his temple. She took his hands between hers and pressed them, running her fingers up his arm to his shoulder, touching her lips to his. She took his face between her hands and looked into his eyes.

"Oh James," she said.

Olivia walked into the great room and Sarah nodded at her.

"It's James."

James looked from Olivia to Sarah. "Will someone please tell me what's going on?"

Olivia stepped closer, studying him. "Do you remember last night, James?" she asked.

"Last night? Last night I…"

"Last night you returned."

Olivia grabbed the hand-held mirror from the top drawer of the wooden desk and held it before James' face. He was stunned when he saw blue eyes staring back from the reflection. He was tempted to ask who he was looking at but he knew. Sarah took his hand and held it to her cheek.

"You're warm," she said. She held her ear to his chest and listened. "Your heart is beating." She held the mirror under his nose, laughing when the glass clouded with his breath.

James walked to the full-length mirror in their bedroom and looked closely at himself, studying his blue eyes, and his flesh-toned complexion, and he watched his chest move. He felt the air come into his body, through his nose, down his throat, into his lungs, and he felt it flow out again. He closed his eyes and allowed himself to feel this, human, and he realized he didn't have to remember any of it. All of it felt right.

"How do you feel?" Olivia asked.

"I feel fine," James said. "I feel as if I've always been this way."

"You never lost touch with your humanity," Olivia said. "Or when you did, you soon found it again. All these years you've kept your humanity intact, so it's no adjustment for you now."

James clasped Olivia's shoulder. "You're the first to cast the spell."

"I'm not, as it turns out. When we were researching the spells we found that over the years there have been other witches who have returned vampires, even a few werewolves. They managed to keep it secret though their accomplishments were documented."

"Why didn't you tell us?" Sarah asked.

"I wasn't sure how this would turn out and I didn't want to give you false hope. For all the successful returns, there were more unsuccessful attempts."

"But this spell worked," Sarah said. She tilted her face up for James to kiss her lips, which he did, gladly. "What do you remember about last night?" she asked.

"I remember everything," James said. "I feel the same, except I'm breathing now. But I remember our life in 1692. I remember Geoffrey."

"Your grandfather," Sarah said.

"Don't remind me." James shook his head. "It's strange because it feels like I'm remembering someone else's life."

"That's the way I think about Elizabeth," Sarah said.

"Let's go see Jennifer, Martha, and Grace," Olivia said. "Let's bring them the good news—James."

"Let me change my clothes," James said. He walked into the bedroom, slipped, and fell to the floor.

"James!" Sarah ran to him. "Are you all right?"

"I'm fine," James said. "I tripped."

Sarah saw a book on the floor and held it up to him. "You must have fallen over this."

"I didn't see it." James took the book from Sarah's hand and laughed.

"What's so funny about that?" Sarah asked.

"I must be nearsighted again."

"I'll take you to the eye doctor and get you a pair of glasses with a prescription. Maybe we can use your old frames. I always liked those." She kissed James' cheek. "Can you hear far away?" she asked.

James closed his eyes as he listened. "I don't think so."

"You have your old human eyesight and hearing back."

James took Sarah's hand. "Are you sorry I'm human again?"

Sarah shook her head. "I thought I would miss the way you were since that's the only way I've known you in this life, but now that I see you like this I see the man I fell in love with all those years ago. I love you any way you are, James Wentworth. I loved you when you were normal, I loved you when you were paranormal, and I love you when you're normal again. Are you glad you're human again?"

"I feel comfortable in my skin, which I never did while I was, well, the way I was."

"Nocturnal?"

James laughed. "Yes, nocturnal. This is the way we were always meant to be."

"I agree," Sarah said. "What do you think Geoffrey will say when he finds out?"

"I don't even know where Geoffrey is. I haven't seen him since the night we escaped."

James squinted in the sunlight streaming through the window. "The sun is bright, but I like it better now than I did when I saw Hempel in my office." He nodded. "I like being awake in the daytime. With you."

Sarah stroked James' temples as he squinted in the stream of sun shifting through the window. "I like you awake in the daytime too. We'll get you some sunglasses when we get you regular glasses."

James nodded. Sitting in the streams of a rare January sun, with his wife in his arms, his daughter waiting only a few miles away, he knew this was the moment he had been waiting for. This was his time. He had returned, finally. He was home where he belonged with the woman he loved. He was only himself, which is all he ever wanted to be.

And he laughed like he hadn't laughed in more than three hundred years.

CHAPTER 21

*E*veryone James and Sarah loved in Salem was gathered in the great room of the wooden gabled house. Olivia, Jennifer, Chandresh, Howard, Timothy, and Martha were there with the Wentworths. They held their celebration at night so their undead friends could be there too. James no longer needed to slink around in the darkness, and he loved standing in the sunshine whenever it brightened those still-snowy March days, though he had to admit, when he was being honest with himself, he still preferred the darkness sometimes. He spent lifetimes hidden in the shadows, the obscurity his constant companion for oh so many years and some habits were harder to leave behind than others. In addition to adjusting to the daytime schedule where life happened at a faster pace, he had to acclimate to eating regular food again. At first Olivia, like a mother tending a child home sick from school, would only feed him vegetable broth. When he was still hungry she gave him applesauce.

"I'm not a baby," James said. "I can eat real food. I have teeth."

The night of the celebration they had several pizzas, James' favorite so far, along with a salad and roasted vegetables. The blood bags had been dumped into the trash and sent away with the stale bread and spoiled cabbage, so James asked Chandresh to provide refreshments for his preternatural guests. James pulled out the coffee mugs and warmed the drink for his friends.

"You look happy," Chandresh said.

"I am," said James.

"You weren't happy before."

"I was happy when I found Sarah again."

"Even then something was missing."

James looked at Sarah, his heart full, his soul grateful for her beautiful presence in his life. "I have everything and everyone I need now."

Chandresh smiled at Jennifer. "I understand."

Chandresh pulled Jennifer toward him, and they kissed, Jennifer certain to flash the sparkling diamond ring on her left hand. She and Chandresh were engaged, and she had eyes for no one in that room but him. Chandresh hadn't forgotten about Jennifer at all when he was gone. He was a man of few words, and he didn't want to propose in an impersonal letter from an internment camp three thousand miles away. He wanted to propose by moonlight near Jennifer's beloved seashore. This was Jennifer's turn too, her third marriage a charm, her opportunity to marry someone not because she wanted him to be James, but because she wanted him to be Chandresh. They didn't leave each other's side all night.

James saw Timothy sitting in a dining room chair before the fire, his night-black eyes watching everyone in the room, settling on Sarah and Martha on the sofa with Grace sitting between them looking as though she followed their conversation perfectly.

"What's wrong, Timothy?" James asked.

"I want to be human again too. I don't want to be fourteen forever."

"I thought spending time with others of your kind in the camp would help you see you're not alone in this," Howard said. He sat close to his son. "There were others there who are also in teenage bodies though they're much older. Some were turned when they were children."

"And they're not any happier than I am," Timothy said.

Howard nudged Timothy. "Did you tell James your good news?"

"What good news?" James asked.

Timothy brightened. "Remember last year when I wrote that novel that was a memoir about my life? Well, the editor remembered me and he found out I was telling the truth, I am a vampire, so he asked to see my manuscript again. This morning he offered me a contract. That, and I'm going to start my own landscape design business."

"I'm so proud of you, Timothy," James said. "You've inspired me."

"How?" Timothy asked.

"I've decided to write about my life as well. I want to capture everything I experienced over the last three hundred years. As it turns out, I'm not going to be around forever, and I want to preserve what I've learned for future generations. I want them to know what I saw, who I knew, where I went."

"Are you going to write it as a novel?" Howard asked.

James nodded. "I think a novel would be best, probably a series. I have a long story to tell, and you'd be surprised at what you can get away with in fiction these days."

"My book is going to be a memoir," Timothy said. "Everyone knows what I am now."

"See, Timothy," Howard said. "Your being turned when you were fourteen didn't stop you from becoming a published author. It's not stopping you from becoming a landscape designer. Now that the vampires are out, people will understand." James grimaced, and Howard shrugged. "Maybe not everyone will understand, but some will."

"Do you think people will understand now, James?" Timothy asked. "You were always so sure they wouldn't."

"The arc of the moral universe is long, but it bends toward justice," James said.

"Doctor Martin Luther King, Junior," said Howard.

"Very good, Professor Wolfe," said James.

"Does that mean you think there's some understanding in our future?" Timothy asked.

"There has always been understanding, just as there has always been madness. People see, they learn, and, when they're inspired, they make things better. We are getting better, even if that's hard for me to admit sometimes. I have a tendency to see the worst that humanity has to offer, but if I'm being honest I can say I've seen things improve. Every generation people fight for their rights, and then others learn better, and they do better, and then we wonder why we didn't know better in the first place. The madness always ends, and we breathe a sigh of relief until some new madness rises to replace it. All madness stems from the same place—fear. When we're afraid we isolate ourselves, separating ourselves from those we fear, and that's when we begin pointing fingers and accusing. It happened in Salem in 1692. It happened during the Trail of Tears. It happened during World War II in Germany and here in camps like Manzanar. It happened when we were sent to Camp Dracula, and there have been countless other instances of madness in between. I might be human now, but I remember everything from my three hundred and fifty years, and I know we've been struggling to learn the same lessons over and over again, from one generation to the next, when the answer is right in front of us."

"What is the answer then, Doctor Wentworth?" Timothy asked.

"We are more alike than we are different. We have the same joys, the same fears, the same pain. That's all we need to know to get along."

Howard held up his bottle of beer as if in a toast. "I couldn't agree more," he said.

Timothy sipped from his mug, his gaze fixed on the fire, his expression intent. When Olivia walked into the kitchen, he stood. "Olivia, can you return me too?"

"Timothy," Howard said.

"I'm serious," Timothy said. "Olivia, I want to be human again like James. I want you to return me."

Olivia hurried to the door as though she were ready to slip away. "Absolutely not," she said. "I will never do that again."

"James is fine. I'll be fine too."

Howard shook his head. "I don't like the idea, Timothy. James nearly didn't survive."

"But he did. Olivia, you're making me stay fourteen forever."

"That was Geoffrey," James said.

"You can fix that, Olivia. I'll pay you whatever you want."

"You can't pay me enough to go through that again. Forget nearly killing James. It nearly killed me."

Timothy followed Olivia around the house. No matter which way she turned, he was there, not backing down. "You have to do this, Olivia."

"You could probably go into business doing this," Jennifer said to her mother. "I bet there are a lot of vampires who want to be returned after this mess with the camps and the watch list. If you charged a fee you could make a fortune."

"I'm not charging anyone since I'm not doing it again."

"Olivia." Timothy tapped his fingers against his leg in an agitated rhythm.

"No, Timothy! Can't you help me, Howard?"

Howard shrugged. "You're on your own with this one, Olivia. My son is stubborn. When he gets an idea into his head he doesn't let off."

Olivia grimaced in James' direction. "Sounds like someone else I know."

Olivia walked through the front door, and Timothy followed her outside and around the crooked oak tree in the front yard, still talking her ear off about returning and how she had to do it for him because she did it for James and that wasn't fair if she did it for James and not him. By the time they were back in the house, Timothy had aggravated Olivia into a frenzy. She exhaled through her lips three times, conscious meditative breathing, to settle herself. When she was calmer, she nodded toward the window. "They're here. They're parking their car by the curb."

"Who is it?" Sarah asked. She looked at the faces of those she loved gathered around her in the great room. "Everyone is here."

"Not everyone," James said. He opened the door, and there was Keiko with Arnie by her side. "Welcome, Keiko-sama," he said. He bowed deeply.

"What are you doing, Professor?" Keiko asked.

"I'm showing you respect as the woman who helped me get my life back."

Keiko bowed deeply. "And I have great respect for you, Doctor Wentworth." She stood back and examined James, taking his hand in hers, nodding at what she saw. "You look good," she said. "As handsome as ever, though I have to admit I like the blue eyes. They suit you better than black."

"I agree," Sarah said.

Sarah hugged her grandmotherly friend as though she would never let go. "Thank you, Keiko. Because of you, I was able to have my husband back sooner than I should have."

"Not only home," Keiko said, "but returned."

"You knew about his return?" Sarah asked.

"He told me about his plan after Olivia agreed."

"How do we repay you for everything you've done for us?" Sarah asked.

Keiko shook her head. "Consider this my payment to the professor for what he did for us seventy years ago."

James handed Keiko a scrap of paper. Keiko studied the words until she flashed her half little girl/half wise woman grin. "You're welcome, Professor Wentworth," she said.

Olivia nodded. "It's like I said. James receives help when he needs it because of the help he gives."

Sarah introduced Keiko all around, and everyone was happy to meet and know this remarkable woman who survived internment and then helped James escape his camp when she hadn't been able to escape hers without years of struggle. Olivia put her arm around Keiko, keeping her close and sharing secrets as though they were long-lost friends. Arnie sat alongside Howard, Chandresh, and Timothy, and they talked about the remarkable old wooden house, the neighborhood, and how Salem was a special place for anyone interested in American history. James smiled when he realized he couldn't hear their conversation from across the room. He couldn't eavesdrop anymore, but he didn't mind. He could hear what any human could hear, and that was enough. He watched the scene before him, marveling, and he knew he was the luckiest man alive. The wooden gabled house was full of people he loved and who loved him no matter what. The only woman he had ever loved was there, laughing, her chocolate-brown eyes bright, her full lips parted, a hot blush along her jaw. She had always been his everything. From the first day he saw her she became his day, his night, his joy, his light. His reason for going on. That would never change.

James tapped a spoon to the wine glass on the wooden table near the fireplace. When he had everyone's attention, he smiled at Sarah, who nodded back.

"Thank you all for coming here," James said. "Sarah and I are well aware of how blessed we are to have such extraordinary people in our lives. We wouldn't be here now without each of you. Jennifer, you hired Sarah at the library in the first place. Without you, Sarah wouldn't have had a reason to move to Salem, and we couldn't have been reunited. Olivia, your motherly warmth and compassion, your seer's wisdom, and your extraordinary abilities, in so many ways you are the glue that held us together. Your willingness to risk it all for me allowed me to take my daughter for a walk along the wharf in the sunshine this afternoon. I took my wife out for lunch yesterday for the first time. Chandresh, we made our acquaintance nearly two hundred years ago along that terrible trail. You've always said I helped you, but the truth is you helped me more than you could ever know. From you I learned that I could still care about someone, and I could still be of some use in this world.

"Howard, how lucky I was to find a connection with someone of a different persuasion when all the world would have us be mortal enemies. I have found nothing but unconditional friendship from you, and I hope you've found the same from me. Timothy, I hope I've been some help for you on your journey as well. I wish you peace as you find your way through the paranormal world. Just because it wasn't for me doesn't mean it's not for you. And if it's not for you, then I wish you luck convincing Olivia to return you." Everyone laughed. "Keiko, what can I say about the beautiful girl with sharp, observant eyes who came to my English class at UCLA wishing to share her love of reading with everyone? I can say she suffered more than others during the war, but she didn't let her wounds stop her from becoming successful in both her career and her family. Your wonderful grandson Arnie is a testament to your strength and your love."

James closed his eyes for a moment, gathering his thoughts, needing to get his words right. "Forgive me," he said. "I thought what I wanted to say to my wife would come easily since I've spent over three hundred years trying to articulate exactly what she means to me, yet I find myself standing here oddly speechless, not because I have nothing to say but because my heart is too full and I can't think how to express the depth of what this beautiful woman has been to me since the first time I saw her here in Salem in 1691. Don't ever wonder if love at first sight is possible because I know it is. I fell in love with this beautiful woman, whom I then called Elizabeth, the first moment I set eyes on her. Even when I was no longer alive in any human sense, even when I thought she was lost to me forever and I would have to linger night after night for eternity without seeing her again, thinking of her kept me going. I hoped, every dawn before I went to sleep, that somehow, some way, she would find her way home to me. I wrote letters to her, keeping her informed of my nights. I spoke to her every day in my dreams. I asked her to come home. And after so long I had lost hope of my wildest dream ever coming true. But one night I woke up and there she was, outside my window, looking at this house, our house, the one my father and I had built for her when I knew she would be my wife. She was every bit as beautiful as I remembered. She looked surprised, yet she looked like she was home, as though she knew in the deepest part of herself that she was where she was supposed to be. I allowed myself to be persuaded that it couldn't be her. Then she learned, as I learned, that she was my beloved Elizabeth after all. Now I have my Sarah here before me, and I am beyond myself with gratitude. I have another chance with the only woman I have ever loved. I'm ready for this new life ahead for our family. Salem will always be a part of me. It has been the center of my life for over three hundred years, and it will be hard leaving it behind."

"Leaving it behind?" Jennifer said. "Where are you going?"

"I received a position at UC Berkeley." He smiled at Keiko. "A professor there has taken ill and they needed someone who knew both Dickens and early American literature to take over his classes for the remainder of the year. I was lucky enough to get a recommendation from a respected Professor Emeritus, Doctor Keiko Sato Ishigura, so I got the job. They're keeping me on next year as well, and hopefully the year after that."

"Are you leaving so soon?" Olivia asked.

"The four of us are moving to California in two weeks," James said.

Martha looked confused. "The four of you?"

Sarah smiled. "I'm pregnant."

Howard nudged James. "You work fast."

James shrugged, but he smiled.

"What can I say?"

THEIR GUESTS CLEARED AWAY after giving their heartfelt congratulations to the three and a half Wentworths. Now the food was stored, the glasses put into the dishwasher, and it was quiet inside the wooden gabled house. Grace was sleeping soundly in her crib, and James and Sarah sat huddled on the sofa listening to the crackling red-orange flames in the fireplace. They were silent, enjoying this time alone without a single worry hanging over them. James was as human as anyone. Any doctor's examination would prove it with his beating heart, his pulse, his breathing chest, and they were left to create their lives however they wanted with Grace and their new baby, living near the California coast, enjoying the sunshine and the fine weather. It wouldn't be the same as the serene Massachusetts Bay, James knew, but he was used to moving on and coming back again. It had been his way for over three hundred years, and it would be his way for the rest of his hopefully long human life with his beloved wife by his side. He kissed the top of Sarah's hair, and she snuggled closer to him. Suddenly, there was a loud banging that startled them both.

"Who is it?" Sarah asked.

"I don't know."

"It's me, dammit!" Geoffrey yelled. "Open the bloody door!"

Sarah let Geoffrey in. As soon as he stepped inside she threw her arms around him and hugged him as tightly as she could. Geoffrey was startled but hugged her back.

"Thank you, little human person. What was that for again?"

"For everything," Sarah said.

Geoffrey looked embarrassed as he pulled away. "Where is the littlest human person?"

"Grace is sleeping," Sarah said, "but you can see her if you like."

"I don't want to wake her, but I don't know when I'll see her again."

"Did you know we're moving to California?" Sarah asked.

"Of course."

"When we move you can come. You can live with us, Geoffrey."

James shook his head. "He can?"

"Are you starting already, larger human person? I thought maybe you'd leave off this being annoyed by Grandfather Geoffrey now that you're no longer that hideous creature of the night I turned you into. Accidentally, of course."

"The accident is that you turned your own grandson."

"Really, now, James. I think…"

Sarah held up her hands, always playing referee for her boys. "Some things never change," she said. "You two are going at it like always."

Geoffrey looked forlorn standing in the center of the great room, staring at the wooden floor as though he didn't know where to put his feet. "I'm the one who should be angry with you, actually."

"How do you figure that?" James asked.

"I gave you the greatest gift any human person could ask for. I gave you forever, James. And you gave it away, for what?"

"For my wife," James said. "For my children."

"You wouldn't have found your wife if you weren't what I made you."

"Now I've found her. She's here. We're together, and we're the same. You're the one who said we should be the same."

"But you're a wimpy little human thing again. You think your life is going to be better now that you're weak? You used to hear me coming miles away. Now you need me to yell at you through the door."

"Like other people," James said.

"But you could die!" Geoffrey said. He couldn't hide his horror at the thought. "Not could, will! You will die! And then what will I do? I'll be all alone. There will be no one left who knows who I am. No one left who cares about me."

"Grace will care about you," Sarah said. "And our new baby, and their children, and their children after them. They'll all know and love Grandfather Geoffrey."

Geoffrey shook his head. "It won't be the same. Even all those years when you didn't know I was watching you, James, all those years you didn't know who I was, knowing you were out there, knowing there was someone I was connected to eased the pain of feeling alone. When you're gone, James…"

"It's going to be all right, Geoffrey."

"And who knows what will happen to that paltry human body of yours. You could break your leg. You could get diabetes. You could get cancer. You could get *constipation*."

"And I could get hit by a bus crossing the street, and an airplane might crash into this house right now. But that's what life is, Geoffrey. Neither Sarah nor I are guaranteed anything. We know the worst can happen, and we know not to take anything for granted this time. We know to cherish every day and night we have together, hopefully for a very long time."

"And what will happen when first one and then the other of you dies?"

"Then we'll come back around and do it all over again," Sarah said.

"We have to," James said. "It's our destiny."

Geoffrey leaned in close to James. He looked tight, menacing, a predator ready to pounce. "I could turn you again, you know. I could turn the both of you, the three of you. The four of you for that matter."

"But you won't," James said.

"Why shouldn't I?"

"Because despite all your bluff and bluster, all you've ever wanted was for me to be happy, and you know being human is what I need to be happy. I'm not dead anymore, and I'm going to live my life to the fullest."

Geoffrey sighed. "Yes, I've always wanted you to be happy." He smiled. "Maybe I'll have that nice red-haired human lady return me too. Then we'll grow old and decrepit together."

"I don't think Olivia would be too keen on the idea," James said. Suddenly, a question that had occurred to him in the night as he fell asleep with his wife by his side popped into his mind. "I wanted to ask you something," he said.

"Anything," Geoffrey said. "No more secrets."

"When you showed up here the first time to ask me about Hempel, did you know I found Elizabeth? You recognized Sarah the moment you saw her."

"I knew you were keeping company with a lovely little brunette human person, but, no, I didn't realize she was your wife until I saw her here. I was quite pleased for you when I realized. I knew how much you missed her, and I understood that pain well. I still miss your grandmother all these years later. Every time I see a plump little blonde I look to see if it's my Becky, but I haven't found her yet."

"Perhaps one day," James said.

Geoffrey opened the door and stopped as though he were waiting for something. He was pensive, so unlike himself without his irreverence.

"It's late for human people who like to sleep when it's dark, I reckon."

Geoffrey walked outside. He stepped away, then paused, stepped further away, then stopped. He turned back to James, nodded, then moved as though he would disappear.

"Grandfather!"

Geoffrey froze, the emotion strong in his almond-shaped eyes as he turned to his grandson.

"None of this would have been possible without you." James laughed at his own words. "It must be later because I'm thanking you, for real this time."

"I am so very proud of you, James. I even forgive you for turning your back on all that is cultured, civilized, and English. I even," Geoffrey graced James with a conciliatory bow, "forgive you for speaking with that silly accent."

"You're more American than you're willing to concede," James said. "I've heard a few Americanisms slip into your speech."

"Rubbish!"

"It's true."

"I understand that as an *American* you're compelled to say so, and I forgive you that as well."

"We're going to have to agree to disagree on this point, Grandfather."

"I believe you're correct, James."

"You will come to California with us, won't you, Grandfather?" Sarah asked. She clutched Geoffrey's hand as though she wanted him to stay.

"Don't worry, little human person. I'll be around. You're not getting rid of me so easily." He pointed at James. "No wisecracks from you, little man."

"I didn't say a word, Bumptybottoms."

Geoffrey looked through the open door toward Grace's room. "You'll kiss her for me, won't you?"

"You know I will," Sarah said.

At a flash Geoffrey was gone.

As JAMES GOT ready for bed that night, he felt a presence in the room. He looked around, expecting to see Sarah but no one was there. He thought he must have imagined it, but the presence was so strong. And then he felt the warmth, the light, and he knew.

"Father?"

He wanted to hear the hearty Shakespearean actor's voice he loved, but he strained and heard only silence. It was the first time he missed his extrasensory hearing.

"Father?" he called again. He saw the flash in the bedroom mirror, the outline of the slight frame, the balding head, the loving smile, the hands folded as though in prayer, the unconditional love that loved James even when he didn't think he was lovable, monster he had become in his own mind.

"I see you, Father," James said. He listened, he strained until the veins between his ears hurt—he used to hear so easily and now at times it felt like such a struggle—but no matter how hard he tried he couldn't hear his father's voice. "I can't hear you. Maybe it's harder now, but I'll keep listening. I know you're there. I thanked Grandfather tonight, Father, and now I'm thanking you. For everything. For loving me when I couldn't love myself. For giving me breath when I returned to human. For being here now. I love you more than I can ever say. I hope to be such a father for Grace and the new baby."

The outline of his father flickered in the dim room. It grew brighter, and brighter still, and the warmth flooded James' body as the light leaned over him and covered him. James smiled, and the light disappeared.

CHAPTER 22

The tour guide looked like other tour guides from witch trial museums around Salem. She was a young woman, college age, her long white-blond hair pulled into a bun and covered by a white coif tied in a knot under her chin. The coif was covered by a floppy bonnet keeping the iridescent early spring rays from her face. She wore brown ankle-length woolen skirts layered over a boned sleeveless bodice and a roll over her bottom, an apron tied over everything indicating a long day of work ahead. She stood near the open green door inside the great room of the wooden house. The crowd of twenty tourists listened to her speech, snapping pictures of the steep-pitched two-gabled roof, the overhanging second story, the diamond-paned casement windows, and the red bricks of the large central chimney peeking over the top. Tourists ran their hands along the asymmetrical façade, touching the long wooden slats of the exterior walls.

"The house has a timber frame," the tour guide said, "and the clapboards are original to the house when it was built by the owner's ancestor, John Wentworth, in 1691." She gestured to the plants and vegetables growing in the plot at the front of the property. "Here you see what the original kitchen garden would have looked like. While this garden was recreated only two weeks ago, many of the newly planted vegetables are the same as the ones you would have seen if you had visited the Wentworths' home in the late seventeenth century." She pointed to an outhouse structure behind the house. "That's a recreation of the outhouse they would have used since they had no indoor plumbing in the 1600s. Thank goodness for modern conveniences." The tourists laughed.

The guide grew serious. She looked at the tourists ranging in age from five to seventy-one by one, certain they understood the importance of what she was about to say.

"This is the very door where, in July 1692, during the height of the terror of the Salem Witch Trials, the constable informed the lady of the house, Elizabeth Wentworth, that she had been accused of witchcraft and she was being arrested. Of course, Elizabeth was horrified since she saw what became of those who were accused before her—many were jailed in horrific circumstances and some were hanged to their deaths. Elizabeth begged for her innocence, as did her husband, James, but the constable came with a warrant for Elizabeth's arrest and he wouldn't leave without her. Elizabeth had been accused of witchcraft, and in those troubled times in Salem, an accusation was the same as a conviction. If others said they saw her specter doing harm, then the people of Salem decided it must be true. Elizabeth was in the later stages of her pregnancy, but that didn't stop the constable from dragging her away. She was chained to a wagon and treated like a common criminal though she was innocent of witchcraft or any other wrongdoing. From this house, she was brought to the dungeon where she lingered in sickness for weeks until she was sent to the jail in Boston, where she died, her innocent baby along with her. While there's no one alive now who experienced the terror of the witch trials, we can imagine the horror. Picture yourself in your home with your family around you. One night the town constable tells you you've been accused of witchcraft and you will be arrested and stand trial. You know you've committed no crime, but no one believes you. Because you're accused you're assumed guilty. If you were in Salem in 1692, how would you have dealt with the madness? Would you step aside and allow innocent others to be condemned? Would you stand up, even at your own peril, to help those subjected to injustice? What would you do if you saw such corruption around you? Would you help Elizabeth Wentworth? Or would you turn away?"

The tourists were silent, their heads bowed as they considered the arrest and death of an innocent woman. The guide stepped further into the house and gestured toward the tourists. "If you'll follow me, I'll show you the interior. It was a grand house for its day..."

The tourists followed the guide inside, murmuring amongst themselves and snapping photos of the great room.

Sarah stood near the curb beside the open trunk of the yellow taxi full with luggage. She listened to the tour guide with a sad heart, then watched the tourists disappear into her house. Her hand went instinctively to the bump where the new baby waited.

"This house has a lot of history for us," Sarah said. "Even with the terrible things that happened here, this house is our home and I'm going to miss it." She allowed her tears to fall freely because when else can you cry but when you're leaving your home, your center point, and you don't know when you're going to return?

James stepped next to her and slid his arm around her shoulders. He sighed, and she loved the sound of it because it was real.

"Are you all right, honey?" he asked. "It wasn't too hard hearing it, was it?"

"I'm all right."

Sarah looked at James' new silver wire-frame eyeglasses and smiled. "I'm just thinking how much I'm going to miss this old pile of wood. I can't believe it was only two and a half years ago when Jennifer drove me home from the library that rainy afternoon and I saw this place for the first time, or what I thought was the first time."

James kissed Sarah's forehead. "That was an auspicious day indeed."

"How much has changed since then, and yet how much has stayed the same."

She took James' hand and led him to the diamond-paned casement window. Inside they saw the tourists snapping photographs on their cell phones or digital cameras. The renovators worked quickly, and in two weeks they restored the house's interior to its seventeenth-century glory—the stainless steel kitchen was replaced with its original wooden counterpart, and the cauldron was back where it belonged in the fireplace. The flat-screen television, the refrigerator, the microwave, and the more modern furniture were all gone, replaced by simple seventeenth-century wooden furniture. The knickknacks were taken down from the attic and restored to their rightful places around the house, and everything looked the way Sarah remembered from all those years before. She was sad to know her modern renovations were gone, yet there was something right, even comforting seeing the house in its original simplicity.

"It's so strange to think this isn't our house anymore," Sarah said. "It's been part of everything about us for so long."

"It's still our house," James said. "The Salem Historical Society has it on loan for the next five years. If we decide we want to move back into the house then we can." James nodded at the wooden exterior. "I bet at some point we'll want to live here again. I know I always wanted to come home."

"And one day the house will belong to Grace and the new baby," Sarah said.

James patted Sarah's belly. "Boy or girl?" he asked. "You were right about Grace. You had her name picked out."

"Boy," Sarah said.

"You said that with confidence."

"I have his name picked out too." Sarah grinned, and James stepped back, laughing at her silly face.

"Do I want to know?" he asked.

"Not yet. I'll tell you when we know for sure it's a boy."

Olivia came around the taxi with Grace in her arms. Grace held her hands out to James, and he took his daughter and held her close to his beating heart.

"You're still coming to visit next week, right Olivia?" Sarah asked.

"Try to stop me. And you know I'll be there for the birth of that baby boy."

"You think it's a boy too?" James asked.

"Sarah has good instincts."

"Thank God," James said.

The tourists followed the tour guide outside into the recreated kitchen garden. They hunched over the plants growing in the front yard plot, touching the green leaves and the sprouts of baby vegetables, reading the labels, and watching their feet so they didn't step on anything green.

"Though she was the wife of a wealthy merchant, Elizabeth Wentworth was the daughter of a farmer and she was more hands-on than other well-to-do women in her position in her day. Though her husband could have afforded to hire as much help as she wished, she continued to keep this garden and she did most of the cooking herself. This garden was recreated with historical accuracy by Timothy Bryston-Wolfe, an apprentice landscape artist located here in Salem."

"About Timothy..." James said.

Olivia shook her head. "Hush, James. I've already told him no. A hundred times no."

"You told me no too."

Grace kicked her legs, ready to stand on her own like the big girl she was. "You're stubborn like your father," Olivia said. "May your stubbornness get you everything you want the way it has for him."

The taxi driver grunted as he eyed the meter ticking on his dashboard. Olivia opened the back door of the taxi and helped Grace inside. She strapped Grace in and patted the airline approved pet carrier where the tailless black cat meowed like her life was ending. When Olivia stepped onto the curb, Sarah pulled her motherly friend aside and hugged her with all her love.

"Thank you, Olivia," Sarah said.

"You're my family, Sarah. I will do anything for my family."

Olivia hugged James, and when he pulled away Sarah saw the saltwater lingering on his cheeks. She didn't need to brush it away. It suited this moment as they left behind their town, their home, and the woman who helped them understand the true meaning of family.

They stood in front of the wooden house with narrow clapboards, diamond-paned casement windows, and a steep-pitched roof with two gables pointing at the early spring sunshine. Sarah stood on her toes, and James kissed her. When the warmth of his lips melted into hers, making her weak from the inside out, she knew that this was the right ending after all. He was unwilling to let her go, ever, and she clutched him closer, unable to break their embrace.

"I shall never leave you ever," he whispered in her ear. He lingered there, his lips on her skin, and she was overcome with the joy of him.

How do you sum up over three hundred years of devotion with a few words? You don't. You allow the truth of your heart to come through the depth of your eyes. With a last look at the wooden house and a final nod to all it meant to them, Sarah climbed into the backseat next to James and fastened her seat belt. She waved once more at Olivia, and the driver shifted gears.

"Don't forget to take the route I asked," James said to the driver.

"It'll cost extra," the driver said.

"I don't mind."

The taxi pulled away from the curb, away from the house where the tourists studied the garden as if it were a new specimen of curiosity. They drove down Derby Street, passing the House of the Seven Gables, the Salem Maritime National Historic Site, and the blue-gray buildings of Pickering Wharf with the Witches Lair. The driver turned left at Lafayette Street for a quick swing around Salem State University, a visual summary of all that campus meant to them, then back left on Lafayette near Pioneer Village, driving past the Grapevine and the Peabody Essex Museum. Sarah recalled everything she had seen in Salem, everywhere she had been, and everyone she loved. She was sad thinking that she wouldn't have the tranquility of the Salem bay beside her every day, but they were moving to the California coast in Berkeley, so she could get to the Pacific Ocean when she needed it. This was a fresh start, James' fresh start, and suddenly, with the exhalation of her breath, Sarah was at peace with the move. She would miss everything about Salem, at least everything about twenty-first-century Salem. She would miss the Federal-style buildings, the quaint New England small town vibe, the Salem Ferry passing leisurely in the bay, and the red trolley cars showing tourists around. Most of all, she would miss Howard, Timothy, and Jennifer. She wished her friend Jennifer luck in her new life with her love Chandresh, and Sarah remembered that she and James would see them in Oklahoma that summer for the wedding. The faces Sarah came to love in Salem flipped behind her eyes like photographs on a cell phone screen, and she smiled when the screen paused on Olivia. I'll miss you most of all, Scarecrow, she thought. My warm, caring, motherly Scarecrow. What would I ever do without you?

"We're leaving Salem," James said as Essex Street became Route 107 S. "Any regrets?"

Sarah shook her head as she watched Salem grow smaller behind her.

"No," she said. "I came here for a reason, and that reason was you. Now that I have you, Grace, and the baby, I'm not tied here anymore. We can go wherever we want, and right now I want to go to California with you." Sarah pressed herself into James' side and leaned her head against his shoulder. "Besides, Salem has been here for over three hundred years, and I have every confidence it will be here three hundred years from now. You don't have to stay away from somewhere because you don't change anymore, James. We can come and go as we please, and we can come back any time."

The taxi merged onto Route 60 E toward Boston and Logan Airport.

James kissed Sarah's lips.

"Yes, we can," he said. "Yes, we can."

EPILOGUE

rofessor James Wentworth walked outside from his Dickens and Theater seminar and stood beside Wheeler Hall. It was a beautiful building, Wheeler Hall, with its French Baroque façade and arched doorways, and he was thankful to be there, at that moment, on the campus of UC Berkeley in the easy mid-April sunshine. He felt the soul-calming breeze blowing the foliage while he glanced at the Venice-inspired Sather Tower, the green steeple pointing steadily toward the cloudless sky, the salty scent of the sea in every breath he took. One day soon he would go back to the top of the Tower, or the Campanile as it was also known, for its exquisite view of the San Francisco Bay, but that afternoon he had an important date to keep. He squinted in the brightness of the day, a bit of the old sting in his eyes until he remembered the sunglasses in his jacket pocket. He was still getting used to mundane things—putting on his regular glasses when he woke up in the morning so he didn't trip over anything, putting on his sunglasses outside so his eyes wouldn't scream, eating lunch around noon so he didn't lag in the afternoon. There was a lot to remember, a lot that was different, and there were the odd mornings when he was disoriented by the sunlight. But then he saw his wife, the only woman he ever loved, waking up beside him, her dark curls tousled, her full lips parted in greeting, her arms stretching toward him, pulling him close. Then he remembered his return, he was home now, and the discomforts became nothing but minor inconveniences.

James passed the Bancroft and Doe Memorial Libraries and he smiled remembering when he and his wife worked at the same college together. He continued around the eclectic Berkeley architecture ranging from neoclassical to contemporary, and he walked down Campanile Way, past the Valley Life Sciences Building to the Grinnell Natural Area. The tree-filled spot was James' favorite resting place on campus, the Monterey pines, live oaks, and redwoods creating a peaceful haven. James watched the students walking or riding their bikes to their classes, their eyes intent on their destination, their earbuds in their ears, and he marveled at how students on the California coast in Berkeley were the same as students on the Massachusetts coast in Salem. They had the same dreams, the same hopes people have always had. They wanted the opportunity to live their most fulfilling lives. They wanted to know they mattered. Some things never changed no matter what clothing or technology was the vogue, James knew.

He sat on a log under the canopy of the overhanging trees listening to the water in Strawberry Creek whisking past and slapping the rocks. He watched two young women sitting on the bridge, leaning on their backpacks as they read aloud to each other. The young women recognized him and waved.

"Hey, Doctor Wentworth," the purple-haired girl yelled. James waved back, and the young women joined him on the log. "What are you doing here?"

"Hi, Stacie," James said. "I'm waiting for my wife and daughter. They're taking me out for my birthday."

"Happy birthday," said the blond-haired young woman. The two young women smiled at each other as though they shared a private joke. "How old are you, Professor?"

James opened his mouth to answer but realized he was stumped. How old was he? It was such a simple question, and yet he had been thirty years old for over three hundred years. Whenever anyone asked, since 1692, he was thirty years old. For three centuries his answer was rote, unthought of, secretly sneered at. But today was his birthday. How old was he, he wondered again. He laughed aloud when the answer occurred to him.

"I'm thirty-one," he said. He laughed again, unable to hide his amusement. "I'm thirty-one today."

The purple-haired girl nodded. "See, Kristi, I told you he was young."

"I said he was young too," said Kristi.

Kristi scooted closer to James. "Doctor Wentworth, I'm glad you took over for Professor Steinman when he had to leave. Class is a lot more interesting with you teaching."

"Professor Steinman used to fall asleep in the middle of his lectures," Stacie said. She rolled her eyes in annoyed remembrance of poor old Professor Steinman. She held the volume in her hand out to James. "Why do we have to read this? It wasn't on our original syllabus."

James took *Several Poems Compiled with Great Wit and Learning* from Stacie's hand. He knew every poem without looking at the words.

"I added Anne Bradstreet to the syllabus when I took over the class. Since she lived from 1612 to 1672 she falls into the category of early American literature so we should cover her. She's an important American writer. *Let Greeks be Greeks, and women what they are...*" His students grimaced. "You don't like Anne Bradstreet?" he asked.

The young women looked at each other and shrugged. "Her poems are a little hokey," said Stacie. "I know she was one of the first American women to receive recognition for her work, but I don't know, Professor. I'm not loving her."

"Listen to this," James said. He flipped to the page he needed and read without looking:

"If ever two were one, then surely we.
If ever man were loved by wife, then thee:
If ever wife was happy in a man,
Compare with me, ye women, if you can.

I prize thy love more than whole mines of gold
Or all the riches that the East doth hold..."

He wasn't surprised when he heard her voice, soft and sweet, his favorite sound in the world:

"My love is such that rivers cannot quench,
Nor ought but love from thee, give recompense.
Thy love is such I can no way repay,
The heavens reward thee manifold, I pray..."

James and Sarah finished the poem together:

"Then while we live, in love let's so persevere
That when we live no more, we may live ever."

James put his arms around his wife and held her close. "Ladies, this is my wife, Sarah." He gestured at Grace, standing on her own with her arms around her mother's leg. She watched the young women with wide eyes like blue-toned jewels which perfectly matched her father's. "This is my daughter, Grace."

"She looks just like you, Professor Wentworth." Stacie turned to Sarah. "Are you an English professor too?"

"A librarian," Sarah answered, "though I'm taking some time off right now." She looked at the book in James' hand. "Are you studying Anne Bradstreet?"

"They think Bradstreet is hokey," James said.

Sarah nodded. "Me too. But if you get past the old-fashioned language..."

"Which wasn't so old-fashioned in the seventeenth century," James said.

"...she expressed thoughts and feelings which we can still recognize. Her declaration of her undying love for her husband resonates today." Sarah smiled at James. "At least it does for us. We read 'To My Dear and Loving Husband' at our wedding."

"That one isn't so bad," Stacie said. "It's kind of touching if you're into syrupy sweet. Happy birthday, Doctor Wentworth."

"Happy birthday, Professor," said Kristi.

James waved his thanks as his students disappeared into foliage and trees in the direction of Hellman Tennis Center. He lifted his daughter high into the sky, her squeals of delight filling the air alongside student chatter and bird songs. He held Grace close to his heart with one arm while he encircled his wife with his other arm, never letting her go, keeping her beside him where she belonged. They made their way toward the West Gate, around Crescent to the Springer Gateway. Sarah slipped James' hand onto the growing bump in her middle.

"Do you want to know the baby's name?" she asked.

"You said you wouldn't tell me until you knew it was a boy."

Sarah smiled. She kept her eyes in front of her, away from James, watching the cars and the students go by, hardly able to contain the laughter she felt somewhere deep within. James stopped walking and turned Sarah toward him.

"Do you know?"

"It's a boy."

"When did you find out?"

"I had the ultrasound this morning."

"Why didn't you tell me?"

"I wanted to surprise you for your birthday."

She threw her arms around her husband's neck and laughed, and James laughed, and Grace laughed. They were picture perfect, the Wentworths, glowing in their joy.

"Are you surprised?" Sarah asked.

"Pleasantly surprised. So what's his name?"

"John Geoffrey."

James shook his head. "Are you serious?"

"Get that puckered look off your face, Doctor Wentworth. Remember, honor thy father."

"I have no problem honoring my father. My pain in the ass grandfather on the other hand..."

Sarah stood on her toes, waiting for James to kiss her, which he did, gladly.

"Happy birthday, James. Where would you like to celebrate?"

"I could go for pizza and a beer," he answered.

"We can do that."

"Beer," Grace said.

Sarah laughed. "Not you, Grace. You're too little."

James patted Sarah's stomach. "Or you, either. John," he cringed, "Geoffrey isn't old enough to drink."

He grasped his wife's hand and kissed his daughter on top of her gold curls. They walked to Oxford Street, the breeze from the San Francisco Bay tousling their hair, and they clustered close, enjoying this moment together.

Which is the way they were always meant to be.

AUTHOR'S NOTES

James and Sarah Wentworth became my constant companions in April 2009 when the vague story of a vampire still mourning for his long-gone human wife first occurred to me. Since then, James, Sarah, and I have been on quite a journey, but it is one that I am most grateful for. Thank you to the many readers from all over the world who have shared their love for the *Loving Husband Trilogy* with me. I know James and Sarah will always have a place in my heart, and I hope they will always have a place in yours. I found great joy in continuing their story in *Down Salem Way*, the prequel to the *Loving Husband Trilogy* set during the Salem Witch Trials.

For anyone interested in learning more about the Japanese-American internments during World War II, I can do no better than to recommend the leader in the genre, *Farewell to Manzanar* by Jeanne Wakatsuki Houston and James D. Houston. The idea for the interviews and some of Keiko's biographical details were inspired by *Farewell to Manzanar*.

ABOUT THE AUTHOR

Meredith Allard is an award-winning author known for the bestselling *Loving Husband Trilogy* and the Victorian novel *When It Rained at Hembry Castle*, which IndieReader named a Best Historical Novel. Her prequel, *Down Salem Way*, earned the B.R.A.G. Medallion and was a semi-finalist for the Chaucer Award in Early Historical Fiction.

A recognized authority on the craft, Meredith is the author of *Painting the Past: A Guide for Writing Historical Fiction*, a #1 Amazon New Release in Authorship and Creativity Self-Help. For over twenty years, she has mentored writers of all ages, helping them find their voices while honing her own signature blend of meticulous research and haunting prose.

When she isn't unearthing the secrets of the past, she can be found in the hills of Southern Nevada with her cats and a cup of coffee.

Join Meredith online at www.meredithallard.com for her weekly blog posts and monthly newsletter.

BOOKS BY MEREDITH ALLARD

And Shadows Will Fall

Christmas at Hembry Castle

Down Salem Way

The Duchess of Idaho

Her Dear & Loving Husband

Her Loving Husband's Curse

Her Loving Husband's Return

Painting the Past: A Guide for Writing Historical Fiction

The Professor of Eventide

The Swirl and Swing of Words: Embracing the Writing Life

Victory Garden

When It Rained at Hembry Castle

Woman of Stones

www.ingramcontent.com/pod-product-compliance
Lightning Source LLC
Chambersburg PA
CBHW031608240626

47153CB00002B/673